The others race for the exit, ready to start their first recorded day. I hang back uncertainly, following Drew, who zips his sweatshirt closed over the XTV-mandated shirt as soon as Kara's out the door.

"Your parents signed the form yet?" he asks.

"I think my mom's too busy getting the check framed."

"Yeah," he says, wriggling a little in his new shirt.

"You okay?" I ask, because I'm not.

He pauses, looking back over his shoulder. "I don't usually wear anything this tight—or expensive. It's weird. This whole thing is weird."

I nod.

"But you're here, right?" His face brightens. "We're in this together?"

I smile back, despite the tightness in my chest.

"It's no big deal," he continues. "I bet it'll be like nothing is even happening."

He pushes open the swinging door, and we both freeze under the stares of the entire student body. They stand on tiptoes, craning to see two people who were, mere minutes ago, unremarkable.

The REAL REAL

A NOVEL

EMMA McLAUGHLIN
& NICOLA KRAUS

HARPER
An Imprint of HarperCollinsPublishers

Library of Congress Cataloging-in-Publication Data

McLaughlin, Emma.

The real real / Emma McLaughlin & Nicola Kraus. — 1st ed.

    p. cm.

    Summary: When Hampton High senior Jesse is cast in a reality television show along with five other, more popular students, drama on and off screen reveals that what the audience and producers want is not the same as what Jesse wants.

    ISBN 978-0-06-172042-0

    [1. Reality television programs—Fiction. 2. Dating (Social customs)—Fiction. 3. High schools—Fiction. 4. Schools—Fiction.]

I. Kraus, Nicola. II. Title.

PZ7.M2236Re 2009   2009002499

[Fic]—dc22   CIP

                                        AC

10   11   12   13   14   CG/RRDH   10   9   8   7   6   5   4   3   2   1

❖

First paperback edition, 2010

TO LOUISA AND ELEANOR,
FABULOUS FROM CHILDHOOD TO ADULTHOOD

"I am not I: thou art not he or she: they are not they."
—Evelyn Waugh

PART I
THE REAL

ONE

"**S**ingle file! Everyone, line up on the LEFT!" Mrs. Gesop shouts to be heard over the din of students crowding into the impractically narrow hallway between the stairwell and the auditorium. "We will let you in when *everyone* is lined up neatly against the wall!" It's a physical impossibility for the hundred-plus seniors of Hampton High to fit along the eight-foot stretch of wall, and as more students step off the stairs we're getting packed in here like panicked cattle. Just open the double doors, lady, and let us in.

Caitlyn wriggles into the air pocket at my right, her face flushed and damp. "What's going on?" she pants, tucking her most recent DIY blond streak behind her ear. "I got to bio late because the Camry wouldn't start—of course I get one semester to park at school, and the crapbox dies every time it snows—and run into an empty room with just the chalkboard saying come here. What does it mean? Is it *terrorists*?"

"It's probably some stupid college thing." I pat her on the shoulder. "And at least you *have* a crapbox."

Caitlyn snaps her fingers in front of my face. "Okay, focus." She flips open her phone to show me the last text she received before the eight o'clock bell. "Rob says Drew Rudell showed up puffy-eyed to cross-country practice this morning."

"*Really.* Why?"

"Dumped over Christmas break. One semester of long-distance love was all she could handle."

"She dumped him?" I grab her wrist to steady myself as we sway in the middle of the bovine huddle. "They were practically married last spring. What is Sarah Lawrence, a two-hour, three-hour drive? For him I would've Roller-bladed that." We reflexively drop our chins to our chests and try to look out through our bangs to locate Drew, while I furtively brush on some Benetint.

"He's behind you," she says. "And, despite said puffiness, does have a certain . . . available vibe to him. Looks like your year of silent prayers and that Santeria candle we bought have finally paid off."

I turn to her, making full-force eye contact. "Find out everything you can before lunch. Did she really initiate the breakup, was there infidelity, and who got custody of the windbreaker."

"On it."

"ALL RIGHT, SENIORS! Since we cannot seem to convince you to line up, I only ask that when we open the doors you move in AN ORDERLY FASHION to the front of the auditorium and take seats. In an ORDERLY FASHION!"

The double doors finally give, and everyone flies down the aisles as if cash prizes were at stake.

Caitlyn and I go directly to seats midway in on the left—for no other reason than that's where we happened to sit day one freshman year, so now that's where we always camp—and slouch back for the presentation. Whatever's coming is bound to be tedious—better be comfortable. "I think I'm going to have to pee," Caitlyn leans over to whisper. "I downed a venti latte after I got the car jumped."

"Caitlyn, it's not a high-powered job on Wall Street, it's AP Bio. Why do you need three shots of espresso?"

"It's good for my metabolism."

I roll my eyes. "I will beat you."

"What? I gave up Parliaments and aspartame, let me have the beans—" She cuts off at the sight of Nico Sargossi, Melanie Dubviek, and Trisha Wright coming down the aisle behind us for the First Day Back Big Christmas Loot Reveal—Nico probably has a new Maserati from Santa/Daddy's dealership parked outside. And Melanie and Trisha are both sporting the same fur vest Victoria Beckham wore to the People's Choice Awards.

"Do you have any idea how many shifts at Bambette I'd have to work to afford that?" Caitlyn whispers into my shoulder.

"Maybe the Hampton branch of PETA'll hit 'em with spray cans at lunch. I'll put in a call."

The Three Graces take their seats across the aisle from us next to Jase McCaffrey, still flushed from morning basketball practice, his black hair damp to his forehead. Nico reaches across Trisha to squeeze her boyfriend's hand. At least I think it was his hand. Can't see from here.

"Think they applied to the same colleges?" Caitlyn asks, referring to Hampton High's own Brangelina.

"They only overlap at six out of nine."

"It's sick that you know that."

"You didn't get the flier?" I surreptitiously fold a piece of gum into my mouth.

Also wet-haired from a post-practice shower, Rick Sachs slides into his permanently saved seat on the other side of Jase.

"What if they get to college," Caitlyn asks as Trisha leans forward to talk to Melanie, leaving Nico to kiss Jase over her rounded back, "and there are other couples there that are at least as hot—maybe hotter—and have been together *twice* as long?"

"Since the womb?"

"Ladies, gentlemen." Our principal walks onstage in front of the slushie-blue velvet curtain, his orthopedic dress shoes squeaking against the polyurethaned wood. "Thank you for joining us this morning." Why is it they always thank us for the mandatory things? "We have a very exciting guest—"

"The president of the New York chapter of *Ornithology*

Today!" Caitlyn whispers with hushed mania.

"Not just to me," he continues into the microphone, his new mustache giving him a certain Dr. Phil *je ne sais quoi*, "but, I suspect, exciting to you as well."

Caitlyn shrugs. It was a good guess.

"Seniors of Long Island's Hampton High School, please give a warm welcome to Fletch Chapman, president of programming for . . . XTV."

There is an audible ripple of "Wha?" as we turn to one another in disbelief. Not *our* XTV? This must be some obscure cable channel devoted to xylophones or X rays.

Looking not that much older than us, Fletch ambles onto the stage in Rock & Republic jeans, a black dress shirt rolled up to the elbows, and Prada sneakers. Okay, this might be our XTV. He takes the mike from Principal Stevens and swings it into his left hand Vegas-style. "Hey, guys." He pauses to flash a big Whitestrips smile. "You're probably wondering what I'm doing here and why I've dragged you away from your calculus and history." We are. Yes. "How many of you watch the show *Park Avenue Confidential* on the CW?" he asks with a swaggering self-assurance that must play well with the ladies.

Almost every hand shoots up, including mine, sacrificing any potential embarrassment from watching the prep-school soap opera for the sake of dialoguing with Fletch. "Excellent, excellent," he says, pacing back and forth in his snazzy sneakers. "So, you get our inspirational jumping-off point. It's a great show, but it suffers from one thing—" He pauses as we wonder, Over-styled hair?

That creepy young dude who's supposed to be the dad? "*Writers.*" Fletch drives the word into the microphone. "It's not real teens talking about real issues; it's a bunch of old farts sitting in a room concocting what they want to reflect back to you as your lives. So at XTV we thought what'd be majorly cool is to create a reality series around the lives of *real* New York high school seniors dealing with the *real* world and *real* issues. And what's more glamorous and fabulous than the Hamptons?"

Oh yeah, you should see me serve Lipton tea to a snowplow driver. Or my mom clean Christie Brinkley's bathroom drain.

I turn to ask Caitlyn with my facial muscles if she, too, finds life in the Hamptons to be a nonstop parade of glamour, but instead I see her nearly levitating with excitement, the corners of her hazel eyes watering.

"I can't tell you any more right now about what we're calling *The Real Hampton Beach* because that's as much as we know. *You* will shape the content of the show. Any questions?"

Sylvia Vandalucci shoots her hand up. "Who'll be in it?"

"All of you." All heads whip left and right as we turn to face what were, just moments ago, merely our fellow classmates and are now our fellow *cast mates.* "That want to be," he hastens to add. "Anyone who doesn't want to sign a release will be given a marker to wear so the cameras will know to keep you out of frame."

"*Out of frame?*" Caitlyn hisses in horror.

"And now we'd love it if you all could come up to the

stage six at a time—" As he speaks, the curtains pull halt-ingly back to reveal six desks manned by equally young staffers in XTV baseball caps. "And take a seat to answer a few questions. After that, we'll be observing you guys for a few days with our cameras as we narrow down who we're going to focus on, essentially who'll be our core cast." At the word *cast*, Principal Stevens's straining smile fades for the first time. "I have to head back to the city," Fletch con-tinues, "but you'll see me again—this is my baby. In the meantime, I leave you in my associate producer, Kara's, capable hands." A pretty, apple-shaped brunette doing herself no favors in thick Elvis Costello glasses shuffles in from the wings, wearing a loose Himalayan blouse over jeans. "She'll be my eyes and ears." Kara gives an awkward wave. "I am super-psyched. And looking out, I can tell we've picked an awesome school," Fletch concludes.

Caitlyn and I swing around to face each other. "Did he just *wink* at Nico?!" she asks, mouth open.

"Or he has an astigmatism."

"In his *pants*."

"All right, students!" Stevens claps his hands. "You heard Mr. Chapman. This is a very exciting opportunity, so let's show XTV what an orderly student body Hamp-ton High has! Let's start with the front row on the right. The first six, let's go! Fill in at the desks! The rest of you can consider this a study hall period. And let's remember, study halls are *silent*."

"Aah," I whisper, tugging out my AP Physics. "This is where it gets boring."

Caitlyn, however, whipping out her contraband nail polish to do emergency touchups, is riveted by the proceedings. I get a Maybelline pen to the ribs when Courtney Metler wriggles her ginormous bra out from under her shirt and lets the girls get some air. And again, twenty minutes later, when she bounds up to the stage and they nearly hit her in the face. Until XTV is presented in 3-D she's probably a no-go. And then again when Gary Sternberg attempts a backflip to his assigned table and Shana Masterson bursts into her glass-shattering version of Mariah Carey.

Caitlyn slumps farther and farther into her chair, finally sliding full to the floor when Tom Slatford starts playing fart music with his hands. "Is it too late to transfer?" she moans.

I slip my hand under her armpit and drag her back up. "Isn't it cruel and inhumane to put us through this when it's so obviously going to be *Nico, the Show*?" I ask.

"Starring Melanie, as Nico."

"And Trisha, as Nico."

"Come on," she says, straightening her gray sweater dress, her look of determination returning. "Maybe they're looking for two minimum-wage-working brunettes who love Pinkberry and think Chace Crawford is just a little bit too pretty. We *have* a shot."

I don't disabuse her of that notion.

At that moment, with a good-luck kiss to Jase, Nico gathers up all her fabulously understated possessions and struts her radiant, lanky everything up to the stage. She's like some wild, exotic animal that roams the hallways:

You might not want to pet her, but you can't pull your eyes away. Her hair is always shiny, her face matte, and her subtle veneer of disdain firmly in place. To be around her is to wonder if she's thinking your sweater gives her a migraine, your Spanish pronunciation grates on her ears, or your highlights are so '07. Tossing her long blond mane, she straddles the interrogation chair like she's about to do a number from *Chicago*. Anyone else and I'd snicker, but when Nico Sargossi does it you actually wish she was about to perform a number from *Chicago*.

Mrs. Gesop snaps at us, and Caitlyn hustles up the steps with me in tow, bras in place, hands in our pockets. I swing my bag to my feet and sit down across from Kara, who's removed her baseball cap and knotted her glossy brown hair above her head with a pencil.

"Name?"

"Jessica O'Rourke. But everyone calls me Jesse, no 'i.'"

"Eighteen?"

"Since November third."

"Social security number?"

I reel it off, trying to catch Caitlyn's eye to see if she might also be having her identity stolen.

Kara sits back, putting a breath of space between the table and her impressive superstructure, which seems to be tamped down in a sports bra. "Okay, Jesse, no 'i,' tell me a little about yourself, your family, activities, who are your best friends?"

"Um, Caitlyn Duggan. She's sitting right there." I point to her, sitting two interview desks over.

"How long have you been friends?"

"When we were little we lived across the street from each other, so our moms traded off child care. You know, each working part-time."

"So your mom works. Anything . . . "

"Glamorous? No."

"Okay." She scrunches up her little ski-jump nose and chews on the end of her pen while I wonder if Caitlyn is re-casting the rusted crapbox as a vintage sports car. "And school?"

"I, uh, like school just fine. I mean, we're all on the home stretch to parole, right? We probably liked it more four years ago."

"Who do you hate?"

"Large corporations?"

"In school." She suppresses a smile.

"Oh." I think for a moment, and she taps her chewed pen impatiently. "No one, really. . . . I mean, you know, trapped with the same people since first grade, some are bound to get on your nerves, but am I, like, feuding with anyone? No, I cannot afford to feud."

"What do you mean afford?" She writes *afford* on her notepad, and I notice the tenacious remnants of brown polish at the base of her nails.

"I work after school at the Prickly Pear, I help my mom at her job on weekends, I keep my grades up so I can get a scholarship—I'll be the first in my family to go to college. I don't have the time not to get along with people."

"Or date?"

"I date," I say defensively. "I mean, not *at this exact second*. Last year. Dan. We broke up."

"Which one's Dan?" she asks, dropping her glasses down her nose to survey the seated masses, her green eyes twinkly when unshielded.

I point over the rows to where Dan sits with his lacrosse teammates, blowing his nose. Probably has another sinus infection. Poor Dan.

"Oh. Okay." She scribbles more notes on the yellow paper. I try again to get Caitlyn's attention, but she's engrossed in her interview, flipping her freshly released hair from shoulder to shoulder.

Knuckles rap on our desk, and I swing my head back to see Fletch Chapman standing over us, a whiff of some spicy fragrance hitting my nose. "I've gotta jet," he says more to his BlackBerry than to Kara. "Everything under control?"

"I think so." Kara nods nervously.

"No 'think.' You want an office on the nineteenth floor? You want us to produce your doc? It's riding on this, babe." He squeezes her shoulder and, with a tongue click and gun fingers at me, he hops off the stage.

"No worries, Fletch!" she calls after him. "It's covered!" She takes a second before she turns back to me.

"Wow. He seems intense." I smile.

"What? Oh. Yes, well, he's just compensating—" She halts, her mouth dropping open. "I did not say compensating. I just meant that he's a crazy prodigy—finished college at eighteen, MBA by twenty—running the network at twenty-four. He's put all his energy here, into this, so . . . I'm really lucky to be working for him. You know, you have a great profile."

"Thanks." I glance down at the stats she's compiled on her pad.

"No, your nose. The side view. Very telegenic."

"Can you tell that to Georgetown?" I ask, trying to absorb this new piece of information about myself. She laughs in a way that suggests she didn't expect to be laughing today. Over her shoulder, I watch as Nico swipes up her interviewer's pen and twirls it gracefully between her long fingers. "Sorry, are we done?" I say, because sitting here, expected to talk myself up not six feet from *that*, feels like a useless exercise.

"Sure. Thanks for sharing, and here's a baseball cap for your time."

I take it, imagining a hundred-plus of them flying in the air at graduation.

We don't hear the first oak tree fall in the adjacent field until lunch. Word ripples fast over the flattened manicotti in the steamy cafeteria. "*Somebody* has donated an Olympic-sized pool to Hampton High," Caitlyn says as she whips upright on our bench from the reconnaissance that extended her to the similarly stretched Jennifer Lanford at the next table.

"Hm," I say, taking this in as I twist off the cap on my Snapple with a dull pop. "Wonder if that *somebody*'s going to tile a mosaic X on the bottom."

"Or hand out our diplomas in his Prada sneakers."

TWO

Stomping my boots on the salted pavement outside the kitchen door at Cooper's, the only two-star Michelin restaurant on the island, I wave good-bye as Caitlyn inches to the exit of the inadequately plowed parking lot. She wriggles her fingers out the cracked window, rocking her shoulders to the beat thumping through the sagging Camry.

I pull open the wood screen and step out of the storm into the bright buzz of the kitchen, greeted by a familiar wave of sizzling garlic.

"Jesssss-ee!" Lester yells over the music as he tempers a stovetop of sauté pans, simultaneously nodding approval to sous-chefs garnishing plates en route to the floor. "Your dad's out front."

"Hey, Lester," I say as he runs a napkin around a plate's

rim, erasing stray drips marring the presentation. "Hey, guys." I give a little wave to the rest of the staff before tugging down my coat zipper. "Wow, it's crazy in here for a Monday." I dump my bag straining with books onto a nearby stack of crates—"*Heads up, Jess!*"—ducking as a laden tray glides over me.

"Sorry!" I say to Angela's retreating back as she passes through the double doors to the dining room.

"The owner's here with the wife's family," Lester reports as he lowers the flame on the *au poivre* sauce. "How's school?"

"Oh. My. God. XTV's doing a show of our class." I shrug off my coat and tuck it over my bag.

"They gonna make you eat intestines?"

"That's called Sloppy Joe Day."

Suddenly I'm grabbed from behind and swung into a salsa by Manny. "Jessica, when you gonna marry me?" He steps me to the front of the kitchen, his sweaty hand working south on my jeans.

"Ah-ha-ha!" I laugh like an idiot because I'm only at Level Three Spanish and I still don't know the polite word for yuck. A busboy hands Manny a dish-filled bucket and I dart away, parking myself in a nook by the walk-in fridge to wait for Dad.

I'm watching Lester carve a duck when the radio suddenly flicks off. The double doors beside me swing open, the orderly chaos morphing into a taut machine as Dad steps in followed by his boss, Cooper, and some old man

I don't recognize, bristling down to the hairs of his cashmere trousers. Cooper addresses the man. "Again, I am *so sorry*. As you've pointed out, this is *my* restaurant and I hold myself *personally* responsible for the lack of lobster. Mike?" he spits at Dad, his eyes conveying that he's pissed. For a nanosecond I debate slipping into the walk-in but opt for flattening myself against the stainless steel instead.

In full triage mode, Dad buttons his blazer and turns from his irate boss to face the kitchen staff. "Lester?" he says pleasantly.

"Yeah, Mike?" Lester whips the bandanna from his back pocket and dabs at his glistening forehead.

"Think you could show Cooper's father-in-law, Swifton, here, how you prepare the *foie gras tatin*? Mario Batali's been after Lester's recipe for years."

"Sure thing, Mike. Right this way, sir." The waitstaff clears an aisle.

His father-in-law safely on the other side of the kitchen, Cooper bears down on Dad. "You like watching me get humiliated, Mike?"

Dad sees me and I see the "yes" straining through his blank expression. He slips his finger under his blue tie and slides it down the fabric. "Cooper, of course not."

"Then what the hell?"

"None of my fish guys could go out with the storm. Lester prepared a number of delicious alternatives as well as a traditional Caesar with fresh—"

"Don't tell me how to do what I do." Cooper's face

condenses, his year-round tan making him look like dried fruit. "I wanted to serve him a Caesar like the one we had in Paris. End of story."

"I'm sorry."

"A gourmet Caesar should have lobster. But I don't know why I'd expect *you* to know that," Cooper mutters dismissively, his grin reappearing as he collects Swifton and passes back out into the dining room.

Dad gazes down at the plastic grid of floor tiles, his eyebrows lifting and lowering before he turns to the frozen staff. "Okay, guys! Cooper's blown his steam. Let's keep the evening moving." Like someone took their finger off pause, the frenzy resumes. Dad rubs the back of his neck and walks over to me. "Hey, kiddo, how was your first day back?"

"Totally weird, we had this assembly and—"

"Crazy night."

"Yeah . . . " My story drains as I see him still nodding to himself.

He puts a hand on my shoulder. "Come, I've got lasagna for you."

"Well, if it doesn't have lobster, forget it," I mug as he hands off the bag packed with dinner for Mom and me.

He lets out a little laugh, glancing through the porthole windows of the double doors to where the Hadleys are cooing delightedly over their first bites of Lester's foie gras.

"Crisis three thousand seventy-two resolved." Dad

sighs. I throw on my coat, pull my bag onto my shoulder, and he holds open the screen door, breathing in the crisp winter air. "Homework status?"

"Halfway there."

"Finish it." His mustache brushes my cheek as he pulls me in for a hug. "So you can be the one dishing the bull—"

"Not taking it." I salute him and step out into a blur of fat flakes.

He smiles into the pool of light from the flood lamp, the white clumps wetting his face, which, for a moment, is really relaxed—not the show of relaxed he offers as a buffer between Cooper and the staff he manages for him. "What were you saying about an assembly?"

"They're making a show about my class. *XTV is making a show.*"

"You're kidding."

"I'm not!" I jump up to him, the excitement to share returning. "They wanted a setting that is, quote, *glamorous.*"

He laughs satisfyingly.

"Thought you'd appreciate that. See ya at breakfast!" I slide the plastic bag containing our dinner to my elbow, fumbling for my iPod as I cut down the alley.

Wedging in my earbuds, I come to a stop at a hip-high mound barring me from the snow-blown Main Street sidewalk. I hoist one leg to straddle the snowbank and swing myself over, the momentum nearly tossing me headlong into the opposite towering plow bank lining the street. "Glam-o-rama." I heave my bag back up my arm, hug the dinner like a heating pad, and shuffle onward in the street-lamp-lit night. Following a row of windows optimistically displaying resort wear, the Corner Gallery, with its canvases of sun-bleached dunes, marks the abrupt conclusion of "town."

I pause where the blinking traffic light spins in the wind like a piñata and run my thumb down the silver disk, scrolling for a tune that'll conjure a heated car of my own. Es . . . Fs—so over every song.

High beams suddenly flood my view, and I squint up at Jase McCaffrey's matte-black Hummer swerving past. Matte, to match the set of gold teeth and Hotlanta McMansion *in his head.* A glowing cigarette flicks out the passenger window, and I catch a flash of long blond hair as a nervous laugh twitters over the revving tires. Unimpressed. By the tires, the hair, the vehicle burning enough gas to light a midsized country for a year. Looking back down, I see I've paused at Gwen Stefani. I press the arrow and "Hollaback Girl" thumps into my ears. Once the taillights have faded, I bump-sway into the snow tunnel abutting the darkened residential street. If I kept going straight, and broke through the southern tip of the Wordsworths' orchid house, I'd be standing in the Atlantic in under a mile, which couldn't be colder than what I'm walking through now. Sheets draped and shades drawn, every one of the estates hidden behind the fifteen-foot hedges lining this "lane" have been sealed tight for the winter.

As the wind dies down and the snow turns to something more *Nutcracker*-ish and less assaulting, I roll up the volume and allow myself to fully bring it. Driveway lights on their nightly timers glow through the drifts, illuminating the intercoms beside each gate. I nod to them like the Harajuku Girls as I toss off a chorus of "B-A-N-A-N-A-S!"

I'm just adding the hip pops when I swing my head into a green windbreaker. "Aah!" I scream. An arm reaches out to steady me. I dart my eyes to the grip on my wrist as it's released, and then up at the sweat-streaked, red-cheeked face of Drew. "Oh my God, you scared the crap out of me," I say as I jerk my head back to toss off my hood, cursing the bag strap and zippered coat prohibiting a similarly casual move from releasing my trapped ponytail. If I was in charge, winter down would come with boy-sensing hair ejector.

"You mean interrupted you." He smiles his half-smile, the one that's been off the market for the last year. As he drops his ski-gloved hands to his knees, I realize he's winded. Right before I realize that my floor show of the last block has been witnessed. By single Drew. And his half-smile.

"Oh, that? That's for Spanish. We're doing skits, and I was just going over my lines as a—"

"Stefani?"

"What? No." My cheeks toast further. "Drug addict." What? Where did I come up with—? Well, the head jerking . . .

"Wow, in French we're only up to ordering wine. *Une bouteille du vin.*"

"Mrs. Gonzalez wants us to be prepared for everything."

He laughs, and the nearby snowbanked driveway lights seemingly flicker brighter.

"Aren't you freezing?" I ask as I point down at the basketball shorts clinging above his bare shins. Boys make no sense.

"No . . . boiling actually." He swipes his bulky gloved hand across his forehead, streaking damp chestnut bangs to the side.

"Must be the gloves."

"I was running. On the beach. Clears my head. And I didn't get much of a practice in this morning." He knows that I know he was dumped. And puffy-eyed. That everyone knows. He bites the inside of his bottom lip.

"Bringing my mom dinner." Changing the subject, I hold out the bag as if he asked. "Last house on the left before the water." Just as he's giving me an *Oh, really?* look, I add, "She cleans it. Most of them actually." I tilt my head to each side of the street.

"Surrounded by all that glamour?" He smiles. A full one. "How can she stand it?"

"That was pretty crazy today, huh?"

"Yeah. The guy interviewing me wanted to know all about my dad's *glamorous* landscaping job. If you're standing in fertilizer, cutting back poison ivy, even in Gwyneth

20

Paltrow's garden, you're still just itchy as hell and knee-deep in shit. And that's in the summer. In winter, he's camped in his Barcalounger with the heat down."

I laugh. "It's so insane to think of them filming at our school, isn't it?"

"Do you think we'll all be in the background?" he asks. "With Jase's flexing bicep front and center?"

"My mom was standing behind Courteney Cox in the 'Dancing in the Dark' video—you can see her for, like, a split second. I'm guessing this'll be like that—an anecdote we can bore people with into our forties."

"Cool." His eyes warm; he nods.

"Yup." I nod back, struck that he is, like, two inches taller than when I took trig with him last year, seated behind him, four rows back, two seats to the left, to be precise. We stop nodding and for a moment stand totally still, flakes of snow falling in the inches between us. His eyes are so brown, and he stares down into me, his brows knitting together and, through the cloud of attraction, I feel a pang of sympathy. "I'm really sorry about the breakup—"

"One of us has to back up—" he says over me.

"Right." I look down, realizing there's no way around each other in the narrowly cleared path. "I'll just—"

"No, I will." He steps backward, and I follow him as his sneakers crunch in the silence. "Don't let me fall." Half-grin. *Don't let me.* And then we're in the plowed driveway, still standing as close as we were in the foot-wide path.

"Too bad your coat isn't red," he says, the cloud of his breath warm against my face.

"Yeah." To do: Get red coat.

"Like you're going to Grandmother's house."

"I totally got that," I lie. "That makes you the wolf," I recover.

"No way, I'm the woodsman who saves the day."

My turn to smile. "Well . . . "

"Back to your Spanish methadone clinic?"

"Look, you never know when you'll need to do a needle exchange at the Barcelona train station."

He laughs and for a moment I imagine the lights watt up so brightly a bulb could pop. I should leave first—on this high note of cute—wipe out the memory of me dancing. Leave! Leave first!! "Well, later." I turn and walk reluctantly away.

"Hey, Jesse?"

I whip around, the width of the driveway between us. "Yeah?"

"Thanks for . . . " He trails off.

For . . . my freak snow show? My down coat sexiness? My faint aroma of warm garlic? "Sure." I shrug, realizing from the flicker of sadness across his face that he's referring to my attempted sympathy.

He tosses up his sweatshirt hood and jogs off, disappearing into the white.

THREE

Mom, Hampton High basketball star circa 1985, tosses the emptied Evian bottle over three rows of seating, and it rims the copper can under the Richardsons' screening room wet bar before falling inside. I cup my hands to my mouth to do a fan roar.

"What does it mean, Jess?" She looks up from her club chair as she finishes the remains of the lasagna on her lap tray.

"Mom, you're *always* asking that." I drain the last of my milk.

"Well, you're saying XTV is coming to your school to make a show, and I want to know what it means."

"I don't know! A new pool for the school and let's see,

um, nothing for me. I'm not *that*." I point up at the glossy bachelorettes on the wall-sized screen anxiously awaiting their rose. "What does *that* mean?"

"That's not having clear goals and good values." She lowers her tray to the floor and stretches her back as she stands. "That's hitching your wagon to a millionaire who'll leave you for the next model." She fiddles with the remote until a green velvet curtain swings across the screen. "No." She presses another combination of buttons, and a matching curtain behind us opens to a wall of frosted windows lining the covered pool. "No again." A different button and the lights come back on. "Thank you. Now, you, please." She aims the book-sized device at the screen and the show clicks to black.

"Think somewhere in West Palm Beach Mrs. Richardson's boobs were getting bigger and smaller?"

"Her brain, more likely." She fluffs up her matching green velvet couch cushions and I do the same with mine, returning the room to its prior immaculate state. Mom pulls her checklist from her apron pocket, and I bend to pile my completed homework into my bag. "Do you want to use the bathroom before I do a final faucet polish?"

"I'm good." I pull on my UGGs.

"Great, you take out the garbage and start the car, and I'll polish while it warms up. Meet you out front in fifteen?"

"With a rose?" I bat my eyelashes, and her tired face breaks into a laugh.

"Zipper up out there." She gathers the aluminum containers and hands me the shiny black bag. "And grab my rim shot?"

I pull out the Evian bottle. "Check." I dump it into the bag. "We were never here."

Mom sighs. "Your homework's done, right?"

"*Yes.*" I pull on my coat and feel through the green velvet folds to the lock on the glass door. Gripping the bag of take-out containers in one hand and my coat closed with the other, I climb through the white drifts toward the Richardsons' garage. The sky has cleared enough for the moon to peek through, allowing me to use the burlap-wrapped topiaries as guideposts to the edge of the property. With the wind no longer blowing, I hear the ever-present distant waves and then something else. Yelling. A man's voice. I round the corner of the cedar-shingled garage and see the growing bone structure of the new mansion on the lot abutting the Richardsons'. The garage's lantern lights spill through a demarcation line of a low hedge onto a Sheetrocked guesthouse all of ten feet away.

"I don't give a crap where you take 'em, take 'em to a goddamn hotel, but to mess with my business—"

"Dad—" another voice pleads.

"So now I gotta go down to the police station and explain that my construction site is secure—thanks for the call—just my shit-for-brains son screwing some slut on a sleeping bag like a homeless bum—"

"I'm sorry—"

I hear the hollow thud of a punch and then a tight growl. "No, what you are is pathetic." A tarp-covered doorway flips open, and I crouch just as Mr. McCaffrey struts out in his Giants leather jacket and disappears around the building.

I quickly stand and raise the lid of the pine bin, using my head to prop it as I drop the bag into the can, wanting to get out of there as fast as possible. But I jerk up when I hear the tarp lift back again, and the lid slams shut. Before I can move, Jase steps out, raking a hand across his wet eyes as they land on mine. A shot of surprise and then his expression hardens, a drop of red trickling toward his chin from his split lip.

"He's not going to tell my mom about this, is he?" a voice calls uncertainly. We both turn to where, teetering in high-heeled boots, the wrong blonde rounds the outside corner of the guesthouse.

"Get in the car, Trisha." He flings his pointer finger toward the Hummer and, with a last look at me, follows her to it.

I stand there for a second watching them go before turning to trudge back to the house, thanking God I'm not in their orbit.

PART II
THE REELS

REEL 1

The next morning, I slide into my seat in calc, half a cold Pop-Tart tucked in my hand. The only two things that make this class tolerable are the knowledge that the time remaining in my life that I'll have to waste in math is now measurable in a countable clump of hours—and illicit blueberry streusel. Streusel that almost goes down the wrong way when Mrs. Feinberg comes in trailed by a cameraman inches from her face.

"Good morning, class." She is as red as the robin knit into her sweater. "I've been instructed to teach as normally as possible, so let's just try to pretend our friend here is invisible and learn a little calculus, shall we?" She turns to the board to write out the equations we were working on yesterday and then pivots to address us, knocking into the camera. "Sir! A little breathing room, please!" But she doesn't get any. Nor is anyone able to pretend he isn't there. Everyone, sporting four-step eyes or unusually clean clothes, depending on gender, speaks theatrically, which is impressive when they're saying things like, "X equals . . . *seven*." Every equation comes out sounding like a declaration of war or a deep betrayal.

The rest of the morning goes much the same. The bright lights atop the cameras crisscross one another in the winter-dark stairwells and hallways like searchlights on the ocean surface looking for survivors. I'm counting the seconds until AP Euro, the only class Caitlyn and I share. She drops her good bag at my feet, the Century 21 Botkier we found on last year's So-Dan's-Not-The-One post-breakup road trip to the city.

"Not you, too." My gaze pans up the bare-legged goose bumps, past her favorite tank top, to rest at the false eyelashes.

"What? I want my grandchildren to see me as a loser with out-of-date jeans and underconditioned hair?" She sits down and opens her notebook.

"Our grandchildren will not be able to get past the fact that we are breathing unfiltered air. Our follicles will be of no interest."

Caitlyn leans in, unsticking the ends of her curls from her lip gloss. "They filmed Melanie Dubviek, like, an inch from her face—"

"Yes, I'm familiar with their techniques."

"—for all of English. *Why?*"

I push up the sleeves of my henley. "Uh, Melanie is very compelling when she thinks?"

Clearing his throat, Mr. Cantone stands from his desk with our papers on the Corn Laws. "I want to start out by saying I'm not impressed."

Lunch is my first opportunity to witness the stars of our class adjusting to their expanded stage. Caitlyn and I wait for a clean tray as the cameras follow the swarm of merging students. Nico walks in first in her skinny cords and wrap sweater, looking exactly like she does every day. So that makes two of us. For opposite reasons. I know there's no way I'll get cast, and she knows there's no way she won't.

As she does every day at this time, Nico twists her amazing golden mane up in a topknot and secures it with one of her many decorative chopsticks. She collects them. It's on her MySpace page. What's not on her page is that the reason she twists her hair up at lunch is that she's a surprisingly messy eater. Taco Day is a good time. Of course, she still looks gorgeous with ground meat all over her face—she has that Cameron Diaz unembarrassable thing going. Which at this moment seems to have spread over to her friends. Which is unfortunate. Because they should be feeling embarrassed. A lot.

Melanie walks in first, looking like a Real Housewife. She is in some middle-aged leopard-print puffed-sleeve something. And it is wrong. Wrong, wrong, wrong. But better than what walks in behind her.

"Are we doing *Rock of Love, the Musical* this year?" Caitlyn asks, tilting her head to the side and squinting to take in the almost-naked platform-shoed glory that is Trisha cutting in at the front of the lunch line. "Oh, baby. Where was Momma this morning?"

"She probably dressed her in it."

"You mean licked it and stuck it to her like a stamp."

We open our tuna-salad-filled pita pockets and start the painstaking process of potato chip integration, to get the tuna and chips to live as one inside our pita world. I am engrossed in fitting as many little chip pieces as possible in the sandwich when I hear the crash, then the sudden silence, and feel Caitlyn grab my arm. "Oh. My. God."

I whip my head up as all eyes (and cameras) converge on two spindly U.V.-tanned legs perpendicular to the floor, one remaining platform shoe dangling precariously off a toe. Suddenly it slips and falls. "AAAAAHHHH!" An agonized scream goes up from the floor, and Nico and Melanie rush from their bench to help Trisha up. Nico gets there first since she's in motion-favorable ballet flats. But Melanie can only shuffle over as fast as her leopard-print mules will allow.

I stand from our bench, now able to see that Trisha is covered in the mayonnaise-based contents of her lunch tray, and blood is gushing out her nose from the assault-ing shoe. The lunch lady rushes forward, but Nico staves her off. "We've got it. Come on, Trish. Little steps." She picks Trisha's shoes off the linoleum before wrapping a protective arm around her to escort her out of the riveted tuna-breathed hordes and tracking cameras.

"Oh. My. God," Caitlyn repeats. "She can never come back here. It's over. After the world's biggest wipeout, she just conked herself with her own platform heel. It was like a public service announcement against high fashion."

"Is that what she was wearing?"

When I push open the girls' room door a few minutes later to wash the fishy aroma off my fingers, I'm met with audible sobbing. I almost back out, but if I try to make it to the one on the second floor I'll be late for next period. As if they'd even notice me in the midst of a PR crisis of this magnitude. I dart to the sink.

Trisha is sitting on the tiled windowsill at the end of the stalls, her head tilted back as Nico swaps the bloodied paper towel for a fresh one, unwittingly tending to the person who was in a sleeping bag with her boyfriend not twelve hours ago. "Mel went to grab you a clean T-shirt from my gym locker. And some sneakers. As soon as she gets back we're gonna take you to the nurse."

"I think i-it's buh-roken," Trisha chokes out in sobs. "I'm s-so em-barrassed. I w-want to k-kill myself. I'll never," she pauses, trying to catch her breath, "make the sh-show now."

"Shhhh." In the mirror over the sink I see Trisha allowing her bare back to be rubbed reassuringly. "Of course we're in the show," Nico says with quiet certainty. "Who else would they pick? We are the glamour. We are *it*."

She coaxes an entitled smile out of Trisha, and I wipe my wet hands across my jeans and jog to Spanish.

REEL 2

The brown pumpkin glop *sliiiiides* off the ice-cream scoop to puddle in the muffin tin as another minute at the Prickly Pear *craaawwwwwls* by. I'll have been scooping from this tub for twenty-four months this June, and the bottom is still nowhere in sight. If only the bejeweled fools paying five bucks a muffin knew this crap was older than the bills they were handing over. God knows it's ruined me. No matter how cute the case or how yummy the aroma, I can't lay eyes on a baked good without flashing to the industrial tubs congealing in the Prickly Pear's freezer.

My job's only perk—to make up for my lost pastry ardor—is the occasional glimpse of Drew corralling emptied shopping carts in the Stop & Shop parking lot across the street. Which helps. A lot.

"Uh . . . Jesse?"

"Yeah?" I push up the rim of my mesh Prickly Pear baseball cap to see Jamie Beth slouching on the bottom basement stair, staring in her vacant, bloodshot Jamie Beth way. "Yes, Jamie Beth?"

"There's, like, a chick up there who wants to know where you are."

I drop the scoop in a bowl of warm water and pick up the huge tray, the muffin glop tilting in each container. "A chick?"

"Yeahhhhhh." She dips her head in a slow nod.

"Okay, well, can you tell her I'll be up in a sec?"

"She wants to see you doing what you"—she stretches her tongue out through her bubble gum—"do naturally."

I hand her the tray, and her eyes widen in surprise as they always do when she finds herself working here at work. "Put these in the oven for me, and don't forget to turn the timer on again, okay?" I wipe my hands on my green apron and jog up the stairs into the little bakery where the Starbucks *Coffee Tunes* CD and dangling baskets competently mask the gross kitchen of frozen crap downstairs. I walk around to the cash register, clearing the stocked display cases, to see a brunette with both elbows on the counter, her head dropped as she rubs her temples.

"Can I help you?"

The woman who interviewed me yesterday looks up, smiling, in the same jeans, same style of loose white blouse, its sleeves exposed beneath a green down vest. "Jesse O'Rourke, right? No 'i.' "

"Yes."

"You look different in that hat. I'm Kara." She sticks out her hand and I shake it.

"Yes, I remember. Sorry, I'm a little sticky. I've been spooning muffins." She raises an eyebrow. "Baking—not sleeping next to them. Sorry, you asked for me?"

"Yes! We want to film a little of the after-school stuff, but just wanted to make sure you were here."

"Yeah, Jamie Beth is a little on the slow-delivery side. She's ten years older than me, so you'd think—"

"I'll take a double espresso, Jesse, actually, that'd be great."

"Sure!" I turn to pull a paper cup from the stack, and when I go to place it under the machine I realize there's a camera about two inches from my face.

"Jesse?"

"Yes?" I follow the voice, leaning around the guy holding the camera, straining to see past a second guy filming the hanging baskets.

"Oh, don't look at me!" Kara waves her hands.

"Sorry!" I whip back to the filling cup.

"Yeah, just try to pretend I'm not here, okay?"

"Sure. Sorry I didn't—"

"And you can't talk to me, either. I'm not here. I don't

36

exist. Sam—the one filming you—and Ben aren't here, either."

I nod and then realize I'm not supposed to nod to people who aren't here, so I do the first thing I can think of, which is pretend that this wretched Norah Jones song that haunts my dreams is undeniably dance inspiring.

"Great, you're a natural, Jesse. Can you just take off the hat?" I shake my head from side to side in time with the music. "The dancing's great, Jesse. Just let's lose the hat."

I grab a napkin and a pen and scribble, *On probation for taking off hat. Owner drive-by spot checks.* I slide the paper onto the counter and tap it with the pen in time with the beat, which is ve-ry slow. I step to the side and see out of the corner of my eye Kara grab the napkin.

"Okay, all right. So . . . just, can you turn it around and pull your hair down around your face?" I do. And then I stand there like a loser. "And my coffee would be great."

I pivot to the cup as the second espresso shot comes pouring out of the machine. I slap on a lid and walk it over to where I left the napkin, wondering what this'll look like on camera. Like I am writing notes and making coffee for my imaginary friend. And that Norah Jones sets me free.

I hear a big slurp. "Ugh, I needed that. Okay, Jesse, so just do whatever you would normally do."

I open the cabinet under the register and take out the gallon of Smucker's, sliding it onto the counter. I squeeze myself past the garbage can and over to the four tables to collect the fake crystal jam jars that were emptied in the morning rush. I carry them back behind the counter. I scrape out the dregs of congealed jelly into the sink. I wash them out. I dry them out. I open the vat. I spoon in new jelly one glob at a time. I rinse off the spoon. I dry it. I put the vat under the counter. I take out the tub of butter—

"For the love of Christ," Sam groans, rubbing his mustache. "It's more tedious than my grad school ant farm doc."

Kara sighs. "Turn 'em off." Ben taps a cigarette from the pack in his quilted flannel's breast pocket and slips it behind his ear.

"Sorry, this is what I do." I bite my lip and look over at her. "It's really slow in the afternoon, so it's mostly getting the place ready for the morning—"

The front doorbells jingle, and we all look over to see Drew pulling off his ski hat as he steps in from the dark street. I am suddenly redder than the Smucker's.

"Go, go, go!" Kara barks excitedly, and two cameras whip up. Startled, Drew steps backward into a hanging basket. Sam squeezes past the garbage can to train his lens on Drew as Kara jumps up on a chair to clear the way. Drew looks up at Kara and opens his mouth.

"Don't!" she and I say at the same time. "We're not supposed to look at her or talk to her," I add.

"Just act natural. Do what you were going to do," Kara whispers.

This seems to kick Drew back into gear. He walks to the register, Ben and his camera trailing after his snow-damp sneakers. "Hey . . . "

"Hi," I say as Kara exaggeratedly swirls her arms from atop her chair. "*Drew.* Hi, Drew."

"Hi, Jesse." He's paralyzed.

"I bet you wanted something to eat."

"Yes." His eyes thank me. "Yeah, I'm here for some, um . . . "

"Hot chocolate?"

"Sure!"

"Riveting," Ben mutters.

"Enough," Kara snipes.

I turn and mechanically pour the Swiss Miss into a paper cup before filling it with steaming water. "Whipped cream?"

"Sure. I mean, yes, thanks."

I spray a circle of foam and then hand it to him. He takes it and we stare at each other, sweating. "Um, that'll be three twenty-five."

"Right." Drew puts down the cup to fish in the pocket of his navy North Face. He hands me a five. "I was going to get muffins."

"Do you want some? I can totally add them to this." I freeze with the bill over the drawer.

"No, I just—I had a joke about . . . packing a basket of goodies."

"Oh." I nod, utterly lost. I hand him his change, my fingertip grazing his palm.

"Thanks." He stuffs it into his pocket and in seconds is

out the door in a clattering of sleigh bells, his hot chocolate left steaming on the counter.

The second Kara and her crew clear the bakery window, I dive for my cell and text Caitlyn. "I'm taking my break!" I yell down to Jamie Beth as I pull on my coat. I wait for an impatient minute during which I hear nothing. "Jamie Beth, that means you have to come upstairs!" She appears at the base of the steps.

"Whatever, I'm coming." She trudges heavily up in her unlaced work boots, and I jog out the door into the little lantern-lit courtyard that abuts the back of the Maiden Lane shops. I climb through the crusted ice to where the snow-filled fountain sits dormant as one of the French doors to Bambette opens. Caitlyn steps out, a blue infant's sweater on her head and what looks to be pairs of matching cashmere pants on each hand.

"Doubling as outerwear," she greets me. "Four hundred dollars an item makes total sense."

"Drew just came into the Pear!" I hop in the snow.

"Drew-Drew?" She hops with me.

"Drew-Drew?" I grab her forearms to steady us as I think for a moment. "Yes. Yes, he is now officially Drew-Drew. He wanted muffins, but then left his hot chocolate and ran off—"

"Aw, did ya scare him with your b-girl do? Thought you were going to get gangsta on his ass?"

"What?"

She points at my turned-around hat and splayed hair.

"Crap." I grab it off my head. "That's the XTV people. Totally embarrassing. They came in to film, and you can't acknowledge that they're there—"

"*XTV* came into the *Prickly Pear* to film *you*?"

"I guess. Unless they're also shooting *The Real Hampton Cosmetology School* starring Jamie Beth."

"They came in to film *you*." Her shoulders drop.

"They're just shooting after-school stuff! They're probably going down the block store by store. I'm sure they'll be in Bambette any minute."

Caitlyn whips the sweater off her head. "Really?"

"Yes!"

"I have to go. Have to lip-gloss." She leaps back through the snow, and I turn to the Prickly Pear. "Jess," she calls after me. "He paid, but he left his hot chocolate?"

"Yeah." I pivot my head to see her silhouetted in the peach light spilling through the French doors. "He said he was going to make a joke about a basket of goodies." I shrug.

"Little Red Riding Hood, you *dork*. Your inside joke!"

I flush strawberry jam all over again. "Our joke is inside! We have an inside!"

"And I have a date with fame." She smack-kisses a baby-pants-ed hand and blows it at me before pulling the glass-paned door closed behind her.

REEL 3

I stare into the microwave, waiting for my egg to puff up like a chef's hat over the edge of the ramekin. It's the small joys. Suddenly there's a pounding, followed by an insistent ring of the doorbell.

"Jess?" Mom calls up from the basement. "Can you get it? It might be Fran returning my steamer."

Six forty-five on a Wednesday morning is awfully early for a steamer return. I pad to the front hall, reluctantly preparing myself to break the heat seal. Pulling my cardigan around my waist with one arm, I open the door, its rubber draft barrier shwooshing against the wood floor.

"Good morning, Jesse O'Rourke!!"

Oh, so not Fran. Unless she now brings television

cameras with her on routine errands. I blink against the lights, trying to look out through the spots in my eyes. "Hello?" I say feebly, still unable to see whom I'm addressing.

"Hey, it's Kara, from XTV." She steps out in front of the cameras, once again wearing the same outfit as at the Pear last week, plus a thin black scarf circled loosely around her neck, like an afterthought. "Are your parents here?"

"My dad's still asleep—"

"Jess," he calls groggily from the top of the steps. "You win the lottery?"

"In a way, yes, she has, Mr. O'Rourke!" Kara shouts past me up the stairs before breaking into a thick cough.

I can hear him slapping down behind me in his slippers, and I pray he's wearing the new pajamas we got him for Christmas and not his worn-sheer Slippery When Wet T-shirt. Nope, it's the T-shirt. Mom appears on the opposite end of the spectrum clutching the neck of her grandma zip-up robe. "Jess, what is all this?" she asks, wiping her hair out of her face with the back of her hand.

"Mr. and Mrs. O'Rourke, congratulations!" Kara opens her arms wide, her exhausted eyes watery above dark circles. "We have selected your daughter to be part of the core cast in our new documentary series, *The Real Hampton Beach,* and we could *not* be more excited!"

Wha-huh?!

"Over the next five weeks, Jesse and a group of her friends will help shape the content of a show offering millions of American high school students an insightful and accurate reflection of the on-the-ground issues they face. It'll be incredible exposure." At the word *exposure* a parental hand grabs each of my stunned elbows. "And, as a thank-you, XTV has arranged for Doritos to donate forty thousand dollars toward college tuition for each of the participants."

At the words *forty thousand* my ears start ringing as I feel Mom and Dad rock me backward and then forward, as if they're about to fling me into Kara's arms and slam the door behind me.

"We just need you to sign a simple parental consent form and the money is yours." She holds out an oversized bright orange check with *Doritos* emblazoned across the top. And my name printed in one-inch letters on the recipient line. Holy. Crap. All three of us lean down and stare at it like it's about to talk to us. A flash goes off.

"We need some time to look that over," Dad says, blinking, his recovered voice raspy. He takes the form from Kara, and she slips her camera back into her vest pocket.

"Of course. We just need to know by tomorrow morning." She presses the check into Mom's hand atop the dryer sheet she's clutching. "Please hold on to this. But don't try to cash it—it won't be cleared for cashing until everyone's permission forms are filed with legal. Okay!" She claps her gloved hands, a big smile breaking over her tired face. "Jesse, there's a trailer parked behind the school cafeteria and, while your parents take today to sign the form, please join us for a super-fun orientation meeting at seven forty-five."

"Oh my God! I can't believe it! And Caitlyn, she'll be there?" I pull my cardigan sleeves down over my bare hands.

"My contract doesn't cover telling you that. But there'll be breakfast! Okay, great, yay!"

She retreats down the steps and hops with her cameramen into the waiting van. As it speeds away to play *Who Wants to Be a Millionaire?* at someone else's house, I shut the door and turn to my parents. We stare at one another in the darkened entryway. "Oh my God. Oh my God!" is all I can manage, my mind already racing ahead to whether this means Caitlyn and I can snag two tickets to the XTV Awards. "What do you guys think?"

Dad sits down heavily on the bottom step, his face breaking into a grin as he laughs in disbelief. Mom leans back against the railing, her eyes welling. "Kelsey Grammer told me about this," she murmurs, hugging the check to her chest. "Last summer. He said if I concentrated really hard on what I want for you and pray every day, that it would happen." She throws her arms around me, squeezing me tight. "Now you can go to any college you want!"

Still in shock, I chain my bike up and pull my cell out of my coat pocket. Nothing from Caitlyn. I leave her a sixth voice mail. Probably trying to give herself a five-minute highlight touch-up before she hits the trailer.

I round the school from the freshly salted parking lot and, sure enough, next to the newly cleared pool site there's a black double-wide with a neon XTV logo painted six feet tall across the side. I knock on the door, but no one answers. I try the cold metal handle and it gives, letting me into what I'm guessing is *The Real Hampton Beach* headquarters. Long, white, tufted benches sit beneath the windows and, just behind, a small kitchen straddles the aisle with what looks to be every single product General Mills makes, from Fruit Roll-Ups to Hamburger Helper.

"Dig in!" Kara cheers from behind me, climbing the stairs, a large Prickly Pear coffee cradled to her sweatshirt chest.

I take two granola bars and sit on the white leather, awaiting my fellow golden-ticket holders. I glance at my cell. Nothing.

The trailer door opens and I look up hopefully.

"Melanie, hey," I say, deflated. "What a surprise."

"You too," she says, but without my sarcastic undertone. She teeters up the three stairs in snow-caked strappy heels and sits across from me to deice her polished toes.

"Granola bar?" I offer.

She recoils. "I don't—you know—*carbs*."

"Right," I say, polishing off the first bar and tucking into the second. God, I hope Caitlyn gets here before everyone else—hate to have to reenact every detail.

The door opens again, and Jase bounds up the steps.

"Howdy, y'all!" he whoops, stopping short when his eyes land on mine and an awkward pause ensues in which I assume we're both flashing back to Monday night—me holding garbage, Jase holding his split lip. Good times.

"Soup! All right!" Avoiding me, he makes a beeline for the Progresso New England Clam Chowder, takes a can opener to it, pours the contents into a bowl, and zaps it in the microwave.

My nose scrunching as the smell of warming clams fills the trailer, I don't even notice Nico until she's standing over me. She kisses Melanie on the cheek and goes to take a seat on Jase's lap. Jase extends an arm holding the bowl around her lithe frame and eats over her shoulder as she lolls her head to one side, unfazed by his proclivities, breakfast and otherwise.

Meanwhile, Kara is shuffling piles of handouts into purple folders and glancing every other minute at her BlackBerry. Where *the hell* is Caitlyn? For the first time I let the sliver of concern I've been ignoring since I left my third voice mail for her grow into a full-blown thought: They wouldn't cast me and *not* Caitlyn, would they?

The door flies open, and Rick pounds up the steps, tossing off a "Dude" in greeting to each of us. Ah, Rick Sachs. A Hampton High phenomenon, all cheekbones and blue eyes. But two minutes into talking to him, you're practically asleep. There's always a sophomore up to bat, but it never lasts. He's a spud. Someday he will just bud off and there'll be a little Rick standing beside him.

"Okay!" Kara straightens up. "We're just waiting for one more."

Shit.

There's no way it isn't Trisha. My stomach dropping, I put down the granola bar on the windowsill. I crook my finger, and Kara takes a step toward me. I crook it again, and she leans her ear down to my mouth. "I just wanted to say I think my friend Caitlyn Duggan would be awesome. She *really* wants it."

I stare imploringly at her as she straightens up. "She'd do a *much* better job at this than me."

"I'm sorry, we're only casting six. We looked at hours of footage from last week, and Network loved you guys. It's out of my hands." Kara shrugs apologetically.

Why?! Why pick me and not her? I mean, you want glamorous? She highlights her own hair! It makes no sense! Oh God, she'll never forgive me. I flash to my parents beaming at that orange check. But I can always work a few thousand more shifts at the Pear. I'll just—stand up and—

The door opens, and I turn to see how bad Trisha's nose looks post-cafeteria crash. But the eyes looking back aren't black and they aren't Trisha's.

They're Drew's.

"Sorry I'm late. I had some family stuff to take care of." Nico and Melanie exchange a look, because, while hot, Drew doesn't register in their circle. Until he started dating someone a whole grade up, these guys couldn't have picked Drew out of a lineup.

"Okay! Gang's all here!" Kara gives a double thumbs-up. "Drew, help yourself to anything from the kitchen."

"Soup's awesome," Jase says, mouth full.

Drew drops onto the bench opposite, gives me a half-smile, and pulls a PowerBar from his pocket. "I'm good."

I sit there. Looking from Kara to Drew, flashing from my parents to Caitlyn.

"Great. But you can't eat that on camera. *Only* General Mills brands." Kara speaks slowly like Mrs. Gesop. "Anything else will have to be *fuzzed out* and that costs our editors *time* and *money*. Got it?"

We all nod.

"Jesse? You have a question?"

"I . . . I . . . " I don't know what to say.

"Okay! Next thing. You'll need to report to this trailer every morning for a check-in. Five, ten minutes max, no big deal." She drops her thick glasses from atop her hair to read from her clipboard. "Now, these are the most important things. We want you guys to spend as much time with each other as possible. This show is about you. The six of you. Six friends—"

Nico raises her hand, looking at Drew, then me. "But, no offense—" she says. I nod, none taken. "—we're not all friends."

"Right, exactly—" I see my in, but Nico plows on.

"Trisha should be here. My father said—" She stops short. "I mean, it only makes sense. What happened?"

"Well, Trisha's blond, and you're blond, and Melanie's strawberry blond, and we couldn't have three blond leads. Network wanted to break it up, give audiences a different type they could relate to—"

"Trisha's relatable *and* she's my friend."

"Drop it, Nic," Jase says under his breath. Nico's breath catches, her cheeks flushing in hurt.

Pulling her pen out of her clipboard's vise, Kara draws herself up. "Okay, any more quibbles with casting? Because I *can* scrap all of you." Still straddling Jase's legs, Nico goes rigid. "As I was saying, there are six of you, and we only have two full-time cameramen, Ben and Sam, and we don't want to miss anything. . . . So, Nico, if you have a choice of going to Jesse's after school, or some random's, go to Jesse's." We catch each other's eye, the idea of her coming over to my house so outrageous we both let out a little laugh. "Laughing together—good, good, that's great." Kara makes a check on her clipboard. "We don't have time to mike you today, so we'll just throw you in with a camera and a boom. You can ask more questions tomorrow when you've gotten the hang of it." She takes in our tense faces. "Relax, guys, you're going to have the time of your lives! Everyone who's done one of our city-based roommate dramas clamors to come back and do a challenge show—they love it; it's so much fun they want to come on again and again." Something on Kara buzzes and her hand goes to her vest pocket. "And now, I'll be right back." Kara steps down the three stairs to the exit and lets herself out, the trailer door slamming shut behind her.

"This is bullshit. Total bullshit," Nico says, pushing away from Jase and his soup, taking a seat on Rick's other side next to Melanie. "How can they do this?"

The door reopens and Kara comes in, trailed by Fletch in an oversized orange Prada parka with fur-trimmed hood. "Jesus fucking Christ, is it cold out there! But gotta hit our air dates, right? My pad's on Fire Island, which I pushed for, *believe me*, but no cars and Network said, 'Eh.' So I'm staying in a hotel the last few nights, and the walls are, like, black—"

"It's hard to keep on top of the mold with the ocean air," I say in Phase One of sweet-talking my way into keeping a best friend—

"So Network rents me a house, and last night the boiler conked out. I cast you guys in a plushie show, and I'm living fucking *Survivor: East Hampton*."

"Fletch," Nico purrs, unwrapping her legs and re-wrapping them the other way in a twirl of streamlined gray denim. "My dad has a little bungalow on the beach we rent out in the summers if you ever need a place," her sweet-talking blowing my sweet-talking out of the water. "It's top-notch." Thank you, Ivanka Trump.

"I'll file that, Nico, but here's hoping the next time I see you we'll be on the other island, the one with tall buildings and my killer office. Okay, so I trust Kara gave you all the skinny on what we're looking for. Just be yourselves.

We picked you guys because each one of you has something special, something captivating." Nico leans forward in her seat, entranced. "I know your forms aren't all in yet, but, looking out, I see a hot cast, and I hope you'll all come on board. Okay, enough gabbing! Go be awesome!" He gives a wave and hops back out of the trailer before I can say a word.

"Guys, I think that's it. Oh, wait, Drew, can I swap your shirt?" Kara looks between him and Jase. "You're both in brown."

"Sure." Drew shrugs, pulling off his coat and T-shirt as he follows Kara to the back of the RV. *Oh, you are so beautiful,* I sing in my head as his rippling everything retreats. He comes out, rippling frontward this time, as he pulls a navy polo shirt over his head.

"And keep the penguin visible—they're a sponsor. Okay, have a great day!"

Nico, Jase, Rick, and Melanie race for the door, ready to start their first recorded day. I hang back uncertainly, following Drew, who zips his sweatshirt closed over the shirt as soon as Kara's out the door.

"Your parents signed the form yet?" he asks.

"I think my mom's too busy getting the check framed."

"Yeah," he says, wriggling a little in his new shirt as he descends the first step.

"You okay?" I ask, because I'm not.

He pauses, looking back over his shoulder. "I don't

usually wear anything this tight—or expensive. It's weird. This whole thing is weird." I nod. "But you're here, right?" His face brightens. "We're in this together?" he asks. I smile back, despite the pain in my chest, because this is not the together it was supposed to be. "It's no big deal," he continues. "I bet it'll be like nothing is even happening."

He pushes open the swinging door, and we both freeze under the stares of the entire student body. They stand on tiptoes, craning to see two people who were, mere minutes ago, unremarkable.

REEL 4

"**J**ust thread it under your shirt," Ben gruffly instructs through his smoker's cough, handing me the jelly bean–sized microphone in the trailer the next morning. I do as told, feeling the icy metal clip pass against my stomach as I weave the wire back out the neck of my sweater. Well, not *my* sweater. My sweater was from Old Navy and—

"It looks like it's from Old Navy," Kara said as she gestured for me to raise my arms over my head.

"Because it is."

"That's better," Kara says now, sipping from her morning coffee and appraising my new Alice + Olivia boatneck, as Ben tries to affix a cold black box, about the size of an individual cereal pack, to the back of my jeans. "You look really good in red, Jesse. Diane?"

The wardrobe mistress sticks her head out from the back of the trailer, a line of pins pressed between her lips.

"Make a note to get more red for Jesse." Diane nods as Drew emerges, shaking out the legs of brand-new Rock & Republic jeans, identical to Fletch's.

"I stapled 'em," Diane mumbles. "But I pinned five more pairs for him, and I'll have them hemmed by tomorrow."

"Your pants weren't XTV-worthy?" I ask as he rips open a Pop-Tart.

We look down at his discarded Levi's sitting in a heap on the floor.

"My pants might make someone, and I quote," he says, smiling in Kara's direction, "change the channel."

Kara sticks her cup in the microwave and hits power. "No one wants to tune in to see their own pants. They want to see the fantasy of their pants."

"Aw, you're wearing fantasy pants," I say, patting his shoulder.

"Ay!" he shouts as Ben affixes the cold black box on the inside of his waistband. The new jeans immediately droop below his boxers from the weight.

Kara looks over, lips pursed. "Tape him."

Ben nods, tearing off a thick strip of metallic gaffer's tape and slapping it to Drew's lower back, affixing the pack before he can protest. Drew's eyes bulge as he tilts his head, looking to me for acknowledgment that he is eight hours away from a world of pain.

Just then the door to the trailer opens with a cold draft,

and Melanie hops up the stairs, her hair expertly barrel-curled, her face pristinely made up.

"There's my girl!" Kara shouts at her arrival, popping open the microwave. "Matte where she should be matte, glossed where she should be glossed. Get miked and you're good to go."

Melanie blushes beneath her freckles as Ben hands off her own cold jelly bean and motions for her to thread it under her chiffon blouse. Which, unlike Drew's pants or my sweater, is probably at a sufficient price point to qualify as a fantasy garment. I have a feeling daily check-ins with Diane might only be on the docket for the two of us.

Shrugging on his coat, Drew turns to Kara. "Anything else you want to stick to me, or can I go to French now?"

Kara bites the edge of her black scarf as she takes him in from head to stapled toe. Suddenly her exhausted face breaks into a smile as her gaze drops. "You are scrumptious," she says into her coffee. "Just solid-gold scrumptious. They're gonna eat you with a spoon."

Although I couldn't agree with her more, Drew nods, the way we do to our deluded parents when they make some grandiose prediction through DNA-colored glasses, and heads to the stairs, to his real life, where no one is currently eating him with anything. At least I hope not.

"So Benjy is hanging on the golf course fence and starts to get agitated. Why? *What* is Faulkner implying?" Mr. Baxter asks. A few arms go up. I turn toward the lofted hands. Not that I actually care who might know the answer; I just want to pivot my face away from the camera hovering inches from my head for a few seconds. "Jesse?"

"Uh . . . " I scramble, so keenly aware of the glaring klieg light practically brushing my left cheek.

"What is Benjy hearing?" he asks with exasperation.

I picture myself last summer on the edge of the Maidstone Golf Club, waiting for Caitlyn to finish with the lunch service so we could hit the public beach. Oh, right. "Caddie?" I pull out of my butt.

"Yes," he says in a pinched voice that indicates accuracy was not his hoped-for outcome. He turns back to the board, leaving me to contemplate what I must look like from two inches away. Are my pores gaping craters? Is sweat from the hot light gushing down my temple like the Rio Grande? This is unbearable. This is worse than the two weeks we had a working camcorder and Dad forgot all the other seedpods blooming into flowers on the ballet studio floor and wandered right into the middle to get a close-up of me. I went from white lily to red carnation in two seconds flat. Yes, despite having a mother who occasionally sings in a Bangles tribute band, I have not been this self-conscious since nursery school.

The bell rings, and I whip my binder into my bag and book it for the door, letting the back of my head be the show for a moment while I pat down my temples with my borrowed red cashmere sleeve. I wonder if Nico is also sweating under the lights. I wonder if Nico sweats. I spot Caitlyn, who I *still* haven't talked to, entering the stairwell, head tucked.

"Hey!" I jog to catch up. She doesn't slow. "Caitlyn, hey," I repeat. She stops on the third step down and turns, her face impassive as people jostle around us to get downstairs.

"What's up?" I ask just as the camera catches up to me, bouncing light off the stairwell tiles. "You would not believe how ridiculous this all is. My head is like manicotti under a heat lamp."

She squints up at me as a trio of freshmen jockey to get into the shot. "I'm late, Jess." She turns and keeps walking.

I scramble down to her, grabbing her sleeve. "Wait. Why haven't you returned my calls or emails? You could have at least texted. Are you totally pissed?"

She stops and just looks at me for a moment, inscrutable. "I had that makeup test for English, remember?" she finally says. "I was busy."

"So we're okay?" I ask, wanting to be relieved.

"Of course," she says, her eyes on the Amnesty International bake sale flier taped above my shoulder.

"Really?" I ask, waiting for a smile.

"Sure. Why? Is this the big *why didn't you return my calls* scene?" Then she smiles. But it is a smile worse than the not-smiling. She pivots and returns to the downstream flow. I make my way back up to the second-floor landing, feeling punched.

At lunch Kara is standing outside the entrance to the cafeteria, hunched over her habitual Prickly Pear cup. She has a walkie-talkie tucked into the back waistband of her black cords, exposing pink cotton briefs. Wouldn't all our lives be easier if the networks got together and made chic pants with an equipment pouch in them? "Ben," she says, addressing my shadow, "Sam's in there, so you can take lunch." He trudges off, lighter in hand, camera dangling at his side.

"Okay, Jess, you're sitting with Nico and Mel."

"Do *they* know that?"

Kara nods.

"Look, can we do whatever it is you're envisioning here tomorrow? I really need to talk to Caitlyn."

"After. They're already on line, so scoot. Doritos!" she trills, which I guess will be her new shorthand for, "*We own you.*"

Knowing there is no "after," that Caitlyn and I don't cross paths again following lunch on Thursdays, I shuffle into the bustling cafeteria with twisted lips. I take my place at the end of the hot dog line and stare at the twelve rows of full tables that run from Loser Town by the beverage dispensers to Hipville at the windows. I have always sat comfortably in the middle, surrounded by other reasonably attractive people, like Rob DeNunzio, Emily Franken, Jennifer Lanford, people who have unembarrassing clothes, decent social skills, and solid senses of humor, but who lack things like sports cars and nose jobs and Elsa Peretti silver. I inch toward my tepid lunch meat and wonder if my ass hitting the orange Formica bench of Nico's table will trigger the beginning of some Indiana Jones–style action sequence. Sand will pour out of the wall, and the whole table will gradually submerge, letting Nico and me into an alternative culture of friendship just waiting to be exposed all these years.

Or she'll finally tell me she hates my haircut.

As the camera sharks over to Nico, I follow, now wondering if this has all been the most elaborate *Punk'd* ever. But across from Melanie and Nico is an empty spot.

"Hey, is this Trisha's?" I ask, pointing to the tray-sized space.

Nico pauses the overstuffed bun to her mouth, already flecked with sauerkraut. "Trisha's MIA, babe. C'mon down." She exposes her palm in invitation.

I rest my tray down, listening for sand. "What do you mean, MIA? I thought she was still recovering from her . . . accident."

Melanie looks up from where she's carefully slicing fruit into her yogurt. "She hasn't returned our calls."

"And her batshit insane mother will only say that she 'needed a break' and has gone to her aunt's in West Palm." Nico pauses to swallow. "What, like, she's Britney and has to hide out and recoup?" She looks to Melanie. "She's our best friend. I mean, I get you're pissed but at least answer your phone. What if I needed her?" I lean forward to commiserate about Caitlyn, but Nico plows on. "She didn't make the show. Get over it." The edge to her voice in contrast to the dulcet maternal cooings in the bathroom suddenly makes me question if she knows about Trisha and Jase after all. She holds up her condiment-smeared hands, and Melanie reaches into her bag and passes her a Wet One. Nico blows her a kiss in gratitude.

"So . . . " I start, knowing I should be bringing something to the table conversation-wise, but the nerves and camera stymie me.

"Wait, is that *Drew* sitting with *Jase*?" Nico asks in disbelief, swiveling her long torso on the bench.

"Yes, XTV has sponsored Adopt-a-Dork Day," I say on our collective behalf.

"I didn't mean it that way." She reaches across and squeezes my forearm with her freshly cleaned palm. "It's, just, what will they have to say to each other?"

"Sex and sports." I shrug.

"Does Drew do either?" she asks, still swiveling and swanning to get a better look. "He doesn't have a MySpace page, a Facebook page—he doesn't Twitter."

"He runs cross-country. And I'm sure Jen broke him in," Melanie quips.

Nico snorts with laughter. Full-on snorts. Someday I would love to be able to be tall enough and blond enough that I could snort and still look cool.

At the end of the day, with my camera-fueled adrenaline flatlining, I push out the front door into the biting air and watch as the yellow buses slowly snake out of the gates. I spot the Camry parked at the periphery of the emptying lot and, ignoring my bike, run over, my bag hitting against my hip. Leaning down on the passenger side, I see Caitlyn staring out the window, the tip of her thumbnail between her front teeth. "You okay?"

She nods but won't look at me. I open the door and slide in. "Cay?" I start to lean forward, but she puts her other hand up in my face. "Caitlyn."

She shrugs, staring out the windshield, her eyes watering as she shakes her head back and forth. "Oh my God," I murmur. "I'm so sorry."

"But I'm . . . really happy . . . for you," she manages as the tears roll down her cheeks, seeping into her white down coat in dark wet spots. "I just . . . want you to know."

"Cay, I know, but—"

"No. Just—I'm happy for you, and I don't think I can really talk about this right now or with you or . . . maybe at all."

She rakes her sleeve across her face, and I feel a cold seep up my chest.

"You *know* I didn't expect this—I'm the last person who would expect this! If it wasn't for the scholarship—"

"I know. I know that. But I can't . . . I've been holding it together for the past two days. I just—need to go home, okay? I'll drop you. But can we just not talk about this?" She grips the steering wheel with the fingerless gloves my grandmother knit for us both last Christmas.

"Yeah, yes, whatever you need." I sit frozen beside her.

She inhales deeply, blinking up at the wilting fabric coming down around the defunct roof light.

"So how was the French test?" I try.

"Fine." She reaches out to push on the radio and Akon fills the space between us. She twists up the volume, underlining how much she doesn't want to talk. Putting on my seat belt, I follow her lead to clear off the windshield condensation with our coat sleeves. She puts the car into drive and, sniffing back her tears, navigates us out of the lot and onto Main Street. As we slow in front of the first stoplight, I struggle with the temptation to jump out so she can roll over me with all four tires.

I grab the knob to lower the music and turn to her. "I wanna shoot myself."

"No!" This just makes her cry harder. "Jesse, no! I'm *happy* for you! I just really wanted this. *Really* really. It seemed like the answer to everything."

"Okay, well, I am reporting back from the front that it is, in fact, literally, a giant, sweaty pain in the ass."

"But I wanted it! I wanted that giant, sweaty pain in my ass!" We stare at each other, her eyes wide, her words hanging between us. She can't help but break into a grin. We both crack up, warmth flooding my chest like someone poked a giant sewing needle through the crapbox's roof to break the tension.

"This sucks."

"So bad," she sighs, leaning her head against the headrest and taking the turn off Main.

I look at her splotchy cheeks, and it is suddenly clear to me that this—this post-needle poking laugh about sweaty butts is how things need to be. The part where she's sobbing and I feel lower than roadkill's gotta go. "Okay, XTV is not going to rain on our last semester."

"Pissing. They're pissing on it."

"There has to be some way to get you on."

"*I* don't have what they want. I don't have the long hair and legs, or the drama or whatever."

"What they want . . . " I twist my lips, racking my brain, as we turn onto Clover Road and I catch sight of the ludicrous Roman fountain that makes a promise the rest of Trisha's sprawling ranch just can't deliver. "Turn around!" I slap the dashboard.

"What?" Caitlyn slams on the brakes.

"I've got the drama to get you cast. Turn around!"

"Jesse, I've got to get the car home so my mom can get to work."

"I have my bike—just turn around before I lose my nerve!"

"Kara?" I call out as I step into the trailer, past the benches, past the kitchen, past the gray bulbs lining the makeup mirrors, to the door ajar at the far end. I stand for a moment between the bulging clothing racks to give myself a two-second pep talk before walking into the blue light spilling from the doorway. "Kara?"

The only illumination comes from a pyramid of television monitors stacked atop a desk, which also currently supports Kara's earphone-covered head. I freeze, mesmerized by the images of us, of school, Drew, me. Oh my God, *me*! For a moment the cameras and mike packs are forgotten, and I feel a panic like I just found myself in a towel on YouTube. Jesse, focus!

"Um, hello?" I tentatively tap Kara's scarf-covered shoulder and she whips up.

"Yeah?" she says loudly, quickly swiping her blouse sleeve over her red eyes before tugging off the headphones. Has she been crying? "Yes, Jesse. What can I do for you?" She puts her glasses back on.

"I was wondering if we could talk for a minute."

"Sure. Can't be any less riveting than the thirty thousand dollars of tedium we shot today."

"Sorry?"

"What were they thinking? The Hamptons in January! But Network wanted a midseason premiere to capitalize on the *Park Avenue Confidential* buzz, so here I am—trying to unearth glamour beneath layers of salt-stained down and fleece. I should get one of those applications to the Prickly Peach, 'cause I seem to have bet my entire career on a bunch of adolescent nothings."

"Pear."

"Huh?" She blows her nose on a Kleenex that looks like it's had a workout, and, looking around for somewhere to toss it, she ends up lifting her right hip to shove it into her cords pocket.

"Nothing. Um, I'm sure I could get you an application if you wanted. The chick who works with me is a total loser. I bet they'd be psyched to have someone with your experience—"

"Jesse." She takes her glasses back off to rub her bloodshot eyes.

"Yeah."

"What do you want?"

"Okay." I drop into the swivel chair next to hers and tuck my hair behind my ears. I decide to give the direct route one last try. "So, I know you think you have, like, all the kids you need for your cast. It's just . . . none of them are funny. . . . They're cool to look at, I guess, but don't people want to laugh? My friend Caitlyn is pretty *and* really, *really* funny—"

"Great. Great. Does she have her own plane? A parent with a Class A drug problem? A six-figure shoplifting addiction? No? Well, then, not really going to help me. You guys just aren't delivering."

I take in the monitors, all of us, even Nico, sallow against our hallways' pea-green tiles. "If you wanted the whole *Park Avenue Confidential* thing, why aren't you filming at a private school in the city?"

"To quote Fletch, '*Those* parents aren't going to bend over for a forty-thousand-dollar check from Doritos.'"

"Oh."

"Sorry, that was rude." She shakes her head in disbelief. "God, I'm exhausted. Listen, I just don't have time. I've got to finish a test tape to overnight to Fletch, and right now I have exactly zero minutes of airtime drama—"

"But I've got drama for you!" I rush, staying just a few breaths ahead of my conscience. "I can tell you about drama, but I think you also really need funny."

She studies my face. "What drama?"

"I just . . . know something between some people in the cast I could tell you about, but only if you promise to cast Caitlyn, which I swear you won't regret because she is *totally* entertaining."

"Okay. Jesse, I can't *promise* to do anything. That's Fletch's call, and he's at Sundance for, like, ten days, so nothing's happening right now except my potential firing." She exhales a slow stream of air. "But I can promise to try."

"Really try? Like tell-him-how-hysterically-entertaining-Caitlyn-is try?"

"Yes. Now what do you know?"

Spit back out to the corridor of darkened makeup mirrors, I fight down the yuckwave set in motion by Kara digging for her cell and yes-ing me out the door. Leaning into the Formica laminate, I try to distinguish actual words in her muffled chirp, try to hear the outcome of my maybe-not-totally-thought-through pitch, try to ignore the intrusive vision of Dad's disappointed face if he knew what I just did.

But what did I do, *really*? What? Told about two crappy people doing crappy things to save an opposite-of-crappy person so she could do a not-crap thing? With me! And get money for college!

I avoid my reflection and turn to where the yellow parking lot light slices through the blinds onto the bulletin board of wardrobe photos of Nico and Jase and—God, why do I even care? They're not my friends. Nico flat-out said so. And Trisha's such a bitch, and Jase's so . . . so— it's not like I told about his dad hitting him. Seriously. It's not my fault Kara's face lit up like I'd given her next week's Powerball numbers.

I push myself toward the trailer door. I mean, I couldn't even answer most of her questions. Like I would even *know* the details! Like I was in the sleeping bag with them . . . ugh. I freeze, my hand on the handle. That's what this feels like, like *I* cheated in that frigid half-built guesthouse.

Suddenly the door whips open, jerking me down the little steps and into the freezing cold. I trip forward, one foot over the other, narrowly missing the icy pavement before I right myself. It's Jase—red-faced and sweat-streaked from basketball. He grips the door wide open against the side of the trailer, his rolled-up mike pack in his other hand. His blue eyes lock on to me.

"Hey!" My voice too loud in the empty lot, I feel my shoulders dart protectively to my ears. "I just forgot to drop off my mike pack, too! That's what I'm doing here."

His expression hard, he stares down his nose, his hand resting on the handle, his stillness implying when I move—he'll leap.

"So . . . so, see you," I sputter. There's no way he could know what I just did.

His chest rises and falls in his damp T-shirt, vapor from his nostrils visible in the frigid air. I lift my foot to walk backward a few feet. He watches, silent. I turn away and, abandoning my bike, not letting myself break into a run, steady with the exception of chattering teeth, make it to the brick columns that frame the exit and then pivot onto the sidewalk home. I don't look back once.

REEL 5

"**W**hat's there to eat in this kitchen that's not on my person?" Caitlyn yells over the music, adjusting the Saran Wrap keeping her wild-honey-and-chamomile-tea-soaked hair from falling into her oatmeal-and-yogurt face mask.

"What's on *my* person." I run my finger across my jawline for some mashed banana to offer her. Declined, I lick it off and join Rihanna in the dance bridge, sock-sliding across the wood floor to check what Dad left for us in the fridge.

"I feel like a mozzarella stick." Caitlyn peers in over my shoulder.

"Well, you smell like a cereal bar." I pull open the freezer door and halfheartedly poke through the tinfoil-wrapped restaurant leftovers. "Let's order pizza."

"Brilliant. How much guilt money did your folks leave?"

"Are you kidding? I'm the one who didn't go to Grandma's 'cause I have to work Sunday. I practically had to pay them. I have, like, fifteen bucks."

"But it's so worth it to spend the night *avec moi*." Caitlyn bats her eyelashes, flaking oatmeal onto the countertop while I grab the phone. "Let's watch the scary one first and then the funny one to calm ourselves down," she mouths over the Blockbuster cases while I rest my elbows on the counter to place the order, careful not to get the phone sticky with banana or the avocado mask in my hair.

"All Johnny Depp, all the time," I say after hanging up. "Jack the Ripper or Peter Pan, it's all good." The timer on the ancient wall stove buzzes.

"You're done!" Caitlyn switches it off and leans over my iPod station to pick our next number. "Go rinse, then step aside, 'cause I've got"—she glances up at the glowing numbers ticking down on the microwave—"sixteen minutes to go until gorgeous."

I give her a thumbs-up before jogging through the living room and up the stairs, pumping my fists in time to the opening bars of Spoon's "Way We Get By," before I realize I'm leaving a trail of conditioning avocado blobs behind. Placing my hands under my neck like a tray, I book it to the bathroom and carefully strip down to rinse off the contents of our Friday Night Spa Date. I'm smashing guacamole chunks into the drain with my toes and debating whether we should actually bake the frozen cookie dough like grown-ups when the shower curtain rips open to reveal a bug-eyed Caitlyn.

"What the hell?!" I scream, wrapping the other side of the curtain around myself.

"XTV," she whispers, her face white at the edge of her congealed mask.

"Huh?" I wipe the water out of my eyes with my free hand. But she's already in motion, kicking off her socks while tugging at the Saran Wrap. Giving up, she jumps into the bathtub behind me, the spray soaking her clothes.

"XTV is in your *living room*," she whispers frantically as I whip a towel off the wall rack and exchange it for the curtain before the whole bathroom gets soaked.

"On a Friday night?" I ask as she moves me aside to frantically shampoo her sticky hair, the bottle flying out of her hands and ricocheting off the tile before I can catch it. "But I thought they want to film us together. We're not together on the weekends. For all I know, Nico locks herself in a cryogenic chamber from Friday to Monday. Cay, just stop for one second and tell me what's going on."

"I was lip-synching. Using the glass patio doors like a mirror and . . . and I guess I couldn't hear the front doorbell over the music. They must've come around to the backyard—the next thing I know I'm not seeing me in the reflection, I'm seeing that woman from the show with her hand raised to knock, just looking in at me like . . . like I'm a *freak*." Her hands pause above either side of her sudsy head, her eyes flitting as she relives the horror. I share her cringe, flashing to what they must've seen with the lights ablaze—Caitlyn's *American Idol* broadcast in high def to Mom's Hummel figurines.

"Okay." I step out of the tub and pull the curtain closed. "Were the cameras on? Was the little flashing light green or red?"

"No cameras." A ball of sticky Saran Wrap lobs over the bar, and I catch it to drop in the wicker waste bin. "It was just that woman—the short, dark-haired one with the glasses."

"Kara?" I jerk my jeans up over my damp legs. "In my living room?"

Caitlyn turns off the water with a squeak and darts her arm out to feel for a towel. "You have to lend me jeans. And earrings." She climbs past me, already reaching for the hair dryer. "Plug in the curling iron." Her voice cracks as she catches her scrubbed raw appearance in the fogging mirror.

"Wait, Cay, this is good!" I grab her wet shoulders. "Fletch must be back! She must be here to tell us you're in!"

"Before my Floor Show of Crazy changed her mind." She tugs open my drawer and grabs a round brush.

"Did she say that?" I whip on my henley. "Did she say she changed her mind?"

"She didn't tell me anything. She just said she needs to talk to you."

"Right! Because I promised entertaining and you delivered!" I pull my dripping hair up into a bun and reach for the doorknob. "See you out there, costar!"

A wide smile spreading across her face, she pauses her manic primping to throw her arms around me, and we both let out a mini-scream before I dart out to jog down the stairs.

Unpeeling my shirt from my damp bra, I round the corner as Kara turns from the wall of family pictures.

"Hey, Jesse! What's up?" She smiles warmly.

"Hey. Not much." I plop down on the couch, aiming for casual.

"I like your enthusiasm." She laughs.

"Do you want some soda or water or something?" Realizing she's not joining me on the couch, I stand back up. "We just ordered a pizza, so . . . "

"Oh, that's sweet." She drops a sidelong glance to the cell phone she angles up with her wrist. "But we don't really have time for that."

The microwave beeps from the kitchen, signaling Caitlyn's masks are ready to be removed. "Sorry, let me just get that." I turn for the kitchen with Kara at my heels.

"Yeah, so, Jesse, I'm sorry I haven't been around for morning check-in this week, but there's been a lot to get organized with the changes. We've *finally* got the whole thing figured out—we'll keep following you in school docu-style. But on weekends we're gonna kick it up a notch, and I'm just really—psyched—to get—filming."

She smacks the Formica counter for emphasis.

"She's in the cast?" I ask. Kara looks at me blankly as the timer beeps. "Caitlyn. You figured it out?"

"Can you—" She tilts her head at the microwave.

"Sorry." I hit the "clear" button.

"I've managed to stave off a migraine for a week now, and I'm hoping to set a new record for myself, you know?"

"That sucks. I mean, that's great? About the record?" *WHAT ABOUT CAITLYN?!*

"So . . ." She purses her lips and tick-tocks her head. "Right. Fletch is flying in as we speak, and he wants to meet with you first thing tomorrow. So, apologies, but we have to put a pin in Caitlyn for tonight, okay?"

"Okay." So not. "But, what does that mean exactly?" I flash to us sticking a cartoon-sized safety pin into my best friend's bum.

Kara shoves her hands into the back pockets of her jeans, her green down vest lifting around her ears, clearly getting impatient with me but trying to pretend she's not. "It means I told Fletch your ideas and he was really psyched. And he's the producer, and it's a creative concept you pitched, Jesse, so it falls under his purview. I'm just the associate producer. But you gave everyone a ton to think about, and it really set us off on what I believe will be a totally compelling direction for our viewers. I'm just really psyched about it. They've tripled our crew, we got an award-winning cinematographer, and Fletch is entrusting me with one of the biggest production budgets in the network."

My heart rises and crashes with her every verb as a cold rivulet snakes down my neck from my dripping topknot. "That's great that you're excited. I mean, I'm glad I could help. It's just, Caitlyn's upstairs—"

"You did more than help! Jesse, you *totally* saved this show." Kara's cell trills and she flips it open, her other index finger extending to me. Can she even open that thing without her other finger popping out—does it happen when she's at home and she just finds herself pointing at her cat? "Yes, we're on our way. . . . I know that, Ben. Crap! Okay, we're leaving right now. Yesyesyes, walking out the door." She flips the phone closed and circles the table to put her arm around my shoulder. "Jesse."

This is awkward. "Yes?"

"Tomorrow. I promise. Now we gotta move. We just figured this shoot out today, and we've got the whole scene set up. You gave us our A and B plotlines, but we gotta do a little C tonight, set the tone, establish dynamics." She walks me back to the living room toward the front door. "The van's outside, so grab your coat—"

"I'll just run and get Caitlyn; she's almost ready." I break from her to head up the stairs. "We're hanging out—I can't just leave her here." But Kara grabs my wrist as her cell rings again.

"Jesse, no! We need to leave *now*. Right now. We're risking running over." She flips open her phone, keeping her hand on my arm and kicking a pair of Mom's boots from the drying mat over to my bare feet. "We're here. . . . Then start with Nico! I don't know, the barrel curls." She swipes up the boots and shakes them in my face to take.

"How about Caitlyn just watches?" I ask as I grab them, stuffing in my feet, trying to catch Kara's eye as she pulls open the front door into the dark night and waves to the street.

"See?" she calls past the porch. "She's right here! We're coming right now."

"Hey, guys." We both turn to see an impressively Blake Lively-ed Caitlyn descending with restrained casualness from the top stair. I beam with pride morphing back into panic as Kara gives a dismissive wave her way before planting one UGG on either side of the threshold to clap at me, "Let's! Go! Let's! Go!"

Caitlyn's made-up face freezes. "What's up, Jess?"

"Um, apparently I have to go shoot some scene somewhere—" The van starts to emit a series of long honks. "But Fletch is really psyched about you, and he's going to meet with me tomorrow about it so—" Kara tugs me onto the porch and slams the door as I scream, "Watch the funny one! I'll be home for the scary! I promise!"

REEL 6

Two hours later, while someone wraps my hair around a huge curling iron one strand at a time, Kara's words—*psyched—new direction—A plot, B plot, C plot*—circle through my head as I try to piece together evidence that I'm going to get the answer I want—*we* want. "Can I just ask?" I toss out into the chaotic mass of powdered pigments and aerosol thickening the air in the trailer. "Why I have so much makeup on just to go into a spa where they're going to take it all off?"

"Welcome to the business, sweetie," Tandy, the makeup maven, mutters. "And you . . . are . . . done. Open."

I lift my heavy lids to see a magazine cover staring back in the yellow reflection. Wow. I bat my fake lashes a few times before raising my hand to touch my bronzed cheek-bones. But before I can confirm that's me in there, it's swatted.

"No touching. From now on there is no touching your face. Ever. Are we clear?"

I open my glossed lips to answer and am met with a blast of hairspray directly to the back of the throat that proceeds to hiss around my head in slow motion like I'm the cornered cockroach in the kitchen who *just . . . won't . . . die.* I hear the trailer door swing open, and a waft of crisp air reaches me through the sticky haze covering my nostrils.

Kara jogs up the steps into view and starts clapping her hands again rapidly, like a cheerleader. "Oh my God! You guys look *amazing*! This is *perfect*. Fletch is going to *flip*."

Nico, looking like the *Harper's Bazaar* version of herself, tugs out her earphones and hops from her chair like she does this every day. Which she probably does. Which would explain why no amount of Prickly Pear–subsidized John Frieda Brilliant Brunette adds me up to that. Melanie looks to her beauty handlers for clearance before following suit in the knee-high suede boots Diane's dressed her in. I stand, unsteady in the white wookie boots she's insisted I wear, and tug self-consciously at the fitted cream cashmere turtleneck that hugs my skintight white cords.

"Jesse," Kara murmurs in disbelief.

Even Nico raises an eyebrow. "You look good," she bestows matter-of-factly.

"It's those cheekbones, the profile," the woman sliding the pointy end of a comb into my hair offers as she lifts my roots in painful little tugs.

"All right, ladies!" Kara shoves her fist into the air and yelps. "We're ready for the first shot of your new reality!"

Our new reality? Nico and Melanie exchange a look of excited anticipation.

After shrugging on our assigned coats and having our copiously lacquered waves lifted gingerly out and over, we fall into line behind Kara down the steps of the trailer and up the walk, through thirty or so added crew members, to Melanie's mom's spa. Well, Melanie's mom's spa's "new reality," which, apparently, is midday instead of—CRAP!

"Kara!" I shuffle awkwardly through the shoveled snow as our threesome parts a clump of teamsters tending to the bulky black equipment. "Kara, I have to call Caitlyn and tell her we're running late. Can I please have my cell back for just one sec before we do this? What time is it even?" I look back to Nico and Melanie, but they just shrug.

"I told you the last three times you asked, no phones on set, Jesse. Unless we need a call or text to be part of a scene and then we'll give you an assigned one. Network rule. I have to have this footage for Fletch to watch tomorrow. Just work with me. Please?" Kara snatches a megaphone from a canvas folding chair, even though we're right beside her. **"Okay! You three go stand by the door and wait for my cue. Remember, it's just a fun Saturday girls' day out. You're swinging by the spa to hang and catch** up from the crazy week at school. We want it just really friendly and girly. Girl time, okay? Natural girl time." She deposits us at the door and kick-runs through the snow to the shadows while somebody scurries behind her with a broom to smooth out her tracks. **"Okay, everyone! And . . . action!"**

I scan the red-nosed faces staring expectantly at us. Screw it.

"What time is it?" I ask into the lights.

Melanie tsks me under her breath.

"*Don't* look out here at us, Jesse! And . . . action!"

"What time is it in real life?" I ask again, sweating into my borrowed cashmere.

"Three minutes after ten!" Ben yells from behind his camera.

"Thank you!"

"Cut!"

"Jesus Christ," someone groans.

"Jesse, I don't want to be stern," Kara calls sternly into her megaphone. **"But the longer this takes, the longer you're here. Got it?"**

"Sorry, just—"

"Girl time. Go."

Nico springs to life. "Melanie, I can't wait for a pedicure, can you?"

"Totally!" Melanie says, pushing open the red door, beyond which the three of us are dumbfounded to find the brilliantly lit spa abuzz with attractive women we've never seen before getting services at every station. I hold my breath for them to break into a coordinated dance number, complete with rolling nail carts. We exchange glances before Melanie recovers. "Hey, Mom!"

Mrs. Dubviek steps stiffly from around the desk, her blond hair wrapped in a twist as tight as her smile. She has on a variation of the same outfit she wears to science fairs and football games, her leopard-print bolero matching the leopard-print pockets on her Just Cavalli jeans. I always imagine her at the Cavalli store, in her clipped Eastern European accent saying, "No, no, no, just give me whole thing—underwear, bra, socks, I take it all." It's her own personal Elle-Woods-grows-up-and-marries-a-Latin-American-dictator aesthetic. "Melanie, Nico, and—"

"Jesse," I jump in as she has one arm around Nico and one around Melanie and has never talked to me a day in her life. "Hi, Mrs. Dubviek." In her defense, I've never set foot in her spa. CVS self-pedis all the way—ugh, Caitlyn . . .

"We're so ready for our pedicures; what's the hot color this week?" Nico drops her head onto Mrs. Dubviek's padded shoulder, the sweet, almost private gesture eliciting a softening in Mrs. Dubviek's taut face.

"How about nice classic Chanel Redcoat?"

"CUT!" Kara's voice booms into the spa with a godlike echo. Everyone freezes. **"Where's the new Essie color? We're supposed to place that! Someone place that!"**

The teamsters in dirty down jackets and baseball hats swoop in around us while two guys in skinny jeans and bowl cuts follow behind them on their hands and knees, mopping at the tracked-in snow with towels.

Mrs. Dubviek squeezes Nico's chin and then wipes the bangs out of her daughter's eyes. "This is good job. Your cousin in Ukraine work herring factory. I proud of my girls."

"Thanks, Mom," Melanie says.

"Thanks, Mamma D," Nico chimes in. "I'm going to run to the bathroom. Can I use the office?"

"Of course, Nikita."

"Can I use your phone?" I add while we're making requests.

"Over there." Melanie points to the front desk. "But I don't think Kara wants you making calls—"

"Great, thanks!" I race around the faux-marble console and, ducking down, pound in my home number before anyone can stop me.

"O'Rourke residence."

"I am sooo sorry. This sucks! Do you want to go home?"

"How? On your skates? My mom dropped me off, remember? She's doing the night shift at the hospital. And I'm not biking uphill on this ice, so don't even suggest it."

"Right. Crap. Well, we're finally shooting this thing, so it shouldn't be that much longer. Do you want to watch the other movie?"

"And get freaked out by myself?!"

"**Jesse!**" Kara booms into the bullhorn, and I stand up

to see the entire spa floor staring at me. **"We're rolling!"**

"What the hell?" Caitlyn says. "Who's yelling at you in surround sound?"

"Gotta go. Watch the movie! I'll be there soon!"

But soon doesn't come. Between the humming "daylight," the clocks perma-set to one thirty-two p.m., and the desperate caffeinated perkiness of a room full of professional extras, time has stopped altogether.

"I'm gonna break out," Nico listlessly observes from where she reclines on her treatment table. I loll my towel-wrapped head, gazing past Melanie to watch Nico hold up a mirror, inspecting a face that has been cleansed, masqued and then made up along with ours no fewer than eight times.

"I can't feel my lips," I offer to the klieg light that hovers brightly above our three treatment tables, like we're about to be abducted by the world's smallest spaceship. Mrs. Dubviek may have finally let them knock down a wall between treatment rooms to accommodate the crew lining every peach marbleized inch, but it took her five masques to shut up about it.

"It's fine," Melanie chimes amenably.

I push myself up on my elbows. "Seriously. How are you so chipper?"

Nico rolls onto her back, adjusting her terry-cloth robe as she rests her head in the foam doughnut. "That's just Mel."

"What?" Melanie shrugs. "It's our job. I mean, better laying here and have this stuff put on than having to be the ones out in the snow waiting to apply it. You two should get magazines." She lifts the cover of *Us Weekly* where Miley Cyrus is ducking into something with someone.

"I get for you." Mrs. Dubviek uncurls herself from the out-of-frame slipper chair, her crossed arms providing a shelf for her cleavage as she squeezes past the crew in her stocking feet.

"Okay, girls," Kara's disembodied voice booms through the megaphone from the other room, where she's encamped behind the monitors. Everyone tilts their heads, listening like Caitlyn's dog when he thinks you said "dinner." **"So here's where we're at: The color of the real facial mask is officially not reading, so we're going to think outside the box on this one. Stand by."**

Zacheria—no last name, just Zacheria (rhymes with digestive distress)—the award-winning cinematographer and officially my least favorite person *ever*, steps in with his black leggings and Hezbollah scarf to hold up his hands in a postcard shape while climbing over our tables. "Jenny!" he hollers, one knee above my shoulder, the other directly on Melanie's. Her eyes tear.

Jenny, the sad, skinny woman who did something really, really bad in a previous life, shoots in with open tubes of . . . toothpaste? wedged between her fingers. "Yes?"

"You are *here*." Zacheria points at Nico's head, and

Jenny drops to her knees and shimmies between the tables to crouch awkwardly with her face level with Nico's. Zacheria stares intensely down at both of them. Nico raises one eyebrow, flinching when he grabs one of the tubes from Jenny and, with a flourish, smears the thick turquoise paste directly onto Jenny's forehead. She smiles as if anointed.

"I have solved this! The aqueous pigments will pick up on the cobalt undertones in the wall. Mother of Melanie! Where is the mother?!"

"Mom?" Melanie calls out. We all turn to the frantic clicking of Mrs. Dubviek's restored mules as she hurries in, a stack of magazines clasped to her chest. Everyone, that is, but her daughter, who's pinned at the shoulder by a madman.

"You have a fountain! Where did I see a fountain?"

Mrs. Dubviek's face lights up. "We do! In the waxing room. I show you!"

"Just a heads-up: I will be un-filmable for, like, twelve hours if you put Crest all over my face right now," Nico says into the air.

"Let's think positive, okay?" Kara pleads from her God station. **"So, toothpaste them, Zacheria, right? Can we get this shot now?"**

Zacheria unstraddles us, using Jenny's head as a railing. "I want that fountain in here!" he screams up to the ceiling. "It's going to be beautiful!"

"Nikita, no complain or they no shoot you so much, yes?" Mrs. Dubviek deposits the magazines on my table and hands one to Nico. "You ice face before bed and be good as new."

"Okay, Mamma," Nico says affectionately. So weird. Was there an adoption I missed?

"Good! Mr. Zacheria, I show you fountain. You will love!" She clicks out with everyone trailing behind her, and the room is finally silent, save the electric hum. I rest my head back and wonder what Caitlyn is doing and if Fletch is on the red-eye, adding her name to the production schedule this very minute.

"Do you think Jase is being weird lately?" Nico turns to us, and I'm thankful that we're all on our backs so she doesn't see my eyebrows dart up.

"I don't think so." Melanie shakes her head while I pretend not to be here. "Weird, how?"

"I don't know. He just seems kind of . . . into me and then . . . not."

"Jase loves you." Melanie pats her arm.

"Yeah." Turning to the wall, Nico curls into a fetal position. "I'm so sick of thinking about this."

Sitting up on my elbows, I fan the well-flipped magazines with my four-time pedicured toes, picking the one with the most headlines devoted to Robert Pattinson. After a few minutes, the faintest hint of a snore fills the room. "Is Nico related to you guys?" I whisper to Melanie.

"No." She flips a page. "Why?"

"Just 'cause your mom and her seem really—"

"I mean, I've known her since we moved to the States

86

when I was, like, two. My mom opened this place the same time Nico's dad bought the dealership land from Trisha's parents," she explains without looking up from her celebrity gossip. Ah, Trisha's parents, now Trisha's mom, who, thanks to her dearly departed third husband, owns practically every commercial property on Main Street. So that's how Hampton High's triumvirate was born: on a Monopoly board. "Nico's always looked out for me."

"Got it. So your parents are . . . "

"Friendly, you know." She shrugs. "Socially. Not exactly vacationing together," she says calmly. And it's only then that I realize what Melanie is *not* saying: that despite her beauty and accommodating personality, and the success of the family business, at the end of the day her mom still pedicures her friends' moms' feet. I think Mel's growing on me. "And *we've* been best friends since forever, and my mom just always really took to her. I don't know. . . . " Her voice trails off. Or maybe my ears are just getting as heavy as my eyes.

"Stay with me, girls! They'll be in to paste you— we're just adding some K-Y jelly for consistency."

"Now, *that's* what this party's been missing," I mutter, and Melanie cracks a smile.

"Isn't it freaky how nobody wears underwear?"

"What?"

"In these magazines."

She flips over the hot-pink cover to check out the latest girl, exiting car in short dress sans panties. "Retarded." She thinks for a moment before returning to the page where she left off. "I don't get why they refuse their makeup for these 'just like us' shots. . . . I mean, you're having your picture taken for a magazine—get it together."

"I know," I murmur, my thoughts drifting to posing in parking lots, my eyes drifting closed before the minty lubing has even begun.

At dawn I find myself back in Mom's boots, slumped against the van with Nico and Melanie. We stare across the snow at the whip-fast dismantling of our "Saturday at the spa" just as Saturday actually begins.

Kara emerges from the well-choreographed frenzy, trudging up to us with her headset around her neck. "Great work tonight, guys. *Great,* great work. Fletch is going to be *psyched*." She sounds so palpably relieved I want to give her a hug. "Okay, so here're your cells." She reaches into the pockets of her down vest and peels blue tape off each one before passing them back. We extend our fingertips from the warmth of our sleeves to take back the devices, each of us flipping them open. Six twenty-two a.m. I immediately hit Caitlyn's number on the speed dial, waiting to get a signal.

"So, Melanie." Kara squints through her glasses. "You can head home with your mom; you're wrapped. Nico, we're going to do some exteriors with you at your house, and Jesse, we need you to stick around, okay? You can wait in the trailer."

Wha?

Melanie blanches. "Did I do something wrong?"

"What? No! No, you were great." Kara lays one hand on Melanie's arm. "There'll be plenty of screen time for everyone, okay? We're really happy with what you shot tonight, Mel."

At that her face relaxes. "Great! It's all great. I had fun. Later, Nic." She pulls Nico in for a quick hug. "Bye, Jesse."

I wave halfheartedly as I listen to Caitlyn's voice mail inform me that my broken promises have filled her inbox and it cannot take my message at this time.

The sound of a door slamming outside startles me awake from where I was apparently forgotten on one of the trailer's white benches. Stretching up in the bright light washing in through blind slats, I look around and register that the makeup station is bare, all signs of Tandy and Diane and their team of magic, gone. I shuffle to the door and push it open, blinking in the sun, struck that no amount of movie lamps could truly replicate this.

"Sorry, have you seen Kara?" I ask the teamster winding up what looks to be the last cable in a now empty lot.

"Over at the other location," he grunts.

"She left? When?"

"Dunno."

"Well, do you know if they still need me?"

"I'm the only one here, and I don't." He hoists the

thick roll onto his shoulder. "Listen, anyone else in the trailer? I got to get it over there."

I stick my head back into the darkened interior. "Hello?" I call. Nothing. "Nope." I pull the door closed behind me and zip up my coat in the bracing air. "So, um . . . if Kara asks, can you tell her I went home? Because no one ever came and got me. So . . . " I watch as he peels up gaffer's tape from the pavement. "Great, then. Bye!"

I head down the steps and through the mess of crispy boot prints to skirt around to the front of the spa where melting ice tinkles from the trees.

I tilt my sweatshirt hood to shield my eyes from the snow glare and zip my coat to my chin in preparation for the long walk home. Home. As soon as I finish giving everything I have of value to Caitlyn in a desperate attempt to win her forgiveness, I will pull on my holey sweats, crawl into Mom and Dad's bed, fire up the TV, and hunker down with marshmallow-packed cocoa . . . ooh . . . or maybe a hot bath . . . maybe get the little TV in the kitchen set up on the toilet seat and bring the cocoa in there . . . maybe rig the DVD . . .

Suddenly a black SUV with tinted windows pulls past me into the driveway. It stops, and the back passenger window slides sleekly down. "Give me natural," I hear as I'm met with a blinding flash. "Your eyes're closed. Whatever." I recognize the mirrored aviators tilted over an iPhone screen. Fletch!

"Hi!" I jog over.

"Jesse, what's up?" He reaches out to swipe fingers, all the while looking at his phone. Registering that he's expecting us to do some street-boy high five, I tug my hand out of my pocket too late to meet his and we awkwardly brush nails. "Come on in." Ignoring my gaffe, he waves his fingers, flexing the word *Killah* tattooed on the fleshy web at the base of his thumb. He would seem to be indicating I should get in the car but makes no effort to move over.

"Sure!" I go around, squidgying myself between the wet hedge and the car to open the back passenger door.

Sprawling on the black leather interior, he greets me with another flash. "Second time's the charm." As the spots clear from my eyes, I see his phone has been custom-spangled with black Swarovski crystals in a skull-and-crossbones pattern.

"Hot, right?" he asks. "Gift from Diddy."

"Cool." I shrug off my hood and attempt to fluff my sprayed-dead bangs. He drops the phone in the pocket of his Prada parka.

"Just wanted a shot for pitching sponsors. Selling young and natural all the way, baby. G, let's do it." He lifts forward to slap his hand on the driver's shoulder—a very large black man in a disjointedly bright pink sweatshirt spotted with Murakami daisies.

His eyes darting back and forth, Fletch splits his attention between me and the flat screen—one of three I can see from here—showing some sort of financial show over the driver's seat. "You ready for all this, Jesse?"

"Definitely. And I'm so glad you're back because I'm really eager to talk to you about Caitlyn. My really hilarious, pretty friend Caitlyn. I talked to Kara about her when you were away, and she said you made a decision?"

He nods, his teeth sinking into his lower lip. Dear God, just make this man say *yes* and I swear I will go directly home and write three letters to Grandma before I even set foot in that tub. "Riiiggghhht," he says. Fasten your walker for some seriously charming communication! "I really dig you taking the initiative to think outside the box about our baby, Jesse. I need that. I need everyone thinking."

"I am!" And now *yes*. Just one little *yes*.

"Man." He laughs as he punches his fist into his hand. "We were in serious need of story line! Something dynamic! I owe you, Jesse, you landed it!"

I did? "Great!" Looks like *yes*, sounds like *yes* . . .

"Now, one more thing." G turns the SUV onto Dune Road. "What I want from you is to really focus on letting your character be bigger. Don't hold back, like, at all."

"My character?" I strain hopefully to spot Caitlyn's white coat in the mass of people milling around the trailers parked in the Beach Club lot.

"Spunky heart-of-gold with a hit of smart to keep it relatable. And here's the money shot, okay? We're meeting you just as you're discovering your dark side. I'm telling you it's a magic combo. Money." I crane my head. There's Kara and the lighting guys and the makeup crew. "Just."

He tosses his hands up. "You know, like, if you're mad, go there. If you're jealous, don't put revenge out of your mind. If you're in love, act on it, you know? Good gets you into heaven, not television. Cool?"

Dude, I have no idea what you're talking about. "I guess?"

"And anytime you want to come by my place to converse about it . . . I think you're about to really blow up."

Sure—uh-huh—sure. "Definitely. So Caitlyn's on the show?"

His face clouds and I get a hint of what Fletch angry would look like. Something you do not want to be in a confined space with, like, say an SUV. "Jesse. I have about two hundred emails to return and twice that number of phone calls to make and that's before, like, *lunch*. Instead *I* chose to come pick you up this morning, *personally*, so I could talk to you, and now I don't feel like you're listening."

"Sorry, no, I am!"

"Cool." He shoots his index finger and thumb at me while reaching inside his parka to retrieve his sparkly Cap'n Crunch phone. "You're getting everything you want. Trust me. The set's down by the water where your new story line is waiting to kick off, so hit the trailer!" Eager to see Fletch's definition of "everything," I reach for the door.

I don't even mind as they re-seal my pores with concealer and re-wave my fried hair. Or when they strip me of my coat in exchange for a mink pullover, skinny jeans, and slouchy suede boots to send me out into the dunes.

Zacheria walks by holding his hands overhead a loaf-sized distance apart and then snakes them down to his hips. "This early light is *scandalous!*"

"It's his catchall for good," Kara translates as she points me toward the water. "Okay, now just walk out to the old lifeguard station. We're going to shoot this one from here—no audio: no mikes, no booms—"

"Cameras are on zoom," Zacheria cuts her off. "Very Cassavetes."

"So you can be more natural." Kara holds back her flapping hair as the wind rolls up the shoreline.

Nodding, I jog against the strengthening breeze about a hundred yards down to the waves, smiling despite the lip gloss shellacking my ponytail. As I reach the old wood ladder, I squint to see Kara wave from the dunes for me to climb up. Careful not to snag the fur on an errant rusty nail, I hoist myself up.

"Cay?" I call out, conjuring Kelsey Grammer's advice to Mom, hoping, praying, willing this into being. I pull myself onto the little deck outside the boarded-up station and wipe off the sand that's blown onto my jeans. "Cay?"

My voice drains away as I stand upright to see my new story line, looking as stunned as I feel.

REEL 7

"**J**ase?"

"Jesse. What the hell?" He scowls, darkening under the XTV bronzer highlighting his impossibly square jaw.

"I was hoping . . . never mind." I slump against the railing, cursing Kelsey Grammer and feeling like a jackass.

"Would you answer me?! What are you doing here?"

"I was sent out here. By them." I point behind me to the dunes and a flurry of down-covered arms wave me away.

"Why?" His blue eyes flicker over my shoulder. "Why would they send *you*?"

"Why would they send *you*?"

"All I know"—he steps closer, dropping his voice—"is

that you spent the night with Nic."

"So?" And then I get what he's implying. Oh my God, my life does not revolve around whether or not you can keep it in your pants! I get a surge of anger so intense I feel heat in my forehead. "Look, I'm tired and hungry and have to go break my best friend's heart now. So if you'll excuse me." I push past him and he grabs my arm, the fur puckering where his fingers meet his thumb.

"Let go," I manage.

"You didn't tell Nico what you saw."

"I didn't tell Nico what I saw," I repeat, as the salty breeze picks up into an audible speed, my ponytail flapping between us like a loose sail.

He squints into my eyes before releasing me. Straightening my jacket, I move to the ladder, stepping over it to climb down. As I watch my suede foot reach for the next rung, I flash to Nico curled in on herself in that robe. "You should, Jase," I yell, my head just clearing the warped boards of the deck.

He crouches, his face incredulous. "Come again?"

"You should tell her." And then it'll be out. It won't be my secret or the secret I sold for a fat wad of nothing. "She deserves to know it happened." And in that moment his flattened expression tells me that it wasn't an "it," it was/ *is*? a "thing."

I drop my eyes and instinctively keep moving. "Okay, whatever, I'm going to go—"

"You don't know shit about me. Are we clear?" His cold hand gruffly takes my chin and jerks my face up to his. "Not a word." And we are no longer talking about Nico. "So go back to town and do what you're good for, cleaning toilets like Mommy."

Tugging my face from his grasp, I clamber down the ladder, jumping off into the sand. Screw him, screw Fletch, screw everyone. Taking off, I look back to see Jase leap the last few steps like Christian Bale in a Batsuit. We both tuck into the wind, trying to get ahead of each other's stride back to the dunes.

As soon as I hit the tall grass, I run toward the trailer to get my stuff so I can get the hell out of here. Fletch jumps into my path from behind the stack of monitors. I open my mouth, but before I can even begin, he pulls me into an Axe-saturated bear hug, screaming, "Yeahyeahyeah!"

My eyes tearing from the fumes, I jerk back to see Jase get pulled in with Fletch's other arm, and we are head-to-head in orange parka.

"Freaking awesome, man!" Fletch slaps Jase on the back as Jase jerks away from me.

"Dude, there was no audio on that, right?" Jase seeks confirmation. "I thought Nico was coming."

"Just mixing it up, Jase. *Man!*" He grabs each of us by the shoulders to give us a vigorous shake. "You two have *it*!"

"What do we have?" I ask.

Fletch blinks at me like I must be joking. "Heat! You two have heat!" he yells as he releases us to clap his gloved hands in hollow thuds. "File that away, Kara!"

* * *

"Caitlyn." My lungs on fire, I push into the ever-empty Bambette, close the door behind me, and slump down the pastel-stenciled wall to catch my breath. "I . . . jogged . . . from the Beach Club . . . in these . . . " I kick one foot out in front of me along the carpet. "Ridiculous . . . " I extend the other. "Boots." I drop my head like Dorothy's scarecrow. "I'm so sorry about last—"

"*So?* He's back this morning, right? Fletch?" She stands from her makeshift reading perch on the cardboard box behind the register, her shoulders and eyebrows lifted in hope. "What did he say?"

I look up at her, prepared to launch into a bullshit speech of why this is all for the best, but she knows me way too well. As she reads my expression beneath the layers of makeup and sweat, her face, her shoulders, her everything—falls.

"Whatever." She shrugs.

"No, wait—" But how can I spin the unspinnable to the one person who's been reading my mind since kinder-garten? "The thing is that, well . . . "

Taking a nearby stack of folded cashmere bibs and shak-ing one out sharply, she commences refolding. "Whatever," she repeats. The cold rock in my stomach overriding my screaming shins, I use the shabby-chic dresser of onesies to pull myself up.

She lifts a hand to stop me. "It's cool, Jesse. I said whatever."

"It's not cool!" I arrive at the white wood desk and put

my hand on hers as she reaches for the next bib. "It *sucks*! And they didn't even have the balls to tell me; they just sent me out to practically get murdered by Jase McCaffrey! Jase, who I apparently have 'heat' with—how scary is that—and I broke out of there *the minute* it was clear that they weren't going to cast you—"

"So you quit?" Her voice is quiet. The CD we're always joking is going to drive her to down the Windex plays Pachelbel's Canon in the space between us.

"No, I . . . " I pull back my hand. "You know I can't turn down this money, Cay; my parents would kill me. I feel so bad—I don't even think there's a word for how crappy I feel. You deserve to be in this show, not that I would wish it on anyone. Oh God, it's so ridiculous. All waiting and having crap slapped on and scrubbed off and 'stand here' and 'say this' with people you don't know, don't like, don't think are remotely funny, and there's, like, a million people there who care *so much* about all of it and, like, a million professional actors from the city—they've got them staying in the B&B behind Saks—and it goes on for, like, hours—"

"Sorry," she interrupts, resuming the rhythm of her folding. "Am I supposed to feel bad for you?"

"That's not at all what—"

"Because *I*"—she flicks a bib at me—"spent the night *alone*." She folds it once. "With your *fish tank*." Twice. She flicks the next one as her nostrils flare. "Oh, and that's *after* the smoke alarm went off from the oven where I was keeping the pizza warmed for you. The pizza *I* had to pay for from your dad's *penny jar* while the guy waited for, like, an hour because somebody took the money in *their* pocket."

"Oh my God, Cay, I'm so—"

"Then, after I stopped it the *first* time, the alarm just went off, like, *every hour* for the rest of the night, and I was totally freaked out after watching the scary movie somebody told me, *promised* me, they were going to come home after. But that somebody did not come home because she spent the night where?"

"I tried to leave a message as soon as they were done filming—at dawn—but your box was full."

"And then when I wake up you're *still* not home. I rode your bike to the spa and there was no one there. Nothing. And I was rattled from the fire alarm and the movie and I was worried. And I didn't know what else to do so I called your mom. I didn't know they were going to have you all night! I didn't know if maybe you had tried to walk home and something or someone—"

A panic bell thuds dully from the back of my head. "You called my mom?"

"Yeah, she was, like, 'I'm getting in the car right now.'"

"When was this?"

"Sometime between the fifth fire alarm and calling the emergency room. Sorry to be worried you were dead."

"No, I'm sorry! It's just—your mailbox was full."

The door jingles open, and a woman comes in with a massive Birkin bag and even more massive *Nanook of the North* hat.

"Weekender," we both automatically mutter.

"I need three of these in an infant size, wrapped separately." She dangles a lime-colored cashmere onesie in our direction while continuing to flip through the rack.

"I have to get back to work." Caitlyn scoots around the table and takes it from her.

"I'm sorry," I say furtively. "I did everything I could."

"So did I." She bites her bottom lip.

"Oh my God, is that the new J. Mendel?" Covetous, the weekender practically steps on Caitlyn to finger my borrowed fur. "*Gorgeous.* I'm on the wait list. Meanwhile I get to spend all my husband's hard-earned cash on shower gifts for my IVF BFFs, lucky me." She turns to Caitlyn. "Are you going to wrap those?"

Caitlyn smiles tightly. "Of course." She takes the onesie and steps quickly to the register.

"The help around here seems a little inbred, if you ask me," the weekender says to me out of the side of her lip-lined mouth.

"That's my best friend," I say loudly. Caitlyn shoots me a *just leave* look.

"Well, I . . . " Red-faced, the woman shakes her head. Not knowing what else to do, I head for the door.

"Oh, Miss O'Rourke?"

I turn to Caitlyn's sickeningly sweet voice.

"You can send your driver over with the seven dollars and fifty-two cents you owe me for the movies. I'll take that in pennies."

"Jessica Taryn O'Rourke."

I fight through the grip of deep sleep to see Mom standing over me, still in her coat, arms crossed, face pissed. "What the hell happened to you last night?"

I wipe away the hair matted to my face and push myself up to sit on the couch. My hand traces the imprint of the phone in my cheek, where I kept it in case she called back after hanging up on me from the road. "I'm sorry," I try again, a yawn escaping as I pull my bare legs up under my bathrobe.

"Yes, so you said. I need a little more than that."

I blink my eyes in a struggle to stay awake. "I'm *really* sorry. The show had me out all night."

"Doing what? What exactly do they need you *all night* for?"

"Filming. I guess they're going to be shooting weekends now, too."

She sits heavily on the La-Z-Boy. "So you were working," she says mostly to herself, staring at me in the late-afternoon light. ". . . Okay." She rubs her hand along the back of her neck. "You really scared us, Jesse."

"Mom, this show's just a lot more . . . " I struggle to put the experience into words for both of us. "I thought I'd be doing my thing and they'd follow and film it and—okay—weird. But not *this*. This is someone else's life. With no *Caitlyn*. I don't know if she's going to get over this." I feel my cheeks dampen, and her expression softens.

She stands and reaches down for my hand, helping me up into a hug. I sink against her. "This is just new, that's all. Just like any job. The whole house is such a mess you think it'll never get clean. But one room at a time and it becomes habit. You're a smart girl; you'll get the hang of this, Jess."

"I don't know if I want to."

She pulls back to wipe my tears with the well-worn sleeve of her down coat. "God willing, you'll both be at schools in D.C. next year, and this'll be no more important than when that boy you both liked asked you to the roller-skating party."

"I don't know, Mom. It's pretty bad." I flash to Caitlyn's wounded face as I circled past her, tugged along by Josh Dupree's clammy hand to LeAnn Rimes telling us she can't fight the moonlight, the only time he acknowledged me all night. All I wanted to do was tell her that up close he looked like a toddler with a blond mustache and smelled like Cheez Doodles and Old Spice. But she didn't return my calls all weekend. It took weeks for things to get back to normal, for the glint of hurt to fully vanish from her eyes.

Mom takes off her coat and folds it over her arm, fingering a tear in the lining. "Just think how much more exciting it is than filling muffin tins and washing them out all day long. You want to be doing that for the rest of your life?"

"No."

"Nobody does, Jesse." She looks up from the dime-sized hole with a tired smile.

The following morning, balancing the stack of Sunday newspapers against my hip, I struggle to get the key into the front door of the Prickly Pear without dropping everything onto the salted pavement. The early sun streaks across the closed storefronts of Main Street, and I note how a fitful night's sleep has done jack to dull yesterday's stings. "Crap." The cold keys slip from my freezing hands and clank to the sidewalk. "Jamie Beth?" I grip the papers and turn to her as she attempts to inhale enough nicotine to fuel her until lunch. "Jamie Beth."

She squints at me over gray smoke streaming from her mouth.

"Could you maybe . . . " I glance down at the keys, splayed beside my sneakers.

Gripping the cigarette between her chapped lips, she scoops them up to dangle before me.

"In the door, please?" I gesture with my chin. She pushes the key in and turns the knob with a sigh, the weight of the papers pitching me inside and onto the nearest wobbly table. The familiar smell of bleach and baked goods clears Jamie Beth's cigarette from my head. So that's something.

"Can you get the coffee going and I'll get the awnings?" I ask, knowing full well that she won't because she's too busy tackling her first priority: slouching against the counter to pick at her peeling nail polish.

No. I do not want to fill muffin cups the rest of my life.

"Jamie Beth? Please?" I plop the box of coffee filters in front of her. She contemplates them.

I duck back outside into the stark sunshine. Twirling the metal pole overhead, I tend to the windows on both sides of the corner bakery, unfurling the striped awnings that keep the sun from amplifying the heat of the basement ovens come noon.

"Jesse!"

I twist to see Drew jogging over from the Stop & Shop parking lot across the street. "You're always running!" What?

"What?" He reaches me, his breath coming out in little puffs.

"What?" Take two. "Hey, what're you doing here?"

"Working." He points at the red apron over his windbreaker. "The cart kid's sick today so I'm on duty."

"Cool. I didn't know you worked there," I lie, leaning into the pole like a cane to steady myself against a wave of nerves because, despite his initial declaration of being in this together, I'm always with Nico and Melanie and he's with Jase and Rick. Other than crowded chaotic morning check-ins, we haven't exchanged more than a "What's up?" since that second day in the trailer.

"Yeah, Sundays in the stockroom. Just helping out my folks with the bills." He looks away, and I wonder just how bad things are. "And, you know, saving for a Maybach." He raises his head, squinting into the bright sky. "I'm working while you're working, so that's probably why you haven't . . . " You know that I'm working when you're working? I pray he couldn't see me gazing from the counter in my fetching Prickly Pear trucker cap—thanks, NYS health code.

"Yeah." We smile stupidly at each other and, staring up at his wind-reddened cheeks, I can't think of a single thing to say. "So . . . " and that went nowhere.

He tucks his hands in his pockets. "It's nice out here this morning, just kinda being out here by myself."

"I can go back inside."

"No." He laughs. "Just with all the filming this weekend."

"What did they make *you* do?" I will my nose not to drip in the cold.

"Oh, I had to go to some pool place in Montauk with Jase and Rick, and we were there, like, *all night* shooting the same thing over and over, which was kind of . . . "

"Weird?"

"Yeah. And then they did, like, all these beach walk things yesterday. So many freaking people."

"Come on, dude." I cock my head in my best Fletch, daring to poke his ribs. "You're not having more freakin' fun than *ever before* doing what kids do?"

"Not bad." He grins.

"You wish you were wearing a mike pack right now, admit it."

He raises a shoulder, his name tag going askew. "I do kinda miss the raw skin and clammy wire."

My turn to laugh.

"Yeah . . ." He looks intently at me. "It's all a little—"

"Much," I fill in. "Much makeup. Much people. Much weirdness with friends . . ."

"You too?" He steps closer and, beneath his flushed cheeks, I notice a small patch of stubble at his jaw that he missed shaving.

"I promised Caitlyn I'd make sure she got cast and yesterday had to tell her she wasn't," I confess. "I feel like I ran over her dog."

"I know." He crosses his arms over his apron. "I was supposed to watch my little brother Friday night and then, obviously, that didn't happen, and my mom came down on me about how I'm getting a big head."

"I see you and raise you." I look up at him and let my hand dart out for a split second to his forearm. "My parents drove all the way to Providence only to turn right around in the wee hours to check local hospitals for my mangled corpse. So they're loving me. It's like this . . . thing that's kind of landed between us and—"

"Everyone. Exactly." He shoves his hands in his pockets

and clears his throat, his bangs falling in his eyes. "Listen, do you want to grab lunch together?" I feel a tremble up my spine. "I can break at eleven fifteen, and we can hit the deli counter and make use of my six percent discount?"

"I can bring dessert." I lift up on the balls of my Converses. "At a full eight percent off, thank you very much."

"Cool!" Smiling, he jogs backward across the street toward the edge of the lot.

"Cool."

Suddenly he stops backing up, and I follow his stare behind me to the XTV van barreling down the street, screeching to a stop between us. The side door rolls open, and I half expect armed men to leap out.

Kara, purple rings under her eyes, leans forward. "Hop in, Jesse."

"Oh, sorry, I can't today." I jerk my thumb at the building behind me. "I'm working a double shift." And having a hot lunch date!

"Yeah, we took care of that. So hop in, we had to get you in makeup five minutes ago."

"You took care of it?"

"We quit for you. Come. In the van."

I step forward, trying to make sense of it. "You talked to my boss?"

Kara drops her head to let out a tortured moan. "My assistant did. It's fine. No more Prickly Crap for you. Now, will you please get in the van?"

Speechless to no longer have a job and crushed to no

longer have a date, I look to Drew, and he shrugs help-lessly.

"You're up at dusk, Drew," Kara yells across the street. "Guys have a five-thirty call at Jase's! Jesse. Now."

"Okay. Okay . . . well, I just have to—" I lift the pole to indicate I'm going inside.

"Whatever, they can bill us for it. Please, Jesse."

Laying it down on the sidewalk, I walk to the van door, murmuring, "You quit my job for me?"

"You can thank me later." Kara reaches out and, in one tug of my hand, pulls me in.

REEL 8

A month later finds me frantically wiping off my face as I stare out the trailer window at the exuberant Friday tide of students flowing to a trickle from the side doors. I have given Caitlyn as much space as I can bear, and today is my breaking point. I miss her so freaking much, and she has to miss me at least a little.

"Later, Jesse." Nico stuffs her towelettes into the small garbage can Tandy holds out and jogs down the steps.

"Later." I give a halfhearted wave as I think I spot— yes, that's Cay's unmistakable streaked blond ponytail swinging. I grab my bag, lob my foundation-caked cloths into Tandy's can, and head for the trailer door. "Thanks!" I call to Tandy. "Bye, Kara!" I yell back to the monitor room as I step outside.

"Seven a.m. call time tomorrow!" she shouts.

"Got it!"

"Hey!" Drew backs up on the pavement to clear the swinging metal. "It's you."

"Hey!" I scan over his ski hat to keep sight of Caitlyn. Crap. She's with Jennifer Lanford. Again. Maybe I shouldn't count so much on the missing part. My eyes dart back to Drew, who suddenly looks like he's not sure what to do with his hands. "Sorry, yes, yeah, it's been crazy this week."

"Every week. We're mike packs passing in the trailer."

I nod—they're only a few feet from her car. "Yeah."

"Right, so I should probably . . . " He points at the door.

Caitlyn reaches for her keys. "I really have to go." I touch the arm of his jacket as I step around him. "Sorry!"

"Fine, but you owe me a muffin."

"Deal." I grin, my heart flicking from excitement to fear as I jog toward the Camry. "Cay!"

She whips her head up from where she's just tossed her coat into the backseat. I wave. She gives me an empty smile. Jennifer turns from the open passenger door to glance from Caitlyn to me with slightly raised, twice-pierced eyebrows that indicate she's been filled in. Great.

"Hey." Caitlyn crosses her arms over her thin sweater as I slow in front of the passenger side.

"Hey!"

We take each other in over the roof. So . . . here goes. "I was wondering if maybe I could, um, hitch a ride. Maybe treat to pizza or whatever. Are you guys hungry?"

"Starving," Jennifer intones. "Those burgers were foul."

Caitlyn sighs heavily. Ugh, I want to be an hour from now, past this part where I'm an awkward stranger with the person I want to tell about it later. "Fine," she says.

"Shotgun." Jennifer lifts the front seat forward, and I lumber into the back, pushing aside the CDs and Coke cans to make room for myself behind her. They get in and Caitlyn starts the car, not meeting my eyes as she turns around to back out of the spot.

"Thanks!" I click on my seat belt. "For the ride."

"So, spill it, Jesse." Jennifer leans around her seat, her leather jacket gathering against the belt. "What's it like? Give me a day in the life."

"Oh no. It's not really—"

"We're dying to know," Caitlyn says flatly as she stares at the road.

"You guys don't want to—"

"We do. Details." Jennifer slices the air between the seats. "We see them trailing you at school. I want the other stuff, these weekend things Caitlyn said you have to do."

So she acknowledges the "have to." "Oh, they suck." I slouch back, hugging my bag.

"Details, bitch!" Jennifer commands.

"Okay, um, well, last Saturday—"

"Valentine's?" she asks.

"Yes. So we're sitting in the trailer at the asscrack of dawn—me, Melanie, Nico, and the nutjob cinematographer guy, Zacheria—yup, that's his name—he thinks he's so artsy, but I swear he worked for, like, *Blue's Clues* before this. Anyway, he informs us that 'we're sick of it all.' And we're like, 'Yes, yes, we are sick of it! Day off?' No. He informs us that we're sick of shopping and spa-ing and eating sushi. What we *want* is to get back to nature."

A smile flickers over Caitlyn's face. Okay, this is good, this is working.

"Cut to twelve hours trying to make the Montauk backwoods look like Mont Blanc."

"Twelve hours?!" Jennifer hoots.

"Three to walk through the trees holding hands and trying to maintain a conversation through massively oversized Gautier earmuffs. We looked ridonculous. And we have *nothing* to talk about because we're never apart for more than forty minutes—" Caitlyn takes a hard left, and I brace myself with a hand on the ceiling. "I mean, unless Nico and Melanie want to explain how to diagram a parabola there's no information they're getting that I'm not."

"Are you like their BFF now?" Jennifer asks like it's nothing.

"*No.*" My turn to slice the air. "No, we are *absolutely* not. It's like people you work with. Friendly, but not—"

"Anyway!"

"Anyway, after a typical lunch of, like, malt balls and Twizzlers, Kara—the producer—announces we're ready, after three weekend shoots of 'fun girl time,' to 're-integrate.' Which means we're snowmobiled to the boys' set, which is the first time I'm around any of them—Rick, Drew, *Jase*," I throw meaningfully to Caitlyn, not wanting to get into it in front of Jennifer. "Awkward, yes. But at least we weren't *chopping wood*. Like the poor blistered, splintered boys. Fletch—the head guy—just stood there in these gigantic moon boots, slurping his Red Bull, yelling at Drew to 'put more back into it.' If Rick hadn't gotten a sliver, like, an inch from his eye, he'd have made them go until they built a chalet. Then, more hair. More makeup. More Doritos. A costume change involving lederhosen. And finally . . . a snowball fight. A *four-hour* snowball fight."

Caitlyn lets out a knowing laugh, and I dare to lean forward between them. "Anybody with half a brain will keep walking when they see one starting. Because you will end up with snow down your neck. You will end up with wet, cold lederhosen where you've fallen down repeatedly in the ambush. You may even end up with a black eye." I pause dramatically, getting into the storytelling, fishing for more laughs. "I got all three."

"Shut up." Jennifer smacks the dashboard.

"I will not. Of course, Nico took every opportunity to throw herself on Jase, while I'm just trying to keep a minimum of one tree between us at all times. Melanie's packing 'em and tossing 'em for all she's worth at every bullhorned suggestion from Zacheria, hitting all of us until Rick winds up and socks her one to the solar plexus, knocking the wind out of her for a good minute. At which point Kara runs over waving a medical liability release form. So, in summary: Nico slapped Rick. Jase pushed Nico. Drew shoved Jase. Jase went to take out Drew, missed, and nearly broke my nose. And that was hour one. Tomorrow we'll probably be going lobster trapping with our bare hands. Jealous?"

Caitlyn turns right on Main and my stomach does a little flip. "Didn't you guys want pizza?" I ask.

"*Yes,*" Jennifer moans, turning back around to face the street.

"No." Caitlyn speeds the final mile to my house. "We kind of have plans." She shoots a look at Jennifer. The look she always used to shoot me. That's *my* look.

"Okay." I tell myself to shrug as she veers into my driveway.

"You're really funny," Jennifer states as she gets out of her seat to let me out.

"Thanks." I climb past her. "Thanks for the ride," I mumble in Caitlyn's direction as, head tucked, I focus on making it inside before my eyes water.

Just as my foot hits the porch steps, I hear a door slam and spin to see Caitlyn marching over, hunched into herself, the skin above her deep V-neck turning red in the cold. "We can't just go back, Jesse."

"I know, I just thought—"

"You can't just tell some Jesse story and expect me to be fine."

"Maybe not fine, but at least talking to me! I hate this. You know what I miss most about Saturdays? Meeting you at breaks to commiserate about lost weekenders with real estate listings clasped to their fur-covered chests."

"But now you have your own fur-covered chest," she spits, her eyes glassy and hard.

"Caitlyn, it isn't my fault that I got this job and you didn't!"

"I can't, Jesse. Don't do this again. It hurts too much." She runs back to the car, and in a blurry moment they've pulled away.

The next morning, after our seven a.m. call time and General Mills Breakfast Of Champions, Melanie, Nico, and I are driven over to the Stop & Shop.

"Yes!" Kara cries into the bullhorn, startling the other shoppers trying to feed their families without coming into the aisle Zacheria commandeered. **"I love it. Now don't look at the prices. Melanie, Jess, stop checking the prices! Cut! You're rich girls shopping for a romantic dinner. Price is irrelevant. Do-over!"**

My heart hung over from my failed attempt with Caitlyn, but trying to focus, I return the packet of steaks to the Stop & Shop meat case, walk back to the top of the aisle, emptying our basket along the way, and begin again.

"Good, great," Zacheria coaches from out of frame.

"Olives! Take olives! And those little pickles! The expensive ones! Yeah! Grab the little pickles!"

At that, Nico and Melanie finally lose it, falling on each other in a heap of helpless laughter.

"Cut!"

"Okay." Kara, ever the pacer, makes her laps behind our three chairs in the trailer as they redo our hair and makeup from the grocery store without the safety net of smocks, careful not to drop anything on our jewel-toned cocktail dresses. "You've shopped. Now you're going to go back to Melanie's house to cook for the boys."

Stricken, Melanie swings around in her chair, getting a green stripe of eyeliner across her face in the process. "*My* house? But it's not—I mean, of course, yes, if you want, but I have to call my mom, we have to get it nice—"

"Oh no, don't worry, Melanie," Kara rushes to reassure her. "We rented a house for the night."

"Oh," Melanie says, swiveling back so the makeup artist can dab at the streak with a Q-Tip. I give an internal sigh of relief that if Melanie's house isn't glamorous enough—and they have an attached garage—ours definitely won't be called upon. And I won't have to run home some night and try to repaint it between four and six a.m.

"So, let's get you gorgeous and get you cooking!"

"Stand back from the steam!" Zacheria shouts into his bullhorn, the sun now setting through Mrs. Richardson's bay windows as I stir the spaghetti. **"Stir from a distance! Jenny, crouch down out of frame and fan her!"** Teetering on my patent-leather platforms, I take two steps back from Mrs. Richardson's antique copper pot with Mrs. Richardson's antique wood spoon. In Mrs. Richardson's French Country kitchen. Which I've been in countless times with my mom and was never supposed to touch anything. Ever.

"Cut! Her makeup is sliding off. Get her fixed up and off stove duty! Can *anybody* cook without sweating?"

"If we were making sushi," Nico retorts. And Melanie shoots her the same knock-it-off look she does any time Nico talks back.

After they fix my makeup, I'm stationed in the breakfast nook with a Wüsthof knife and olive-wood cutting board. Which I think is only supposed to be used as a cheese tray. Every slice of carrot makes a thin groove in the wood.

"Kara!" I call out as they're re-lighting the kitchen. "Are you sure I can use this?"

"They signed a form, Jesse. We're clear."

"Okay, you are making dinner for the guys, and go!"

Nico, Drew, Jase, Rick, and I all nod on fumes of enthusiasm from where we're seated at the massive mahogany table. Melanie once again delivers her line: "I'm so glad you guys liked the pasta. Dessert is from this really cool Doritos recipe I downloaded from the Doritos website, www.doritosdelights.com. It has a delicious key lime center and a crumbly Doritos crust—"

A loud stomach grumble interrupts her. We all cut our eyes at Drew, who shrugs apologetically.

"Drew," Kara moans, her bullhorn momentarily at rest in her lap.

My non-dining dining companions slump forward in our straight-backed Napoleonic chairs while the food stylist appears to spray more baby oil atop Melanie's outstretched pie. To keep up the gleam. The same gleam that has been sprayed on all our food tonight. I am starting to wonder how many brain cells I could really lose to baby-oiled garlic bread and if I would really miss them.

"I can't work like this!" Zacheria screams from the minstrel's balcony above the table.

"Drew, just . . ." Kara wrings her hands in exasperation from the nearby monitor station. "Hang in there. We're almost done with the 'pie' scene, okay?"

Drew sighs. "Yeah, I need to eat something that's not in quotes."

"Seriously. That pizza smells killer." Rick strains to see the spread on the craft services table just out of shot.

"Can't we at least nibble on the stuff we cooked?" Nico twists around to blink into the wall of lights.

"I'll get it right this time, Kara," I hear Mel offer from behind my chair.

"Remember, don't say the line exactly how I said it. It sounds forced." For the first time Kara makes little effort to cover her frustration. "Just give it your own spin, Melanie. The clock is ticking."

"Sure, no problem!" I turn to see Melanie nod with a frozen smile, her green eyes sparkling in panic. The more frustrated Kara gets, the more Melanie freezes up.

"She says she gets it, but I'm not hearing it," Zacheria mutters.

"Sorry, I'll definitely do it this time."

Eager to help Mel out and get this over with before my stomach joins Drew's in a chorus of protest, I whisper over my shoulder, "Just say, like, 'This pie from doritosdelights. com rocks! You guys have to check out the site.' And then I'll ask what else is on the site, okay?"

"Exactly, Jesse!" Kara booms, reminding me that I traded in effective whispering when my parents signed the XTV consent, just like the Richardsons traded in the safety of their cheese tray.

"Thanks." Melanie's cheeks redden under her foundation.

"Sorry—no, I think she's doing a great job—"

"Melanie, sit. Jesse, up. Change of plans. Take the pie and we'll start the scene from the kitchen."

"But I really think Melanie—"

"Take the freaking pie to the freaking kitchen, Jesse." Jase grips his hands around the table lip, the linen puckering.

"Please," Nico implores. "I'm going to faint, seriously."

"No, it's fine." Melanie steps forward to hand me the cold porcelain dish, and I push up and around her as she studiously smoothes the emerald satin of her skirt to sit.

I scurry through the double mahogany doors and wait in the trashed kitchen, grabbing an abandoned clammy fusilli from a nearby strainer and snarfing it down as Kara yells, **"Action!"**

I push through the doors and walk to the head of the table, where everyone stares at me expectantly over the flickering candelabras. "This pie *rocks*. It has a key lime center and a Doritos crust. We found it on doritosdelights.com."

"Cool." Drew gives it his best. "I love that site."

"It's dope," Jase helps.

"Totally!" Nico lifts a shoulder coquettishly at Jase. "I get a ton of after-school snack ideas there."

I slide the pie onto the table, and Melanie brings it home. "Hey, after dinner, let's hit my parents' Jacuzzi!"

"Cool!"

"Yeah!"

"Let's do it!" We all cheer like we're on Nickelodeon.

"Cut! Moving on!" Kara says the magic words. **"I love you guys! Okay, break. And into bathing suits."**

"Girls, no pizza for you, or I'm going to have a camera full of tummy bloat," Zacheria warns from above as we scoot back our chairs and scramble over one another to descend on the crew's food.

"Nico!"

Nico looks up from the fray, Cheez-Its crumbling out of her full mouth. "Yeah?"

"Hair and makeup." One of the faux-hawked assistants reads down his clipboard.

"Two minutes," she begs through chipmunk cheeks, spraying bright orange flakes.

Melanie and I offer sympathetic smiles, but continue shoveling in anything not-pizza from the trays.

"*Now*, Nico."

Nico manages to grasp two handfuls of gummy worms as she's hurried away toward the library serving as trailer.

I take advantage of the distraction to swipe a slice from the open box and, knowing the layout, dart around the feeding frenzy and into the back hall. Saliva filling my mouth in anticipation, I take a few steps into the cover of the dim sconce lighting and sink my teeth in. Oh my God. Cheesy, salty, bready, baby-oil-free heaven. I slide down the wall to the black-and-white-marble tile, savoring every bite.

"Busted." Two John Varvatos Converse appear in my carb haze, and I look up to see Drew. He grins.

"If you tell on me I will have you killed, and I'm not even kidding." I hastily swipe a napkin across my chin. "There's a felon who washes dishes in my dad's kitchen—he has crazy sympathy for having to eat on an institutional schedule."

"Don't worry, O'Rourke, I value my life and don't really see you as the tummy-bloat type. They said there was a bathroom back here?"

"Down the hall." Savoring the compliment, I pull in my legs so he can pass, my patent leather heels squeaking across the marble. "In the paneling." I point a few feet down the green silk brocade panels bordered in shiny wood.

"Where?" He looks from wall to wall.

"Between the painting of the hunting dogs and the painting of the hunted pheasants. It's hidden."

He steps closer to the wall and runs his finger along the molding. "Because rich people don't want people to know they go to the bathroom? Ah-ha!" He locates the groove and swings open the door.

"It's like a status thing."

He tilts his head at me questioningly, brown hair flopping.

"That's my theory and I'm sticking to it."

"You have . . . " He walks back toward me.

"Many theories. Rich people like: appliances they don't use, curtains they can't close, pets they don't play with, and bathrooms they can't find."

"No." He leans down and gently wipes my chin. "Sauce." He slides his finger over the napkin wadded in my hand while I die a silent death.

"Thanks," I manage.

"Sure." He smiles, his face staying low next to mine. I breathe carefully out of my nose, willing my nostrils to mask the pepperoni.

"This the shitter line?"

Drew jerks up, and we both look over at Jase, tugging

at the starched collar of his borrowed shirt.

"Just gimme a sec." Drew steps to the hidden door. "You should tell him your theories," he offers before closing it.

Jase leans against the wall opposite me as I dab the napkin over my whole mouth and chin. "This blows," he summarizes after a beat of me nodding with pursed lips.

"It does," I concur.

"I mean, I thought they had an indoor pool."

"Right, that's the bummer." Not the two hours we just spent not eating.

"Everyone on this street has an indoor. My dad's building one with a waterfall next door. Next to the guesthouse."

I stand up as the person I'm avoiding brings up the subject that makes me avoid him, lest we have any more "heat."

"Pizza was decent," he continues his review.

"Yeah." I straighten the hem of my cranberry satin minidress to cover the tops of my thigh highs.

"So, sorry about your nose," he says to me. I look up, and he looks to the painting above my head. "I was gunning for Drew. My pitching arm must be off. Good thing spring training's coming up."

"Whatever, it's fine." I give a shrug in that brown-bunny-turning-white-in-the-snow sort of way. "Tandy fixed me up."

He drops his blue eyes to mine for the first time, his

smile spreading. "You just had me all distracted in those lederhosen. They let you keep those?" He drums the wallpaper behind him.

"That's silk." Reflexively I point to his greasy fingertips as my mind registers and then tries to reject his comment.

"What, this your house now?" Straightening, he shoots me a withering glower.

I fold my napkin into little squares while glancing back at the wall that's sealed up over the boy I want to be talking to. The one who's nice, funny, hot, and nice. "No, I just . . . " know that my mom spent six hours trying to get a speck of mud out last Easter, so ten fingers covered in pizza grease—

"You just *what*?" he prods, leaning in to lower his voice. He gives me a look that makes me wish we could go back to the minute before when he was only being sleazy. "Why does Fletch keep asking me about Trisha?"

"JESSE!"

"Sorry, gotta go." Never so relieved to hear Kara yell my name, I dart past him to get suited.

An hour later finds the six of us, girls in strips of couture swimwear, boys in board shorts, huddled together in the sunroom, its curtains drawn. A shivering mass of spray-tanned gooseflesh, we wait in darkness to be released through doors held shut by crew guys in down jackets and ski hats. I keep from freezing by focusing on the rippling profile of Drew's shoulders all of an inch from my nose. Hello, Drew's shoulders.

"**Jase?**" Kara requests, via bullhorn, from all of two feet behind us.

"Yeah?" To my horror, the head atop those shoulders swivels around, catching my glazed-over eyes mid-fantasy. Not Drew. Not even close. His gaze locks on mine for a moment before a slow smile twinges Jase's lips. The clouds of air cease puffing from my lips. Tilting his head the tiniest bit forward, he lets his gaze boldly wander down over every inch of me. I am suddenly breathless as I feel an involuntary hot capillary dilation creeping up my stomach and chest.

"**Crap, I can't see you in the dark. Jase, raise your arm and wave it around!**"

I shake my head, knocking his pheromones out of my nose and my brain back into place. Hello, he's an *asshole*. I step away, into Melanie, who pushes me back off her toes. Jase darts out a hand to my hip to steady me as he waves the other overhead for Kara.

"Great. I want you up front so you can be the first on the patio. Jase, then Nico, then everyone else."

With a last cocky smile he releases me to step forward, and we all shuffle around to let him and Nico take their places.

"Nice suit."

I look up from the invisible palm print Jase left to see Drew—rippling muscle, but *nice*. "Thanks, I had no idea crochet held up to chlorine," I whisper.

"And . . . action!" The doors whip open to a blast of light and frost as we shuffle forward into a six-kid pileup.

"*Trisha?*" I hear Nico. "What are you doing here?"

I step out from the huddle to see, standing on the top step of the steaming sunken Jacuzzi, an airbrushed version of Trisha Wright: gold string bikini taut over flattened bum, triangle top straining over two freshly installed C-cups, and a nose and cheekbones that make her look like a five-years-older someone else. Someone generic. Someone *Girls Next Door.* She lets out a squeal and dips to splash water in our openmouthed direction, dousing the guy holding the fan to keep her hair extensions waving.

Sweet Jesus. The A plot has arrived.

"Come on in, guys! The water's *hot!*"

Jase backs up a step, missing Rick's high five. "Yeah!" Rick recovers into a fist pump. "It's got cup holders!" He jogs over the icy slate patio to grab a soda from the nearby cooler and hop on in. Drew follows, and, with a furtive look at Nico, Melanie pads quickly behind him.

"Jase!" Camo-clad Zacheria waves him on from the bushes and, finding his smile, Jase follows into the frothy water.

But Nico just stands there, rigid as everyone passes, her breath coming out in little puffs in front of her pale face. "Come on," I say, sliding my hand gently around her elbow. "It's freezing out here."

"Right." She starts walking next to me, our feet

stinging. "Right," she says again, seeming to shake it off as we arrive at the tub.

"Damn! This joint is boiling," Rick says as Jase settles back into the circular bench.

"Your skin just has to adjust . . . to the heat," Trisha coos before dunking under and surfacing in Jase's face. Nico stops dead, one hand on the railing, one foot in the water. Trisha whips her hair across Jase's chest to spin around and sit on his lap, her back against him. "So, Nico, miss me?" She rests her extensioned mane on Jase's neck, her implants surfacing over the bubbles.

Nico appears to be speechless.

"Well, you know, it's been pretty hectic," I answer, tugging Nico down the steps into the stingingly hot water behind me. "School, I mean. Has been hectic," I add for the cameras. Melanie scoots over to make a spot for her, but Nico just stands there, eyes locked with Trisha's new blue contacts, which, over her naturally brown irises, make her look like she's not really in there. Nico looks at Jase, but he just shrugs as if Trisha has a gun on him. I then look to Melanie, the resident Nico expert, but she's in a baby splash war with Rick. Because off-camera Zacheria is pointedly patting the air in front of him.

"Nico, you want to sit down?" I try as I lower myself on the bench next to Drew.

"I do." She stares at Trisha writhing slowly on her boyfriend—Trisha, arching her back, pursing her lips, her body angled for Jase, for Nico, but ultimately for the cameras sticking out in the nearby hedges. What, did she get a tutorial while on the operating table?

"Nico?" Drew says suddenly, moving over to create space between us, twisting that pizza slice in my stomach to life.

Her face radiating gratitude, she turns her full, God-given blond everything on him and, striding through hip-high water, sidles between us, slipping an arm around his waist.

Jase's brow darkens. Trisha swivels around to face him, upping the ante, and I, I am as frozen as if I were buried in that snowbank a foot away.

"Cut! Now, that's television!" Kara cries into the frigid steam-filled night. **"Trisha, you're a *trooper*! Gold star for coming in before your stitches are out!"**

Having dispatched Nico and Melanie twenty minutes ago, Jenny raps on the metal siding of the van to cue the driver to take Trisha and me home. I huddle into the corner, my wet, chlorinated hair starting to harden in the cold, wishing I lived in the same direction as Drew. But I don't. Nico does. Nico, whose rescue Drew came to. What *was* that?

The van pulls out into the empty street. "That was *amazing*!" Trisha gushes, slowly peeling off a false eyelash. "Wow." Sticking out from below her swing coat, her bare legs straddle the tote between her strappy-sandaled feet. "The wardrobe and the crew and the lighting! The makeup lady even shaded my stomach," she prattles in delighted disbelief. "Has it been like this the *whole* time?" But she doesn't stop for me to answer. "Wow, you're *so* lucky." She reaches down into the tote and pulls out a packet of makeup remover towelettes. "But I'm lucky, too! I mean, I couldn't believe it. There I was in West Palm— recuperating." She points to her face. "Because I didn't make the show, and, as my mom said, I mean, *hello,* wake-up call! I'm just sitting there, letting the new me heal, and Fletch comes a-knockin' talking about dynamic new story lines. Mom says I manifested it." She wipes the white cloth across her face, and it comes away thick with concealer, revealing a yellow-and-black marbleized web of bruising across her skin.

The driver's cell rings in the silence and he answers it, listening for a few moments. "Will do," he says before hanging up.

"He wanted me ASAP." Trisha resumes her update. "But not even tattoo cover-up worked a week ago. This is so much more awesome than I thought it would be!"

The van lurches going over a pothole as it does a U-turn.

"I know I've missed a lot of school, but, whatever. I'm a legacy at Goucher." Trisha reaches under the nape of her neck and unclips an extension, holding a glob of wet hair. "This is totally going to kick Jase's ass in gear. Did you see the look on his face when he saw me? It's ridiculous. He just stays with her out of convenience. But being chosen for this has to show him how big his world can be. And how *great* we are together." She unclips another clump of hair. "And screw Nico. Let her find herself some nobody. Drew Rudell. He wants to sit next to her? Perfect. Done."

The van parks and, unable to pull my eyes off her, I fumble for the handle. *So* not perfect. *So* not done.

"Okay! Well, see you on set!" She smiles, and I can see a small black wire peeking out of her nostril.

"Yeah," I say, desperate to get away, unable to believe, in a futile effort to get Caitlyn cast, I've thrown Nico onto Drew's lap. With my thrust the door roars open, and I blink out at the unfamiliar driveway. "Um, sir?"

"Yeah."

"This is Nico's house. I'm on Belvedere."

"Nope, Kara called. You're both getting out here. Sleepover shoot."

Trisha and I look at each other, confused. And then Ben's van pulls up behind ours.

REEL 9

With Trisha at my heels, shielding her raw face from Ben's camera with her bag, I tentatively push open Nico's front door. "Hello?" We step into the two-story entrance hall, squinting as Ben's light is refracted in every prism of the chandelier, multiplying and magnifying the glare. He drops the camera to his side, but the reflection off the polished pink marble isn't much better.

Trisha rushes past me and opens a door to a powder room under the sweeping staircase. "I just need to, um . . ." *Put your head back on?* Face tucked into her chest, she disappears inside.

"In here, Jesse!" Nico calls from the double-wide doorway to the left. "Take your shoes off! And no smoking in the house!" This, I assume, is directed at human-ashtray Ben.

I follow Nico's voice into her living room. Not how I ever imagined I'd get here—not that I imagined I would. Standing in front of her hulking flat-screen, I pause between the brass-trimmed glass shelves and the mushroom leather sectional to stare at the portrait over the mantel. I knew Nico did JCPenney fliers and the like when we were kids. There she'd be, sitting in our Sunday circular, twirling a pink umbrella above her daisy-patterned sack dress. But here she is in a black velour sweatshirt popping against a bright blue background, her hair blowing back from her heavily glossed lips. I'm about to shout into the kitchen to ask if she's still modeling, but then I realize the Nico in the picture is flat-chested. It couldn't have been taken later than sixth grade.

Ben and I find the fully developed Nico with her damp hair pulled into a bun, emptying the contents of the Sub-Zero onto the flecked granite countertop under Sam's watchful gaze. "Where's Mel?" I ask.

"Oh, Kara dropped her off first. It's just us." Quality time with you and FrankenTrisha—awesome. She pulls a copper pot down from a rack above the stove and squirts olive oil into it, lighting the flame. "Chicken cacciatore over linguine?" she asks, turning to the chopping board and hacking apart a carrot with vicious determination. "I ate, like, that entire thing of gummy worms and I'm still starving."

"That sounds great. But I can also totally have toast. It doesn't have to be fancy." And you really don't need to know about my bogarted slice of pizza.

"I sautéed the chicken this morning before I left. It's no problem," she says, sounding like one of those drama exercises Mr. Brauer made us do in tenth-grade public speaking, where you're thinking *Die, motherfucker, die*, but the line is offering someone a doughnut. Flipping her damp hair over her shoulder, she fills the pasta pot from the special hot-water nozzle, the steam deepening the red in her cheeks.

"You sauté chicken?" I ask, attempting to lighten the mood.

"I don't strike you as the Rachael Ray type?" she responds edgily, going to the fridge and pulling out a half-empty bottle of white wine. "Dad likes to eat as soon as he walks in the door, and if I don't leave tennis practice till six that doesn't give me much time." She twists off the cork and pours herself a glass. I watch the liquid hit the rim, hoping it can achieve what I can't.

"Um." Ben clears his throat, tilting the lens to the floor. "If you, uh, put that in a water glass, a tinted one, and keep the bottle out of frame, we're golden."

She obliges with rolled eyes. "Want some, uh, apple juice?"

"No, thanks," I say, eyeing Ben. "Apple juice gives me a headache." As she stirs the pasta, I look around the joyless kitchen, the stainless-steel appliances and more mushroom leather in the breakfast nook, bringing out the gray in the terracotta granite. Our fridge might be yellow vinyl, but at least its covered in photos of my Halloween costumes and our cousin's Christmas cards. At least you know we live there. "You know, my dad's fine with it." It takes me a second to realize she means the wine.

"Don't address me," Ben says, his eye on the viewfinder.

"Don't address me," she mimics, the corners of her mouth turned down.

There's a sudden clang as he accidentally hits the hanging pot rack with the boom.

"Uch, *do* you mind?!" she lashes out.

"So, where is your dad? Is he home?" I leap in. "Would he like to join us maybe?" Or perhaps we could wake the neighbors?

The sauce bubbles on the stovetop and, taking a breath, Nico adds the chicken before reaching over and hitting play on the answering machine. "Hey, baby." A man's voice fills the room. "Sorry I'm out. Sal wanted to try bottle service at that new club on the North Shore. But in the morning I'm gonna take you for eggs Benedict, and you can tell me all about XTV's next big star. I'm so proud of you, Nicolina. I told Alec Baldwin about you today and he was very impressed. I'm seeing a guest spot on *30 Rock*. . . . " He kisses into the phone and hangs up.

"So, Alec Baldwin . . . that's really cool," I say, like he doesn't come in once a week for muffins.

"He's thinking about the new Aston Martin," she says into the pot.

"Your dad's out clubbing? Right now my parents are sound asleep after rubbing Vicks on each other and watching Conan."

"That's funny." Thank you. She takes a deep swig of wine. "He likes to dance. That's how he met my mom. At Limelight." She ladles up the chicken, and I take my plate to the breakfast nook and dig in, relieved to have something to do while she fixes herself a helping and leans against the sink. "You remember that iodine commercial where the woman holds up her finger and the scar disappears?" She re-creates the pose.

"Yeah."

"That's my mom," she announces with pride, her face finally relaxing.

"Wow," I say with a full mouth. "That's really cool," I repeat inanely, eager to fan the relaxed flames. "So . . . she lives in the city?"

"They're not divorced, if that's what you're thinking." Her lips remain apart, but the smile falls out of her eyes. "Not . . . legally." She slides into the seat opposite me, shrugging. "One day she was in the middle of making me lunch and just put her purse on her shoulder and walked out."

"Oh my God, that's awful. I'm so sorry."

"It's fine," she says, her voice and expression fully flattening. "The last time I saw her I was ten. She took me to the zoo." She picks up my used napkin and wads it into a ball. "I Google her sometimes. Or look her up on IMDB. See if she might be working. She did a spot on *Law and Order* a few years ago."

"Nico, I don't know what to say—"

"Then don't." She narrows her eyes at me and, even though by all appearances at school I've been "let in" as the Fourth Grace, I'm reminded this is a limited-time guest pass.

"Right."

"Hey," Trisha calls softly as she comes padding in wearing low-ride sweatpants and a tank top, her face intact, her extension-less hair twisted into a chignon. I inhale hard as Trisha wraps her arms around a rigid Nico, resting her head on Nico's shoulder. "Smells amazing, Nic."

Nico waits for a moment before slinking out of her grasp. "Kara didn't mention you were coming, too." Nico beams at the camera, which probably can't detect the now nuclear level of tension that fills this kitchen.

"Yup." Trisha shrugs awkwardly as if this is, in and of itself, an answer. Still smiling broadly, Nico pulls a plate from the cabinet and slings another portion for her.

"Thanks." Trisha takes it, placing it down on the island to grab the wine bottle tucked next to the cookbooks. Nico pulls a water glass from the cabinet and hands it to her without meeting her eyes. Trisha fills it to the rim and takes a long gulp as Nico leans back against the counter.

Trisha clears her throat. "It was fun to hang out."

Nico nods slowly, staring at her intensely. "So, where you been, Trish?"

"Down visiting my aunt in West Palm." She slides her near-empty glass onto the table.

"Funny, the last time you took me down there I'm pretty sure I got reception." Nico clatters her plate into the sink and squirts Williams-Sonoma dish liquid from the stainless-steel caddy of matching hand soap and lotion. "Trisha always used to take me and Mel on vacation with her," she informs me. "Or at least call when she didn't."

Trisha lets out a hard laugh. "But Nico's been busy. Right, Jesse? Would have been pretty hard for her to get away because of the show, don't you think?"

Ben sighs, "Girls."

"Because of school," she corrects, both their eyes flashing with an equal tenor of hurt.

"Well, this chicken is amazing," I offer feebly.

"You should have called me back," Nico says quietly.

"You should have gotten me cast."

I shake my head as Ben lets out another exasperated sigh. "Oh, she couldn't—"

"Shut up," they both spit at me.

"You should know better than to throw yourself at my boyfriend." Nico takes the wine bottle from her and pours the rest down the sink. "You just look cheap. And desperate. Desperate and jealous."

"No." Trisha's acrylics grip the granite, her face reddening as what looks like years of the unspoken is surging to her mouth. "What I look . . . is *awesome*." Nico turns around. "I'm as hot as you are now, Nico. I'm not your lame sidekick. Mel can have it. And I'm not going to tiptoe around you and your freaking moods for another freaking minute."

"Fuck. You."

"Yeah." Trisha sucks in her lips, wiping a splash of mascara from under her eye. "I'm sure he will." She strides out, and a moment later we hear the front door slam.

Nico whips around to the sink and flicks on the water. She reaches for a switch and the garbage disposal grumbles to life. Her head falls. I stand, debating my next move while her shoulders shake, and then all at once it's over. She turns everything off and, pulling her sleeve across her eyes, turns to me. "Those onions were crazy, huh?" she says cheerfully, reaching out for my plate.

"Yes?" I say, wondering if this is Trisha's code name.

"I always cry like crazy when I'm chopping onions."

Oh. "Yes, yeah, me too. It's awful."

She drops our dishes into the dishwasher and closes it. "You know what, I'm crashing. Can we call it a night?"

"Sure," I say. Really? We can't stay up till the sun rises having cozy, uncomfortable talk?

"Great. I have a queen. You can sleep with me."

I wake at seven in Nico's bed. In Nico's pajamas. With a sleeping Nico clutching my hand. And a worn stuffed unicorn in her other. I twist my head, seeing in the daylight four walls of collages capturing three lives entwined. Melanie, Trisha, and Nico flying down a Slip 'n Slide, watching fireworks, riding ponies, turning thirteen, their arms around one another's shoulders, grinning from baby teeth to missing teeth to braces to Whitestrips.

Then, on her armoire, on her dresser, in sterling frames—Nico and Jase in fallen leaves, in swimming pools, in front of Christmas trees. And on the bulletin board over her desk—the notes. Short but copious, and all signed, *Love, Your Jase*.

Slipping my hand slowly from her grasp, I try to reconcile the Trisha from these pictures with the Trisha from last night. And the Jase from the guesthouse with this Jase who smiles adoringly at Nico in every image.

And then I flash to his hand on my bare hip. And try to reconcile that.

And then to Drew. For whom I need everyone else to reconcile their everything else and keep Nico focused on Jase if I'm even going to stand a chance.

REEL 10

"**J**esse!" Mom calls from downstairs early the next Saturday morning, a slight warble in her voice. "I think you should get the paper today!"

I look at my tired eyes in the bathroom mirror, the zits Tandy manufactures and simultaneously hides every day with her layers of makeup.

"Jess?"

"*Really?*" I cry out indignantly from a whole floor away, my mouth full of toothpaste foam.

"I'm dipping French toast and my hands are all eggy. I just heard it hit the house! Get it before the cold makes it damp!"

Rolling my eyes, toothbrush in mouth, I stomp down

the stairs, open the front door, and reach down to swipe the *Sunday Star* from the doormat when something purple catches my eyes. I straighten up to take in the four-foot-high white teddy bear sitting on the porch's old wicker rocking chair, a fresh lavender rose in its mouth, an envelope in its hand. I step over the doormat, the late February wind slicing through my thin cotton pajamas. Through the living room window I can see my mother squeezing her hands together in vicarious maternal excitement.

I look around in the chirp-filled stillness. Nothing. No van. No cameras. Tentatively I extract the envelope from the velour paws and open it.

On the florist's card is printed, beneath the glittered illustrations of flowers and hearts, *Let's get away from it all, just the two of us. Drew.*

Get away. With me. Drew. Me. Not Nico. Take that, FrankenTrisha! Yes. *Yes!* "Yes!" I cry out, toothbrush aloft, bouncing up and down on my porch, the invitation clutched to my chest.

"And cut."

I freeze.

"Moving on!"

I pad down the steps, around the side of the house, and under the porch, where I find Kara crouched low with puffy headphones on, watching a monitor. "Great. That was just *great*, Jesse. And thank God, because it only took two friggin' hours for your mom to notice the bear on your porch." She takes off her headset and, stepping

142

out through the hole in the lattice, straightens, beaming, despite bloodshot eyes that belie her exhaustion. "And Fletch owes me twenty bucks. He said Jase. But I said, no, our Jesse is a Drew girl. I wish we could've gotten this sooner, but we were waiting on Trisha. We had to make sure that was going to go off as planned before we could even start following a secondary romance. Now that we have our love triangle, we can focus on you and Drew. It was *fantastic*. With the bear and everything. And we got *lots* of profile. You look so great. You're gonna *love* it."

I look down at the fake invitation I just did a Snoopy dance over, mortified.

"So," she barrels on, consulting her clipboard. "First you're gonna go get dressed, and then I'm driving you over to the spa. You have a date with Drew tonight—"

"A 'date,' you mean." I rabbit-ear my cold fingers.

"It's Valentine's Day—"

"Two weeks ago." I point my toothbrush at her. "I spent my Valentine's Day getting beaten in lederhosen."

"Tonight." She reaches down to unplug the headset from the monitor and winds the cord around the metal. "If we shot it on the actual V-Day, it'd have cost a fortune to rent a location. You have a date to get ready for. A real date. With a limo and a restaurant and everything. Regardless of who initiated it." She looks at me, and what is sitting between us is the full hand I've just shown, all hearts. "Besides, you might be interested to know the color of the rose was Drew's idea."

Chin lowered, mouth pursed, eyebrows knit, Kara stares at my breasts. And stares. And stares. I feel myself flushing deep pink to match the dress. Behind the ten-foot felt screen behind her I can hear Jase and Drew and the crew setting up for the shot. I reach for another Twizzler, capping off my lunch of Twizzlers, the only "food" I can eat in Zacheria's proximity that doesn't invite bullhorned commentary. "I don't get it," Kara says finally to Diane. "Jess, unzip the dress." I do, letting it fall to my waist. "She *has* breasts. Where do they go in that dress?"

"Can we change it?" Diane asks, lifting out a hot pink tutu from a Cynthia Rowley bag.

"No. Viktor and Rolf are paying to have it in the episode. Can we add some cutlets?"

"It won't take a bra. I could sew one in?"

"No time." Kara checks her phone. "It's after five thirty. The sun's set. Tape her. Just be careful of the paint." I twist once more in the mirror to see the lavender hearts that run up my spine into my hair, the color I requested to match my lavender toes, wondering with an eager twinge if the night will reveal them. I let myself imagine for a moment being on *The Bachelor*. Not the not-having-good-values part. The part where a TV show enables you to have your first kiss on a secluded exotic beach or in a hot air balloon. Where they pay for your ten-million-dollar dream wedding. Where a little staging, a little TV magic, could make this "date" our first.

Walkie-talkie to her mouth, Kara exits our little make-shift dressing area set up between Mr. Wooten's pool table and Mrs. Wooten's monkey-patterned couch, and Diane hands me two silicone blobs that look like—

"Cutlets," she says, jerking her head toward my palms. "That's why they call 'em that. Hold 'em up."

I do, and she pushes my hands closer together, creating monster cleavage. Then she pulls out a roll of lingerie tape and wraps me like a burst pipe.

"Ow," I say as she catches my skin.

"Honey." She snorts. "Just wait till it comes off."

She finishes and gives a good squeeze before zipping on my dress. Ho-ly cow. I look like Angelina.

"You should totally get implants," she says admiringly in the mirror.

I shake my head. "I don't yet know what I'm going to do with my life, Diane. But I'm hoping being shaped like a barbell could only be a hindrance."

"Okay." She tilts back the screen, and I step out into the Wootens' baronial entry gallery. "Tah-dah."

"Shhh!" Kara holds up her finger, and I see through the forest of lighting equipment Nico, in a strapless red velvet sheath, doing Kara's "fun" take on gender reversals and coming to pick up Jase at "his" house. He looks surprisingly at ease in his black suit, even between takes, as Zacheria instructs Jase to shift the flowers to his "upstage" hand. Nico seems to be gripping his other one tighter than she held mine in sleep a week ago.

On the fifth retake of closing a door, Jase loses his patience. "Dude. Isn't this a little ridiculous for Valentine's Day? Last year—"

"You took her to Denny's and gave her a thong from Victoria's Secret? Riveting. We're doing Valentine's glamour the way every teenager wishes they could.

"And . . . rolling!" Kara shouts.

Nico reaches back into the Wootens' entry gallery to sweep the red fox stole from the side table. She flings it over her shoulder and shuts the door. A few moments later I hear a car start.

"And cut!"

Zacheria stands up from his green folding chair. "Gorgeous! Let's get the setup flipped to the side door and take it again with Drew and Jesse! Where are Drew's flowers?"

A sneezing Jenny comes running over with a bouquet of pink roses.

"Great. Jesse! Where's Drew?"

"Here!" He emerges from the baronial library doors on the other side of the foyer, and Kara thrusts the bouquet into his hands. I step forward as she spins him by the shoulders and suddenly we are almost nose-to-nose with only the fragrant blooms between us.

"Hi," he says, blushing in his gray suit.

"Hi."

"Guys, let's move!"

I pull on my Viktor & Rolf evening coat, and Zacheria

146

leads us to the service entrance at the Wootens' mudroom. He walks outside and looks back from the garbage cans as the cameras arrive, holding his hands up, framing the door.

"Drew, Jesse!" he barks. "You're going to stand here. If we crop it well, it'll look like the front door to a mansion. Ben!"

"*Drew.*" I turn to him mock-stern. "You're going to sit on the toilet. If we crop it well, you'll look like you're sitting at a fancy French restaurant."

"*Jesse,*" he says right back. "You're going to get in the fountain. If we frame it right, it'll look like an Olympic pool."

We lean against each other in hysterics, eyes watering. "Wait, wait," I say, my hand on his shoulder, my other holding my stomach. "I can't ruin my makeup. I don't have the patience."

We straighten up, panting. "It does look good," he says. "Pretty. I mean, you look pretty."

"Thank you. I dig your tie." I touch one of the tiny heart-holding penguins.

"Thanks. It's mine."

"I cannot say that about a single thing on my person."

"Drew, over here." Zacheria commandeers Kara's bullhorn. **"Get *out* of the limo. *Walk* to the door. Jesse, you wait. *Wait* for a beat. Feel it. *Feel* for the moment. Like you're not standing there. And then answer. He'll give you roses. Take his arm to the limo—sparkle, sparkle,**

fairy dust—we'll pick up filming when you arrive at the restaurant in the city. Got it?"

I nod and shut the Wootens' back door, waiting for the moment that'll make it seem like I'm not waiting. And then, when I arc it open, though I know it's powdered Drew in the product placement suit, and though I know Jenny just handed him the flowers, I lose my breath, I lose my place. And I let him take my arm all the way to the limo. He opens the door for me, and I slide in for a real date, at a real restaurant.

But we get no farther than the end of the drive before the limo suddenly does a U-turn and goes back to the Wootens' front door, where Kara and three production assistants pile in. Kara plops herself between us while the other three squash in across and commence swapping black nail polish and chattering about East Village rents, Williamsburg bars, and Greenpoint STD clinics. Drew and I stare out opposite windows, studiously ignoring words like *itchy* and *ooze* that get bandied about our heads.

"It's awesome to be out of the van," Kara says, slouching down. Within moments she's snoring—and drooling—on my shoulder.

Three hours of epic over-sharing later, the limo pulls up at a large town house on Fifty-second Street in Manhattan. "The Twenty-one Club!" a refreshed Kara cheers off her third bottle of Frappuccino in ten minutes. Nico and Jase's limo is parked ahead of us. "I love this place," Kara says, smiling up at the wrought-iron porch on the first floor, lined with small painted jockeys. "Real old New York. Fletch wanted something in the meatpacking district, but I'm, like, that could be anywhere. And since I won a certain bet about you this morning"—she pokes me in the side—"I got to pick." Blushing, I follow her out of the limo and onto the sidewalk as the crew runs lighting equipment and sandbags inside. "Bacall and Bogart had their first date here. Howard Hughes hung out here. Alfred Hitchcock—the real deal."

I pick up the hem of my silk dress and follow Kara down the steps, under the ornate wrought-iron awning, and into an old-fashioned saloon, the ceiling blanketed in model airplanes from the twenties and thirties. We weave our way through the cashmere-wrapped customers having a warming drink to the small stairwell and up past three flights of dining rooms. "We took the top floor. Thank God it's off-season. Okay, you guys can pop a squat here." She points to a banquette by the stairwell. "We'll be shooting you in shifts. Nico and Jase are having their romantic dinner through there." She points stewardess-style to quilted leather double doors a few feet away. "We've been covering it with a skeleton crew, but now we're really going to load in. Stay quiet. We'll let you know when we're ready to have you guys start your date." Kara disappears through the doors.

Left alone, Drew and I are suddenly both fascinated by the framed nineteenth-century melon prints on either side of us. Because it's one thing to be told to dress up, to give flowers, accept flowers, but to have it described as *our* date right in front of us is mortifying. Falling somewhere between fake invitation Snoopy dance and the inspection of my disappearing boobs.

I slip off my coat and we take our seats on the tufted peach toile beneath the low-lit chandelier as Ben and his team run past with equipment.

"So," Drew says, fidgeting with his cuff links.

"So," I say, fidgeting with my bracelet.

"What did you do for Valentine's last year?" he asks.

I pivot away from him to stretch my legs out long on the banquette, my dress's slippery fabric fanning toward the floor. "Caitlyn and I made a red velvet cake and watched *The Notebook*. You?"

"I bought my ex some pricey chocolate from that gourmet store in Bridgehampton. Then we got in a fight and she threw it out of the car."

"See, now that's real," I say, surprised he's brought her up and hoping he might say more about her fight-instigation and irrational snack defenestration.

Suddenly we both sit straight up, cocking our heads like rodents.

"*French fries,*" Drew says, identifying the captivating aroma. "God, I'm starving."

"See if they're eating—see if they're done—ask when we eat." I propel him to action.

Drew Scooby Doo tiptoes to the quilted doors to look

through the porthole windows. He lifts the felt flaps the crew's taped up over the glass circles and stares in.

"Well?" I whisper.

"We're screwed—they're only on their shrimp cocktail."

"*That we can see.*" I scamper over to him. "This might be the third time they're eating it. They may have had steak and dessert and now they're re-doing the appetizers. You never know. Let's see if we can order something to eat while we wait."

He spins to me. "Okay, you." He takes my elbow and gently guides me back to the banquette. "Sit tight." With a salute he disappears down the stairwell.

I do. I sit tight and swing my heels, listening to intermittent Zacheria outbursts of **"Hate it!" "Loathe it!" "Crap on it!"**

"Tah-dah!"

I look up at a beaming Drew standing in the stairwell doorway carrying a tray with two metal plate warmers stacked atop each other. He brings the tray to the table and whips off the warmers with a flourish, releasing a burst of savory steam to greet me. "Twenty-one Burgers. Their specialty."

"You. Are a genius." I reach out for the golden bun, slavering to shove the entire thing into my watering mouth.

"Wait!" He twists to the next table and whips off the white tablecloth in one toreador move. "Turn around." I spin my back to him.

"Whoa," he murmurs. "Nice ink."

After a split second of confusion, I remember, darting my finger to feel the rough texture of the body paint. "Thanks."

Clearing his throat he continues, draping the yard of fabric over my silk front before going to a pile of lighting equipment and returning with a metal clamp. He secures my bib and gestures for me to eat.

"Good call," I admire from under my white damask poncho, grabbing a crispy fry.

"I was afraid if you got grease down the front Kara might beat you to death with her clipboard." He squeezes in beside me as he lifts his burger to his mouth. "That would suck."

We happily inhale the food, pausing only to steal Cokes from the crew's nearby Igloo cooler. "Cheers!" he says, tapping his can with mine.

"Cheers."

"To the weirdest Valentine's ever." He grins.

And to my best.

"Look at her!" We startle at Zacheria screaming in the bullhorn from the other room, presumably at Jase. *"Look at her adoringly! Compliment her dress! Tell her she's beautiful! Say it again! Sound like you mean it!"*

"Love her! Act like you love her!" Drew mimics as he wipes off his hands and tosses his napkin on the table in disgust. "God, *what* does she see in him? He's rude to the makeup people. He's totally arrogant. He's stolen, like, three shirts from wardrobe, and it's not like he can't afford to buy them. Seriously, he's such a douche."

I nod, tensing.

"And she's so impressive."

"Well, he's a hot douche," I level back before I can stop myself. Impressive? *Really?*

"You think he's hot?" He looks at me intently.

"No, I mean, but obviously she does. Maybe in a caged-lion kind of way."

"And that's why she puts up with him? Because she wants a predator as her boyfriend?"

"Drew, I don't even know her. I have no idea why she does what she does."

"But you think he's hot."

I think *you're* hot! "And *what*, other than the fact that she looks like Heidi Klum, is so *impressive* about her?"

He stares at me for a second as I'm wondering how this conversation went so wrong, so quickly. "This is stupid," he says finally, then gets up and strides to the door, leaving me to sit alone with the cooling platters in an increasing cacophony of take seventeens and do-overs.

I dejectedly spin the miniature Heinz bottle, *impressive* looping in my head. I want to go back five minutes. I want to take a deep breath, but the tape braces my rib cage together.

This *is* stupid.

"How about I steal us a sundae from the magic food well you found downstairs?" I try.

"I'm full, but thanks."

I try to raise my arms, but the tape pins me. "Sorry, but can you . . . " I twist, pointing at the out-of-reach clip on my bib.

He walks over and I lean forward, willing back the ease of a few minutes ago. I feel the tablecloth release around me like an untied bikini.

"You're free," he says quietly, dropping the clip into my hand.

Suddenly Fletch charges through the swinging doors so hard they catch open. Practically vibrating, he stops just short of knocking over the chilled remains of our feast as I jump up. "Nico! In here," he growls.

But Nico, surrounded by dozens of dining extras, doesn't make a move from her chair.

"NOW!" Fletch bellows, his face sanguine as the Persian carpet.

Slowly Nico lifts her napkin to the corners of her immaculate mouth and dabs before setting it down next to her untouched food. Pushing back from the table, she glides languorously away from a glazed-over Jase, who sits forward to reveal—*Trisha*? Yes. She's sitting at their table, her nose job facing Rick—*Rick? What are they doing here?*—her boob job facing Jase.

Nico passes our dropped jaws on her way to Fletch. "Yes?"

"You're upset. Your rival for Jase's affection has just crashed your date by showing up with Rick, who she's using to make Jase jealous, which, in a subplot, will come between their bromance, having serious repercussions." As Jase and Rick shrug at each other, Fletch crosses his arms tightly over his star-patterned shirt and rocks back on his heals. "Nico, we're shooting you storming off in a whir of hurt. Understand? Go back to the table and let's get this in one take."

"But I'm not upset," she says, slicing her words as she stands firm before him. "I trust Jase. It's *fine*."

"Fine?! Fine makes *them* turn the channel, *me* earn scale, and you a *nobody*." His last word whitens her. "So. Go back to the table and give me my scene. Now."

Her expression faltering, she turns to where Trisha has just pulled Jase's handkerchief from his breast pocket and is dabbing it against the imaginary sweat on her cleavage. Shoulders splayed, head rigid, Nico walks gracefully back to the table and takes her seat, her eyes locked on Jase. Trisha, tucking the square back into his pocket, also locks eyes on Jase—who reaches out for a roll and bites into it without a look to either of them.

"Jase." Nico's voice is airy, belying her struggle to stay put. "Tell them. Tell them I can trust you. Tell Trisha to stop embarrassing herself."

Jase's jaw tightens as he looks to Fletch, to me, to the bloody filet on his plate— and I feel myself gauging along with him what could be planned next, how far Fletch will go to get the scene he wants. "Let's just get this over with, Nic," he pronounces, his voice slightly hoarse with defeat.

155

Trisha sidles closer to him, hitting Nico with an unmitigated look of triumph.

Nico just blinks at them, a slideshow of shock and rage flashing across her face.

"And nobody got that, I suppose?" Fletch screams. The guys shrug, their cameras dangling in their hands. "Goddamn it! You should be rolling *all* the time! At least I could've edited that down! Fuck this." Fletch spins to us. "Drew!"

"Yes?" Drew takes a small step forward.

"Scratch the date with Jesse. Go to the bar where you'll run into Nico, be her shoulder to cry on."

My stomach drops. Not so much at the concept, but at how brightly his face lights up when he hears it. "Okay. Now?" he asks, darting his eyes to me.

"Uh, yeah," Fletch says. "Jesse, you go wait downstairs." Fletch claps his hands and people start packing up the equipment. While I stand there dumbly, Kara tentatively brings a stunned Nico her stole as Jase jumps up from the table, yanking down the knot of his tie. With big smiles to the crew, Trisha grabs her wrap like she's leaving a *Dancing With the Stars* audition she's nailed.

"I guess we should head down," Drew says to me, turning around to check his bangs in the antique mirror.

"Yeah." I pick up my coat and walk to the stairs, my heart sinking with each step. "Good luck with the, uh, consoling."

We both arrive at the landing. "She deserves it," he

says. "That was pretty shitty. So—Jase and Trisha—how long has that been going on?"

"I have no idea," I say, eyes on the Persian runner.

"Do I have anything in my teeth?" He shows them to me.

"Nope. You're ready for your close-up."

"Thanks." He jogs off toward the ground floor, leaving me to collect myself against the floral wallpaper.

And all at once Nico is on the step above me, shaking her head abruptly like she's jarring herself back. I watch as she continues slowly past, sinking down each stair.

"Nico!" I call after her, unsure what to say next. "That was really shitty," I try. "Fletch is really shitty. But—"

"But *what*?" she says to the railing.

"I—I like Drew."

She stops for a moment. I stare into the back of her twisting blond waves. And then, without a word, she disappears down the steps.

"Where are we going?" I hear Jase ask as everyone else starts down in a loud rumble. "That's kind of bullshit to send my girlfriend off to, what, cry on Rudell's shoulder? I don't know how I feel about that."

"Good," Fletch says, taking the stairs two at a time right past me. "That's good."

I slump down after Fletch, Jase, Trisha, Kara, Zacheria, the P.A.s, and Ben, all the way out through the fire door and onto the sidewalk, back into the bitter cold. As I clasp my coat together, Trisha shrugs hers on over her heart-patterned minidress. The van pulls up.

Fletch raps on the door and it slides open. "Trish," he says, extending a hand to help her hop up.

"What?" she asks as she huddles against Jase. "I don't understand. I'm not going with Jase?"

Fletch smiles to himself as he takes her elbow and half tosses her up onto the van seat. "Nah, Trish." He looks up at her bewildered face, her heavy makeup caked from her performance. "You're too easy." He slides the door shut with a thud and raps on the side again to send it off. "Jase, come with me. Jess, stay here." Fletch and Jase walk back under the metal awning, and I stand shivering, the thin silk doing nothing against the cold. I hear Jase raise his voice: "I'm *not* your bitch." I turn around to watch, but red velvet catches my eye, and I look up into the first-story window where Nico sits at the bar. I stand on my toes to get a better view. And I do. Of Drew, smiling warmly as he slides his arm around her naked shoulders. She nestles into his chest. Ben and Zacheria come through the fire door, carrying more equipment. They're not even filming yet!

All I want is to call Caitlyn.

Hot, tight tears roll down my face as the limo pulls up and Jase approaches, rattled and angry, Sam's camera on his heels. He stops short when he sees me.

"What happened?"

"Nothing," I choke out, squinting in the camera light. "I fucked everything up. Please, just get me home."

"I have my car." He spits out his fed line with one last

hostile glance back at a beaming Fletch and opens the limo door. I throw myself in, not caring, just desperate to be out of the camera's view. Jase slams the door against the hot light, and we pull away as I finally allow myself to cry for what I've lost, huddling into the corner, praying this is really it, the night's really over. We're not going to circle back and start again.

But we barrel straight across town to the Midtown Tunnel, and soon we're underwater.

I feel something brush my forearm and lift my head to see Jase holding out the Trisha-scented handkerchief from his breast pocket. I take it and blow my nose as the sooty white tiles blur past. He pulls a flask from inside his blazer and takes a long swig before passing it to me. I gulp back the warm whiskey. "Thanks," I choke out through the burn as I hand it back to him. He takes the polished silver from me, and I realize his eyes, which were unavailable to a naked Trisha and desperate Nico, are locked on me.

"Long-ass day," he murmurs.

"Yes," I say, feeling the warmth of the drink spread across my chest. I let myself lean back against the leather bench as we exit onto the Long Island Expressway, the dark familiarity of it, the low buildings and night sky. He lies back, too, rolling his head toward mine. I turn to the window, and he reaches down to lift my foot onto his knee, sliding his finger under the silk sling-back to release it from my heel.

It drops to the carpeted floor with a thud. We both

glance down at the light from the highway lamps glinting off the lavender polish. Getting a hold of myself, I withdraw my foot, tucking it under me. But he reaches out his hand to run his thumb along my damp cheek, his eyes on my wet eyes. And our breath catches.

He pulls my face to his. And we sink into each other. His mouth hard on my mouth. Kissing me. Kissing him back. Making a choice. Making a mistake. But at least in control of our lives for a whole two and a half hours.

REEL 11

"*Oh, the tide is high, but I'm holding on,*" Trisha trills along with her iPod as the seven of us climb down from the white airport minivan. We make our way toward the marble-floored three-story domed entrance of Cancun's Las Vistas Five-Star Resort and Casino.

As they roll in their product placement suitcases, I hang back from the person I hooked up with seventy-two hours ago, his best friend, his girlfriend, her best friend, her nemesis—and Drew. Inside I let the warm ocean breeze that wafts through the open space seep into my chilled body, which has gone from the unheated XTV van to inexplicably air-conditioned JFK to the air-conditioned plane to the air-conditioned hotel shuttle. Under the spray tan, my ears are blue and, despite two straight days of scrubbing, those stupid painted hearts are still faintly visible, although Kara's promised me they won't "read"—so there's that.

Jase and Rick take pink drinks from a tray by reception and down them, while Nico and Melanie sniff theirs. Rick reads the little card and grabs a second. "Guava juice, cool."

"Take a seat on the couches while I get you all checked in." Kara lifts yet another embroidered cotton peasant blouse—which someone *must* have told her is her best look—and removes our passports from the pouch she has taped to her stomach. "And I just want to take this moment to thank you all again for your amenability. Believe me, I was as thrown as you were to get this trip green-lit at ten last night. But Fletch's schedule moved around, and the only time *convenient* was this week. I'm sorry I had to get you all out of bed. I'm sorry I had to spray-tan you myself. I'm sorry I cannot get my fucking boss to approve the production plan more than eight hours out. It's not like I've seen my boyfriend in two months. It's not like I had a doctor's appointment—fuck—that I haven't even canceled."

Ben pauses his load-in to rub her shoulders, and she smiles in gratitude, fumbling for her phone. For once probably equally as exhausted as Kara, I gladly sink between Trisha and Melanie into the puffy white leather and rest my eyes. Trisha and Melanie, who I also managed to sit between on the plane, and who I plan to keep bookended around me for the rest of the trip. I don't care that Trisha's perfume makes me want to gag or that Melanie hums without realizing it.

"Okay, guys, follow me."

We wheel our Tumi suitcases *label out* to the elevator and, as Jase swats Nico's ass and she lets out a giggle for Trisha's benefit, I squeeze between T&M and make myself small for the ascent to the penthouse.

"Okay, here we are. For the next four days this'll be your home base." Kara opens the door to what could be a living room, or it could be a snake farm. I don't notice. All I see is water. Beautiful, bright water. Not like what we have at home, which is dark as denim and choppy and freezing, even in the dead of August. This water is crystal blue, warm, and calm. I step out onto the marble balcony that runs the length of the room and smell the dense bougainvillea encircling the pool fourteen stories below.

"Why is no one down there?" Trisha asks, peering over the rail.

"It's not spring break for another month, dumbass," Nico retorts.

Kara purses her lips, pushes her glasses back up the bridge of her nose, and continues. "Okay, a few ground rules. Absolutely NO swimming in the pool," she instructs as she opens one of the bedroom doors. "The chlorine will dissolve your tan in seconds. Girls, you're in here. Boys, across the way." She points to the wood-paneled door on the opposite side of the parrot-patterned couches.

Nico, Trisha, Melanie, and I follow her into a large room with two queen-sized beds. "This is where you're starting, at least." She shoots us a suggestive glance. For Kara. Which is like sexy squirrel.

"Mel and I are sharing," Nico says, tossing her Tumi duffel on the bed closest to the window.

"Great," Trisha sniffs, looking at me. "Just be careful." She cups her breasts. "These are still sore."

"I'll try not to feel you up in my sleep."

"Wanna swim?" I ask Melanie as I stretch awake on the poolside lounger. After a full morning of pretending to buy diamond-encrusted jewelry in the lobby of the Ritz-Carlton under Zacheria's critical lens, I'm thrilled to be back in my own bikini shooting b-roll. "Maaan," I mutter in annoyance as I un-stick my AP Physics book from my tummy where the black ink has transferred to my skin via sweat and suntan lotion.

"Kara said no. Plus, I don't want to reapply the SPF." She lifts her head from where her folded arms are serving as a pillow. "I swore to my mom I'd be covered. Fastest way to early aging."

"I'm making you a T-shirt with that on it." I scratch my hair, my luxuriously unstyled hair.

"Well, it's true." She settles her freckled cheek back down to her forearm.

"We've been filming outside for two days." I touch my palm to my reddening chest. "Aren't we tan enough underneath the spray? *They* didn't bleach out." I stare through my sunglasses across the aqua pool to where Nico sits perched atop the tiled bar, her legs extending into the water between Jase's submerged stool and Drew's. Behind a potted palm six feet away, cigarette dangling, Ben seems to be refocusing his camera on Nico's caramel thighs glistening against Drew's caramel shoulder. I hate her.

Then Jase swivels around in our direction and lifts his umbrella-covered drink in a long-distance *cheers*. And back to hating myself. I give a stiff wave I'm hoping will convey *stop looking at me*. But he continues staring with all the subtlety of Chuck Bass as he sucks on his straw. Uck. Although, I guess I should be grateful that he's kept his acknowledgment of what happened in that limo restricted to pervy looks and hasn't actually spoken to me.

"Well, I'm waiting until Kara says we can," Melanie, thankfully unaware, announces over the music from the speakers nestled in the clay planters behind us. Drew cracks up at something Nico says—probably she's noting that this is the fourth time they've played this song since breakfast. Either that or I'm now dreaming in Jimmy Buffett. Nico looks eagerly to Jase, but thankfully he's returned to cheering the NASCAR broadcasting from the TV under the dried palm awning. I watch Nico watch Jase, a flicker of sadness weighing her face for a moment before Drew swats water on her thighs and she squeals adorably.

I flop back in my chair. I could use a day off from how perfect she is. Just, like, one. A mental health day. Twenty-four hours where her breath smells, her hairline is wonky, and she gets backne.

"So, no on the swimming?" I ask, pulling off my glasses and sitting to twist up my hair. My awesomely product-free hair.

"No until we get permission."

"Happy baking." I hop across the few feet of broiling cement to the pool's edge.

Melanie props herself onto her elbows and slides her sunglasses back on as I plunge. "How is it?" she asks enviously.

"*Awesome.*" I dunk back under, enjoying the moment of hearing nothing but the water against my eardrums.

"It is kind of nice not to have to wear those mike packs for b-roll," Melanie murmurs as I surface.

"Seriously," I second as I swim over to hold on to the wall near her chair. "Lounging around this place between scenes rocks." Minus the avoiding Jase part, who's always with Drew, who's always with Nico, who's always with us. Which leaves sleeping, hiding under homework, and talking to Melanie.

"We're still working," she reminds me, tilting her scarf-wrapped head in the direction of Sam's boom hovering over the conversation at the pool bar.

"Thanks, Mom." I splash at her.

"I'm just saying!" She leans over her chair to sip ice water from a straw.

"Don't worry, I wasn't about to take my top off." I kick my legs out behind me.

"Speaking of." Melanie raises an eyebrow to the massive red clay doors that lead from the pool to the lobby. I squint to see Trisha emerge from the shadows, one hand gripping her water bottle, the other's French fingernails pressed to her brow.

"Let the party begin," I mutter as she spots us and begins teetering over in her cork platform mules. "I found her snoring on the floor outside the bathroom when I got up to pee around five. Where'd you guys go, anyway?"

"Señor Frog's. It was fun! Even the crew danced. You should come with us tonight."

"I'm still hungover from playing quarters with Rick and Ben the first night. Plus I have to take three tests the day we get back."

"That's what your T-shirt'll say. And then we did karaoke in the lobby bar. Fletch got on a Jay-Z kick. I gave out around three. I have no idea what time Trisha made it up."

"'Sup, bitches." Trisha gives us her new signature greeting, her voice gravelly. "Kara said these are our seats? *Why?*" She lifts her hand to shield her massive Kanye striped sunglasses as she surveys the sea of mostly empty chairs surrounding the mostly empty pool. "Of course we have to come here *before* spring break. Of course the place is dead."

"This is where they want us to sit. It's where the shot's set up." Melanie rotates onto her back and re-smoothes the towel beneath her.

"Well, I want to lay out over there." Trisha points at the lounge chair positioned closest to the bar, in Jase's direct sight line.

"Why do you have to be such a drama?" Melanie sighs.

"Why do you have to be such a kiss-ass?" Trisha fumbles

in her gold Marc Jacobs bag to withdraw a pack of Camel Lights.

"Because my mother can't just write a check for someone to rearrange my face," Melanie retorts calmly as she closes her eyes.

Trisha covers her flicking lighter and takes a deep inhale. "Jealous much?"

"Hey, guys!"

We look over to see Kara shoving through the huge doors, flip-flops flapping. A tray of Coronas in one hand, she also holds a Styrofoam cup to her chest over her new tropical uniform of V-neck white T-shirt and frayed army shorts.

"I had to," I say apologetically from the chlorinated water as she arrives at our chairs.

"What? Oh, fine. You're tan enough."

In one move, Melanie tosses off her glasses, whips off her scarf, leaps up, and dives over my head.

Kara peers at us from under the brim of her XTV baseball cap. "Uh, Trisha? No." Kara circles her coffee cup in front of Trisha, who reluctantly drops her smoke in to fizzle. "This is a round on Fletch," she says, offering up the beers. "Since most of you guys're legal down here. And now if you want to sit closer to the boys that would also not suck. Fletch isn't thrilled with the seventh-grade dance vibe we've got going on here." Trisha takes a beer and a lime slice. "And a heads-up that Fletch and Zacheria are finalizing the rest of the week as we speak, and we're gonna shoot some really exciting scenes tomorrow now that you guys've had a chance to chill, loosen up."

Melanie surfaces next to me. Holding on to the wall with one arm, she wipes the water off her face. "I love this pool."

"Beer?" I ask her, reaching for the one Kara has set by the ledge.

She shakes her head. "Not eighteen yet."

"Good girl," Kara says. "So I need to plan you hanging for your last afternoon of b-roll. Maybe I can get a volleyball net."

"Does it have to be as a group?" I ask. "I mean, can't we split up and do different things?"

"Or we can play volleyball . . ." Melanie tries, like this might get her the A on this pop quiz.

"Great." Kara scribbles on her clipboard. "We'll set up some sporting equipment for you. And, Jesse, please, no more footage of you behind a textbook, okay?" Kara tucks her pen over her ear and circles around to update the bar crew.

"Told you I could sit over there. Later, bitches." Trisha totters off after Kara, readjusting her C-cups.

"Was Trisha always this charming?" I ask Melanie as she scissors her legs beside me. "I mean, she seemed this charming from afar. Just wondering if this delightful love of a girl came with the boobs."

"She's just Trisha. Only now she's just Trisha with a lot to prove. I mean, everyone knows they cast me and Nico and not her the first time. Whatever. I don't let her get to me." I watch her focus on her watercize and think back to all those framed pictures in Nico's room, Mel and Trish looking as close as Nico and Trish. Were their friendships just alliances of convenience that kept them in charge? Or was it real and XTV simply exposed the inevitable cracks that crop up after fifteen years? Exposed and exploited. With my help. I hold on to the side, spinning myself to face the water, wondering for the first time if Caitlyn had been cast, would XTV still have found a way to split us up?

"Do you let anything get to you?" I ask Melanie as Trisha forgoes the walk-up side of the bar to hunker on the edge of the swim-up side, her lot-to-prove squeezed together at Jase's eye level. Nico notices. Drew notices her noticing.

"Sure. I just don't let it get in the way."

I nod, deciding Melanie knows more than any of us.

The next afternoon, in my fourth costume change, I step into the frostily air-conditioned elevator and cross my arms over the chocolate-zebra-print organza tunic. "Cover-up, my butt." I jerk my finger into the lobby button and huddle in the cold, cursing the freezing gold bracelets that have been copiously stacked up my arm. Who goes for a walk on the beach with this much jewelry? Or this much makeup? A hooker hoping for a passing yacht?

I miss yesterday afternoon. I miss laying around in my own suit, the one that stays put on my ass without double-sided tape, and sleeping. By the pool, in the cabana, in the room. I don't care if it makes for bad television. It makes for great Jesse.

A floor down the doors open to the sky-view gym, and Drew steps in, startling when he sees me. "Hey." He pats off his face with the towel around his neck and hits the penthouse button.

Oh, you remember me? "I'm going down."

"I'll take the ride." He drops the towel and leans back against the railing. "Barbie Jesse returns."

"Yeah." I hold a fake nail to my new extensions. "Can't say I missed her."

He smiles. The elevator opens to a maid with an overflowing laundry cart who waves us on. The doors close.

"So." Drew turns to me, clearing his throat. "Did I do something?"

"What? No. What do you mean?"

"I just mean you seem to vacate wherever I am, unless there's a camera making it mandatory."

I shake my head like I don't know what he's talking about.

"Jesse?"

"Just making more room for Nico." I shrug.

"Oh." He loops the towel over his neck and holds both ends, pulling it taut. "I thought maybe you were just making room for Jase."

"What do you mean?" I feel the heat in my cheeks and am thankful for heavy concealer and dim elevator bulbs. "I don't hang out with Jase."

"You said he was hot." He stares at me.

"Nico's thighs are touching your shoulder!" I sputter.

"What?"

"Nothing."

"Okay . . . just, Jase was talking shit about you, that's all."

OhmyGodOhmyGod. "Does Jase talk anything else?"

The doors open to the spa level. He waits for me to say something—but what? Yes, I hooked up with Jase? Yes, I cheated on my faux friend. My faux friend who seems to be lining you up as a backup even though—and maybe because?—I told her I liked you.

"I have to be down at the beach for my stroll with Trisha," I say miserably. "Where we've been told she's going to confide her growing feelings for Rick."

"Fine. I'm gonna grab a steam before my shoot." He steps out and the door starts to close before he darts his hand in. It rolls open. "Jesse."

"Yeah?"

"We need to just hang out," he says decisively.

I lean into the open button.

"Go for a walk with me tonight. I hear there's going to be fireworks, and I'm sick of seeing Trisha get hosed down at the clubs."

"What time?" I ask as the door starts to beep and to my total surprise his face lights up like it did for Nico. Maybe brighter.

"Without the cameras. I'll sneak out of the club and meet you down by the cabanas at, like, eleven thirty."

"Eleven thirty at the cabanas!" I repeat giddily as the doors force their way closed.

* * *

That night, having fulfilled my obligation to Zacheria with a Dior-clad trip to the casino with Melanie, I sit under the full moon on the sand among the striped canvas huts, pressing my lips together and questioning the relatively low stickiness factor of just one coat of gloss. I am completely losing the ability to gauge appropriate makeup application. Getting ready in the room, I stared at the fresh crop of freckles on my nose and felt like a total loser because I can't operate an airbrush machine.

Whatever. Drew said "Barbie Jesse" with a tone. A tone that implied un-Barbied was better, and so here I sit on a striped deck chair, in a pair of Melanie's navy short shorts and my stretched-out white sweater, listening to the waves while scanning the hotel horizon in search of my date.

What time is it? The moon is definitely a lot higher than when I got out here. But if I go all the way to the lobby, I might miss him if he walks back from town on the beach.

Wait—there's a clock next to the pool bar TV.

I swipe up my leather flip-flops and corner around the cabanas—slowing when I hear Trisha's piercing giggle. I squint down to the silvery waterline to see her up to her calves in the waves, twirling her dripping tank overhead like a lasso. She lets it fly, attempting a swerving striptease for someone sitting in the sand. At this point you'd think her sales pitch would be having the rare treat of seeing her with her clothes *on*.

I turn away, head up the steps to the pool area and toward the blue light of the bar, which illuminates the turquoise water surrounding it. I cock my head at the melody coming from the potted palm. Yes, here we are again in Margaritaville. Making my way around the periphery of the glowing water, I bend to check the time cloaked in wavy shadows—12:05. Is he not coming? Could he not get away without the cameras? Is that him down on the beach with Trisha?

"Hola." The bartender puts down his novel and walks over to me.

"Hi. Did you by any chance see the boy with brown hair from our group"—I gesture to the empty chaises he and Nico have been camped on for the last two days—"head down to the beach?"

"I haven't seen anyone. Sorry, miss. I make you something?" He picks up a cocktail shaker and tosses it from hand to hand.

Why not? "Yes."

"Something sweet?" He grabs a tall tiki glass and juggles them together.

"Something strong."

Staring into the melting ice crystals, I'm not sure how many minutes have passed when I hear, "Nico, please."

With a coldness moving up my chest fueled by the alcoholic slushie I've just downed, I set my emptied glass on the cement and follow the low voices along the hedge to the gurgling pineapple-shaped hot tub on the terrace's edge. Rounding the corner to see Drew's back, I dart behind the cover of the leaves.

"I told you I can do it, too. Watch!"

I look past his broad shoulders to where Nico teeters on the tub's steps in the white tank dress that just barely grazes her butt. She drops her hand to cup the water, conjuring Trisha. "Come here," she demands softly.

"Nico, we need to talk." He sounds sad. I know, it must be so tragic for you that she's still in her dress.

"You talk. You talk and talk and talk." She jerks back on the step, and he bolts forward. Her hand catches on the metal rail, and she swings around like a rag doll into the bubbles, the white cotton soaking through to reveal the black lace of what's beneath. "Whoops!" she exclaims.

He bends down, says something I can't hear.

"Or this." She pulls his face into a kiss so deep the breath is knocked out of me.

Double-fisting, I carefully slide my two emptied tiki glasses on to the entry table in the dark penthouse. The warm, salty air billows through the open balcony, sending the sheer curtains flapping laterally over the couches. I swerve over to see Melanie passed out on her bed. I should wake her up, tell her what I've seen! No. I have to . . . screw. Him. Just screw him. I'm going to tell Jase, how about that? I'm going to . . . I register that my hand is slapping against the boys' bedroom door. Well, good. Because Jase can answer and I'm going to—

He pulls back the paneled wood and raises his hand along its side, cheeks flushed, shirt off. I hear Rick snoring in the dark behind him.

"Jase," I start, tequila warmth swimming in every direction along with shards of that kiss. "I . . . I wanted to—"

"Me too." He slides his hot hand around my waist and pulls me against him, his lips taking mine.

I bushwhack through the thickness in my head. "That's not—this isn't—"

"Okay." And just like that he releases me and closes the door.

I stand in the dark living room, gulping for air, my skin on fire. Suddenly the room bursts with a series of brilliant crackles from the beach outside, fireworks echoing off the stucco walls around me. I go to knock, but before my hand touches the wood, the door opens.

"Nico and Drew in the hot tub," I say, my eyes wetting. "I did." I nod my head. "I told Kara about you and Trisha. Back at the beginning. And now it's messed up everything, and I'm sorry. But I didn't—I never told her about your dad." His face set on mine, eyes smoldering, Jase walks toward me as I back up into the living room, feeling behind me for the suite's guest bathroom doorknob. It gives, and I reach out to him, my fingers catching at the belt loop of his shorts. We tumble together onto the cool tiles in the darkness inside, stopping only to reach up and push in the lock against the rest of them.

REEL 12

"**W**ell, aren't we a talkative bunch," Kara comments, carefully keeping her balance as she steps between Nico's and my legs to grab a seat at the pointed bow of the speed-boat we've been on for the last twenty minutes.

Last night's tiki binge leaving me redefining hungover for an entire generation, I squint up at her through my borrowed Chloé glasses and grip my bench seat as if this might steady the hammering in my head from all the lift-ing and dropping over the white waves.

"I think you all could use some coffee."

"I think we all could use some *not going so freaking fast.*" Nico turns to the guy driving the speedboat while he chugs on his loathsome cigar. "Can you slow down, *por favor!*"

"No, please." Drew pats the air at her not to scream and pivots himself back out to face the water. Jase snores like he's gargling furniture on the bench next to me, his iPod blasting in a tinny thump in time with my throbbing. I close my eyes to shut out the three people I would most like never to look at again for the rest of my life. Mistake! My stomach lurches.

"Oh, Jess, by the way, we got a fax from your mom this morning. You got into Georgetown."

"What?" I say, the information sinking in through the fog of pain. "Oh my God! Can I see it?"

"What? Oh God." She pats her pockets. "Oh shit. I may have thrown it out. Sorry—it said you got into George-town. Congratulations!"

"Thanks! That's—wow! I need to call my parents. Do you have cell reception out here?"

"Sorry. No communication till we land back at JFK." She pulls her tube of zinc from her pocket and slicks a pink strip down her nose. "Fletch is really strict about that."

"But I'm the first in my family to—I have to—can I fax them back at least?"

"Those are his rules. Fletch is going for total immer-sion while we're here. I'm so sorry."

Total immersion? It's one thing to force us to pretend to be best friends; now we have to make it look like we're orphans?

"I'm sure Fletch will want a scene of you celebrating somewhere chic when we get back—on us."

I flash to Mom and Dad sitting with the acceptance letter, no way to talk to me, and my stomach starts cramping double-time.

"There!" Kara waves at the driver. I open my eyes to take in the massive catamaran we're slowing to approach.

"That doesn't have a bathroom," I say with alarm. Here's what I need: water on me and in me that is not salty and a flushing toilet. Not bobbing canvas stretched out under a rapidly clouding sky.

"Okay, we'll be in the speedboats out of frame, filming around you guys. So head on over to the brunch they've spread out for you four in the middle and enjoy!" We glower at her and one another. Kara lifts her bullhorn and clicks it on. **"I said, enjoy!"** she bellows.

Jase startles awake.

"Drool." I point with disgust at the trickle on his chin. He wipes at it with the shoulder of his T-shirt, and we all stand to unsteadily make our way to the ladder. To enjoy, exclamation point.

This must look awesome. Seriously, I bet Kara's thanking every minute she spent getting that film degree. Who wouldn't want to watch four green teenagers on four different sides of a catamaran, alternately hurl and moan?

I just want the ride to stop. I want my own bed, but I'd happily settle for a piece of cement in a jail cell if it came with steady horizon.

"I'm supposed to talk to you now." I open my eyes to

see Drew sit down next to me. He drops his head back against the metal frame and closes his eyes, grimacing.

"How'd I get so lucky?" I curl back into my ball.

"Kara boated over and yelled it at me with her bull-horn."

"I heard," I say, eyes closed.

"Fine," I hear him say angrily. What the hell?

"What the hell's your problem, Drew? I was at the beach, you know. I waited for you."

"You sure about that?"

My eyes fly open. "So you hooked up with Nico and you're pissed *at me*?"

"Nico was wasted, and I had to take care of her. She was wasted because Jase has been ignoring her."

"That's not my fault," I say quickly. "Besides, you don't need Kara yelling at you with a bullhorn to cheer Nico up."

"Nico was wasted." He sucks down water from his bottle and lowers it between his crossed legs, his face twisting in disgust as he looks down at me. "And you have a fucking hickey, Jesse." He gets up and uses the sail ropes to unsteadily walk to Nico's corner. I look down to where he's pointed, to my hip bone, where the black Asian disk holding together my bikini bottom has shifted just to the left of . . . oh God, a hickey. I lift my face over the choppy water to hurl whatever possibly could be left.

An hour later, Jase and I stand in wetsuits, watching the speedboat race toward a nearby island with Fletch,

180

Zacheria, Drew, and Nico for a heavily lit romantic stroll as the threatening sky suddenly darkens to match the inky chop of the surrounding surf.

"So, where are we going to snorkel?" Jase, relatively energized by his little nap, turns to Kara. "One of those cool reefs or downed sub sites near shore?"

"Here," Kara says, studying a combination of her GPS and clipboard.

"Here?" we both echo.

"Like, right here?" Jase repeats shakily. "We're in the middle of nowhere. It's probably even too deep to scuba here. I mean, what about sharks?" He grips the base of the sail overhead.

"I'm sure there are no sharks." Kara forces a laugh as she scans the water behind us. "Are there?" she asks under her breath to the guide next to her.

"I mean"—he scratches at the back of his leathery neck—"I think we'll have a better time inland, but—"

"It's just b-roll." She drops her GPS into her backpack and zips up her fleece. "We don't have time to set it all up again inland before the storm."

"There's a storm coming?" I shiver.

"Oh my God, you two need to relax. Come on, the sooner you're in the water, the sooner you're out. Jesse?"

"And then we can go back to the hotel?" All I can think about is a hot shower. Right now I'd shoot a man for a hot shower.

"Yes." Kara takes my hand and guides me to the edge

while holding on to the sail with the other, the wind whipping our hair every which way.

"Fine," I sigh, pulling my spit-filled mask down and feeling it suction to my face. "Let's get this over with." I take one last look at all three cameras pointed at the stretch of black water in front of us and jump in to—FREEZING! "Freezing!" I sputter to the surface. "My legs are going to crack off!"

"KICK!"

"ENJOY!"

"YOU'RE HAVING FUN!" Everyone yells down at me.

My teeth chattering, I flop my feet behind me in the plastic fins for all I'm worth and, shakily shoving the snorkel into my mouth, put my face down to look into the water. Total mistake. It's dark as hell and goes down forever. Screw sharks; a Transformer could be stretching up on its tippy toes and would still have a mile of cover to eat me.

I whip my face up as I hear a shriek and see Jase surfacing a few feet away in a splatter of hysterical splashing. "Aah! Aah!" Water flies everywhere, including into my snorkel. I spit it out and take a breath while the spaz flails closer.

"FUN, JASE, FUN!"

Screw this. I kick my fins out toward the ladder while my arms still have enough circulation to guide me, and suddenly Jase is climbing on to my head like a crazed puppy. "Stop!" I scream, trying to throw him off.

"Sharks! Sharks!" he squeals.

"Sharks?" I manage, salt water flooding into my nostrils and mouth as I fight to stay afloat with Jase literally scrambling up onto my shoulders. I feel two hands reach down and lift me up and into the boat. Jase is plopped next to me. The two of us sputter, cough, and shake as we try to get a full breath.

Kara looks down in disgust. "In the film world, you guys wouldn't last two minutes." She tosses towels at us.

"There were sharks?" I chatter to Jase.

"In his head." The guide un-sticks the masks off our blue faces. "But now you know how far you can carry your boyfriend here."

I am woken from the darkest depths of dreamless sleep by Trisha's laughter. Moaning, I pull the pillow from under my head and hold it over my ears, trying to sink back to where there is no Kara, no cameras, no everyone. The mattress starts to vibrate under me from blasting music in the next room.

"Come on, bitches!" The bedroom door slams open. "Last night in Me-hi-co! Make it count!" The overhead blares on, and I open one lid to see Trisha running over to the window to yank Nico's hand. Sleep mask dislodged, Nico turns to me, blinking awake as we both register the people making their way noisily into the penthouse.

"Trisha, what the hell?" Drew stumbles through the

rapidly growing crowd to our bedroom doorway with Jase and Rick, bleary-eyed, behind him. "It's four in the morning."

"Dude, we have to be on a plane in a few hours," Jase croaks. A bunch of local guys shove the boys into the room as they roll a Corona keg the three feet to my bed, its metal lip scraping the tile.

"No!" Melanie whips off the covers and marches over to them. "Not in here. Trisha, at least keep it out there."

Trisha drops Nico's hand and spins to Jase. "You're no fun anymore. None of you are!" Trisha crosses the room to tug up the face of the guy pumping the keg and plants her lips on him, his eyes bulging in surprise. She throws her arms around him and his friends cheer, gathering as he tosses her gruffly onto our bed. I roll out and onto the floor, crawling away as more people cram in from the living room for the show. Standing, I dart along the stucco to where Melanie and the boys huddle by the bedroom door. A swerving man grabs Nico around the waist and she pushes him off, her unicorn tumbling to the floor as she jumps behind an alarmed Jase.

We look through the chanting melee to see Trisha's leg suddenly flop limply over the side of the bed. Drew pushes Melanie, Nico, and me into our bathroom and, pointing to Rick and Jase, the three dive in to get her. Shouting erupts as I scramble toward the bathtub, clutching Nico and Melanie as Trisha stumbles in, her arm dangling over Drew's neck. Jase throws the door closed, and Rick locks it, the two of them sliding down with their backs braced against it as men yell and pound. Drew flicks on the light. Melanie starts to cry. Nico, white-faced, clutches her hand as she stares at the shaking door with wide eyes.

Trisha curls up on the floor as Drew slides the bathmat under her head. "Jase left and Fletch left and nobody . . . nobody . . . " She passes out.

"We have to get her out of here." I feel for her pulse like they do on TV. "She needs help."

"She's just passed out," Jase says, still catching his breath as the door shakes behind him. I pull a towel off the rack for Nico, and she drapes the thick terry cloth over Trisha's legs before sitting Melanie down next to her on the tub's edge. Jase pulls up his knees for better leverage. The thumping of the music gets louder, and we hear glass shatter.

"Making themselves at home," Drew huffs from where he stands, leaning his weight against the shuddering wood over Jase and Rick.

"My jewelry's out there," Nico says quietly.

"So are our passports and wallets," Drew adds. "Doesn't this bathroom have a phone?" He looks back over his shoulder.

"It doesn't. No phone, no hair dryer." Melanie lifts her head from Nico's shoulder and reaches for some toilet paper to wipe her eyes.

Nico smiles thinly. "So calling on that's out, too."

"I'm just saying because the boys have one and we don't," Melanie sniffs.

"What about Kara and them—they should check on us," Nico tries.

"Not till breakfast. That's in, like, three more hours." Rick knocks his head back against the finally still door.

More glass breaks. More cheering. And there's the sound of women laughing. "Great, they're inviting the whole country over," Rick mutters.

"This sucks." Nico feels her naked ring finger. Rick, then Nico, even Melanie, everyone starts to nod.

"It does," Drew agrees.

"I thought it would be different," Nico murmurs. "Instead it's just . . . " She trails off.

"So why are we doing this?" Jase asks as I re-prop up Trisha's head. "So we can spend our golden years beating the crap out of each other for a measly few thou on a challenge show?"

Trisha's eyes open to half-mast. "I want my senior year back," she moans into the bathmat. Nico blinks at the ceiling.

I look around the room at the seven of us. Scared. Exhausted. In way over our heads. "So all in agreement. If we get out of this bathroom in one piece, we're quitting?"

Everyone's hand shoots up, even Trisha's.

REEL 13

My spine aching from fits of cramped sleep on unforgiving terra-cotta tile, I grimace as I shift to find a non-ouchy position in the bucket chair where I landed a half hour ago. At dawn, we finally emerged into our only recently abandoned but thoroughly trashed suite. Standing there in the mess of bottles and feathers, staring at all that was left of our belongings—Trisha's tin of bruise concealer and my splayed physics text—no one talked about our pact. No one talked at all.

Which brought us silently here, to the lobby—in our pajamas.

I wearily watch as Kara reaches the potted fern by the couch, pivots sharply on her heels, and does an about-face, her cell clamped in her tensed hand. In twelve paces she'll hit the table of gratis guava juice and pivot again. Nico digs her own hollow-eyed groove between the rattan coffee table and the bellhop station. Rick crosses her path on a diagonal, and Mel and Trisha make parallel lines on the far side of the concierge's desk. The only people not pacing are Fletch, who's completely horizontal with his feet up on the coffee table, and me, because there's no path left.

Oh, and Drew.

Drew, who, now that crisis has been averted, is sitting as far away from me as the square footage of this massive atrium will allow. If he had shoes, I'm confident he would have chosen a seat in a lobby down the road.

"No. We have to be able to leave the country *today*!" Kara cries, slowing to a stop to restate our case for the thirtieth time. "It's not these kids' fault their room was robbed." She shoots another glare at the serenely smiling staff behind the desk. "You have to help us. . . . Well, then, have the ambassador call me back. . . . You said that twenty minutes ago!" Slamming her phone shut, she beelines for Fletch, tapping the splayed *Maxim* serving as his sleep mask. He startles awake beneath earmuff-sized Bose headphones, and she manages to keep it together while he slides them off with a loud yawn.

She crouches beside him, and I watch her face contort as they whisper, her voice rising, "But, I only went along with pushing drinks because you said they'd be watched!"

"They were watched." Fletch sits up, cracking his neck

with a quick side tilt of his head. "And you need to check your tone."

Stung, she lowers her voice again. "I meant chaperoned. Safe."

"Grow up, Kara, they're fine." Fletch jumps to his sneakers and turns to us. "Aren't you fine? Melanie?"

"Yes?" She freezes by the potted palm.

"Aren't you fine? I mean, it got rough for a few minutes, and you lost some shit, but it's insured and nobody's dead, right?"

Melanie looks from Trisha, who circles an ashtray like one of the crushed butts might morph into a fresh Marlborough and land lit in her bruised mouth, to Nico, who continues to run her hands across her bare wrists and fingers.

"I guess," Melanie says quietly. I watch as Jase notices Nico's distressed gesture. He reaches out to touch where her Rolex and Tiffany links should be. She looks at him for a moment, and he pulls her into his chest. I cast a sidelong glance to Drew, but his face is unreadable.

"Actually . . . " Rick trails off, his hand swiping his bangs where the cupped brim of his Yankees hat should be.

"Yes?" Kara nods. "What did you want to say?"

"We're done." Go, Rick.

"Yes." Fletch nods in agreement. "Thank you! So, chill out, Kara, and let's get—"

"No." Rick clears his throat, resting his hands where

his sunburned hip bones peek out from his shorts. "I mean we're really . . . "

"Done." Nico crosses her arms over her sleep tank.

Fletch tilts his head, his eyes squinting in confusion.

"I think—" I stand up. "What Rick is trying to say is that we quit."

Fletch grins like Tom Cruise, a bracing blend of rage, hysteria, and glee. "I beg your pardon?"

"We quit." Nico stands to her full height in the hotel slippers we've been given. "No more filming. We quit."

"You quit filming?" he echoes.

"Yes," Jase affirms with his arms around Nico's waist. The rest of us chorus in agreement.

Kara stares at Fletch, her breath held along with ours. Fletch studies each of us as we wait to hear which direction that grin is going. And then he doubles over laughing. Laughing. "You're done. You *are* done."

We look at each other—are we declaring our independence to an idiot?

Kara throws her hands up and stalks out to the driveway.

"Do you need us to explain this more . . . slowly?" Drew stands up uncertainly.

"No!" Fletch wipes his eyes. "You quit something that's *over*. Shoot's done. Spring break is the last episode. You're done."

We're done. The information sinks in. I root my slippers to the tile to keep from running over to grab Drew's shoulders and screaming, *We're done*!

"Okay." Kara reappears in the tiled archway, the morning sun streaming in behind her, her hand cupped over her cell. "Mr. Hollingstone called in a favor. Someone from the embassy will meet us at the airport and allow you to board. And someone from XTV will meet us at Immigration with the Xerox copies of your passports that I left in New York."

"So we can leave?" Nico asks from her reclaimed nook in Jase's arms.

"We can leave."

PART III
THE REAL REEL

REAL REEL 1

"*Attention, Target shoppers, don't forget to ask your sales associate about all the exciting benefits of applying for our REDcard when you check out. Happy shopping!*"

Two weeks later, I'm slumped over a red plastic cart in the towel aisle while Mom labors over a wedding present for Dad's cousin. Norah Jones resumes crooning from the loudspeakers, returning me to feeling like I'm covered in muffin glop. Like none of it ever happened. Which, if I squint, it almost never did—Nico and Jase are permanently lip-locked, Nico and Melanie have closed the Trisha hole with an inseparable seal, and Rick is, well, Rick. None of which bothers me—it's as if we were in the same class or homeroom or lab section and now we're not. Weird, maybe. Melancholy, perhaps, but not troubling. Which is the opposite of whatever it is I feel when Drew pretends not to notice me as we pass in the halls. And double that whenever I see Caitlyn, who, despite my obvious solitude, refuses to even break stride for my hellos.

"White or cream with little flowers?" Mom asks from where she's surrounded by piles of both on the linoleum.

"*Mom*," I moan into the crook of my elbow. "I don't know. I don't know what their bathroom looks like. We've been doing this for an hour. Just pick something."

"I think I remember them saying something about a seashell motif."

I push away my hair from where it's fallen into my face. "Then get her the cream."

"With flowers, though? Will that go with the shells?"

I whip my head up and shrug.

"Hey, you wanted to come." She points the folded terry cloth at me. "Make yourself useful."

Being done is simultaneously euphoric and not. Euphoric, because I don't have a perma-parameter of cameramen. I can go where I want, do what I want, with nothing adhered to me—hair, nails, mike packs. And not, because I have no perma-parameter of cameramen distracting me from the fact that the two people I want to go anywhere or do anything with think I'm a Capital A asshole. After weeks of reserving so much energy for the eightieth take of my reality, I'm lost without the direction.

At least in school the bells have been my Kara. *Jesse! Go to English! Jesse! Go to Spanish! Jesse! Go to physics!* But when the three o'clock bell rings, the afternoon stretches into the evening with no Prickly Pear to go to, no Caitlyn to talk with, leaving me way too much time to replay Cancun in nauseatingly slow motion.

"How about a light green or blue, like the ocean?" I roll the cart with my forearms slowly down the long aisle.

"Carol? Is that you?"

We both look up to see a mink-encased Mrs. Cortland striding toward us with her uniformed maid in tow, pushing a cart brimming with clinking glassware.

"Hi, yes!" Mom darts her hand to check her hair.

"I'm throwing a dinner for the McMillans at my house Easter weekend—they're bringing the children, so I'm stocking up on the non-crystal this time."

"Very smart. Mrs. Cortland, you remember my daughter—"

"Jesse, of course! Everyone's talking about this new show that's been shooting in town. And I hear Jesse is one of the stars. How fabulous for you, Carol. I don't have to look for a new cleaning girl, now, do I?"

"We're very proud." Mom smiles. The maid just barely rolls her eyes.

"Actually, I've been meaning to call you. We're planning a fund-raiser tea at the Maidstone this summer, and it'd be such fun to have Jesse come and speak."

"At your club?" I ask. This is a woman who used to make Mom leave me in the car with a coloring book so as not to "upset" her cat. Mom darts her eyes to me.

"That sounds great."

"Fantastic! I'll be in touch. Oh, it'll be such fun!" She

claps her gloved hands together, her ostrich bag swinging back and forth off her elbow.

"Fun!" I echo.

"Well, I'm off. Bye, you two!" She strides past us, and her maid follows with a withering gaze at Mom.

"Seriously?" I turn to her.

"Never thought I'd see that day," she murmurs, stunned.

"The day you'd see Mrs. Cortland in Target or the day you'd see Mrs. Cortland in Target and she remembers my name?"

"All of it. Wow, Jesse." She turns to me like she's not sure if I've been replaced by a pod person.

"What am I going to talk about at her club?"

She opens her eyes wide and then rubs her hand down her face. "You can think about it while you pick out a wedding card for your cousin."

"Me?"

"Yes. And then you can think about what you'll say when she asks you to join her club. Leave the cart, and I'll meet you at the register after I pick a damn towel set."

I salute her and, shoving my hands in my jacket pockets, weave through the familiar aisles, wondering when things will get back to normal between her and me. Between anybody and me. Out of habit, I cut a quick left and duck into the makeup section, where Caitlyn and I have logged a quarter of our lives trying samples that might reinvent us as runway stars. I catch sight of myself in a sliver of Maybelline mirror, startled by my unmade-up face. I pull down my bangs and push forward to the card aisle as instructed.

"Cheesy or sarcastic?" I ask, holding out the two options as I shuffle-jog up to where Mom is unloading cream towels onto the conveyer belt.

"*Jesse O'Rourke?* Oh my God, are the cameras with you? Are they filming?" Sara Brady leans out of her register corral to look wildly past me. "*Nathan!*" she yells three registers down to Nathan Lozario. "*XTV is here!*"

"Oh no—" I wave the cards in front of me. "Nope, it's just . . . me, actually."

"Oh." Her shoulders fall. "NEVER MIND!" she informs a frantically preening Nathan.

"Sorry," I say, placing the cards atop the towels.

"That's okay!" Sara recovers. "It's just cool to see you! In person, I mean. I see you constantly on the commercials. The premiere's this Sunday, right? So psyched! Hey, let her pass," she orders the old lady ahead of us and her ten cans of Fancy Feast.

"Oh no, that's fine, we can wait." Mom waves the lady on.

"No! Seriously, come up. Come on, Jesse," she says, pulling the bewildered lady's cans to the side and holding them hostage until Mom moves her towels forward and we reluctantly squeeze past.

"I don't understand." The woman snaps her coin purse shut. "Are you closed? You didn't have a sign up. Is there a sign up?"

"Lady, just wait," Sara says through gritted teeth that break into an ingratiating grin as she scans Mom's towels. "You can always jump ahead on my line, Jesse. Seriously. And tell Nico and them it's cool."

"Thanks." I dip my chin into the top of my coat, trying to remember if we ever had a class together. Maybe gym? Ninth grade? Eighth?

"Do you think you'll be back?" she asks, handing Mom her credit card.

"To Target? That's pretty much a sure bet." I go to take the bags from her, but she holds firm.

"Oh my God. I can carry these out for you, please."

Mom and I look back at the fretful old woman staring at her cat food. "That's okay, it's pretty light." I have to wrestle the plastic handles from her hand.

"Are they filming in the parking lot?"

"No." Mom takes the other bag.

"Oh." Her shoulders slump. "Well, bring them in, okay, Jesse? You can use my employee discount if you bring them to this register!"

"Sure!" I wave as we hustle toward the electronic doors. "I should have told her we're done filming, but I didn't have the heart." I turn to Mom, who's officially over it.

She passes off her bag and pulls the keys from her purse. "I'll get your limo."

REAL REEL 2

Early Sunday morning, I shut the car door and lean down to give Dad a last wave good-bye.

"We'll be watching at the restaurant!" he shouts with a big smile, doing a K-turn on the tarmac to exit through the metal gate of East Hampton Airport's private runway, not a place I ever imagined I'd be in a million years. Tucking my hands in my down vest, I cross to our familiar trailer, parked beside its corporate twin, a small plane with the neon XTV logo emblazoned on its side.

I climb the steps to find Kara sitting with Diane on one of the benches, sharing their morning coffee. "Hey, stranger! How ya been?" Kara greets me, wearing—not a peasant blouse.

"Kara! You changed."

"What? Oh." She looks down to where the black wrap dress ties at her side. "Diane hooked me up."

"It looks great."

She blushes. "Thanks to the stress of running this little operation I now have a waist. Premature gray hairs. And a waist. Nervous?"

"Kinda."

"You're the first to arrive." Just like the first day. "Let's get you into wardrobe."

Diane stands as the door opens, and Melanie hops up the stairs, ready to roll—hair wet, face clean and prepped. "My pro."

I'm about to give her the same small smile and tentative wave that have encompassed all our interaction of late when she throws her arms around me. "Jesse! Isn't this exciting?!"

Within twenty minutes, the van is filled with the seven of us, girls hugging, boys roughhousing, everyone trading camera phones to capture our last tour of duty and egging one another on to greater layers of MAC foundation. Despite the estrangement of the last few weeks, I allow myself to be subsumed in the camaraderie.

"I'm going to miss this," I say wryly to Melanie.

"What?" she asks through taut lips as her liner is applied.

"Smelling like I bathed in Aussie Sprunch. The unexpected woohoo of excitement when the cold metal mike pack brushes my lumbar spine. Getting up at four. Getting to bed at four. Good times."

"I'm going to be sad when my eyelashes grow back," I hear Nico chime in from the leather bench where she's contentedly snuggled at Jase's side. "I've gotten used to the nightly depilation when I pull off the false ones."

"I'm going to miss wearing borrowed clothes that smell vaguely of other people and whatever stressful situation they wore them in," Drew pipes in from where Diane staples the hem of his last pair of fantasy pants.

Rick turns from the kitchenette, downing a handful of Doritos. "I'm going to miss Zacheria. His little fingers. His little toes."

Smiling, Kara pulls her coffee from the microwave. "Okay, enough reminiscing. Here's the rundown." Everyone leans out to get our last set of instructions, seven styled heads aligning. Kara puts her mug on the counter to read to us from her binder, her freshly manicured nails fanning on the underside. "In a few hours, once everyone is camera-ready, we'll be boarding the jet to South Beach, where we've set up a second XTV beach house location adjacent to the private airport. You will disembark *on camera* and take your seats on the stage to watch the premiere *live* with America. We'll be split-screening the show and your reaction shots. How real is *that*?" She weaves a hand through her blown-out hair.

"Kara, when are you going to tell us what it's like?" Trisha pleads from under an aluminum roof of foils.

"How'd it come out? Do we look amazing? There's going to be a party back in New York, right? 'Cause my mom knows a lot of celebrities she could get to come."

"Owning the building they shop in is not the same as knowing them," Nico scoffs, suddenly breaking the family reunion veneer.

"It's better than having their asses sit in your bucket seats. Bite me."

"Well," Kara continues, "let's see how this premiere goes first. And to answer your question, Trisha, I think you'll be really pleased. It's—"

"Glamorous?" Jase finishes with a girlish lilt, and we all groan.

"Yes, it actually is. We've created a really engaging, sexy show, and I think you're all going to be thrilled with how audiences respond to it."

"So, people are coming to an airport to watch us watch ourselves?" I ask.

"We're giving out beer cozies."

"Of course," Drew says, his head emerging from the sweatshirt they've given him, shaking out his chestnut hair. I want to reach over and touch it.

But I wait until we're three thousand feet up and everyone is distracting their preshow nerves with magazines and iPods. After his sixth Coke, I see Rick finally head to the bathroom, and I seize the moment to attach Mel's terror grip to the armrest, unbuckle my seat belt, and walk nervously up the aisle to Rick's vacant spot.

"Whoa," Drew says as I slide in past him.

"Good. A syllable in my direction. I'll take it."

"I'm not *not* talking to you." He tugs the emergency procedures brochure out of the seat pocket ahead of him and flips it open.

"Well, since Cancun you haven't, in fact, talked to me so—"

"Look, Jess," he lowers his voice, leaning close. "You're doing whatever it is you're doing with Jase."

"It was *one* night." I say what I want to be true, looking down at the Prickly Pear muffin in my hand that I brought to give him as a token of my contrition. "I thought you were with Nico," I whisper. "I saw you guys at the hot tub. I thought you were hooking up—"

"Jesse, let's not, okay?" He cuts me off, shoving the brochure back in the pocket. "Look, the shoot's over. We're weeks from graduation. So let's not . . . complicate things."

My stomach drops as if the plane had hit an air pocket. I played through this strategy all night. Muffin to smiles to bathroom makeout. Not . . . "Complicate things," I repeat while he crosses his arms and closes his eyes like he's already moved on to better, less complicated things like napping. "Right. Sure."

The *occupied* light goes out, and the bathroom door opens. I stand, locking eyes with Nico two rows behind, who gives me a sympathetic look. With an embarrassed smile, I squeeze past Drew's knees.

Kara is right behind me, holding herself steady with the headrests as the plane dips forward. I'm grateful to have an excuse to close my watering eyes as she pokes each person in turn with a powder brush, talc puffing and suspending with the dust particles in the orange sunset streaming through the little windows. "Okay, my fabulous stars!" she calls out as we coast to a stop on the runway and I force myself to bring my shattered attention back. "Hair fluffed! Sunglasses off! Sweatshirts off! Earpieces in! Don't be nervous. Just be yourselves!" We insert the plastic buds and remove all our protective shields as Kara releases the door to a rush of hot, heavy air that fills the cabin. Hot, heavy air and screaming. Screaming?

Her kohl-rimmed eyes widening, Trisha skibbles past everyone and out onto the stairs first.

"Come on!" Kara waves at the rest of us, and we shuffle forward nervously.

I suddenly feel Nico running her fingers through one of my barrel curls. "There," she says. "Perfect." Smiling, she squeezes my arm. I find a smile in return. "Good luck out there."

"You too." I duck through the door and straighten on the top wire step. Out of practice, it takes a moment for my eyes to adjust to the blinding brightness of the lights. I shield my view, almost stepping back into the plane when I realize there are *hundreds* of kids packing the stretch of palm-bordered lawn XTV has cordoned off. Actual living, breathing people—about to watch—whatever it is this is about to be. Suddenly the reality sinks in that this hasn't been a home movie for Zacheria's sole benefit.

"*Hamp-ton Beach! Hamp-ton Beach!*" their chants echo off the tarmac. This is *a lot* of enthusiasm for a beer cozy.

"And we're walking!" Kara's voice reaches me through the din, and I return my focus to putting one heel in front of the other as I shakily descend the little steps and follow the red carpet.

"Here they are!" a disembodied game-show voice reverberates from the ten-foot-high speakers on the stage. **"The brand-new stars of *The Real Hampton Beach*!"**

Keeping my eyes trained on the back of Drew's head, I follow our line to the edge of the stage, up the three steps, and take my seat on the last folding chair on the side, where we can see the audience and the screen at the same time. **"And now, *live*, the world premiere of *The Real Hampton Beach*!"**

I pivot to the screen, keeping my spray-tanned knees carefully together. The spotlights on us are bright, fading the images. That and I'm sitting way too close. And off to the side. But I get the gist.

As Wilco plays, I see the sun rise on the surf.

I see our school.

I see Jase shooting hoops.

I see the store banners on Main Street—Gucci and Tiffany and Tory Burch.

I see Nico leaving her McMansion, getting into her Maserati.

And I see me stepping out of the Richardsons' red-lacquer front door. Like I own it. Like I'm richer than Nico.

"*Smile*," Kara's voice pleads in my ear.

I see us shopping, getting pedicures, eating sashimi.

Then it's Nico and Jase over and over; the happy, sexy, gorgeous couple, looking like a Valtrex ad, lit to perfection by Zacheria and loving life.

Then Trisha standing in snow-patched sand looking forlorn.

I see Jase running with springer spaniels in the distance. Springer spaniels?! *Whose?* What day was that?

Then the moon cross-fades into a red stoplight cross-fades into a cherry on Nico's tart.

I see Jase and Nico not talking over the tart at Cooper's.

I see Jase standing in snow-patched sand looking forlorn.

Then footage—darkly grainy, like it was shot on a surveillance camera—of Jase and Trisha at the guesthouse where I saw them back in January, before any of this. The snow is gone, though, the house has siding, she has boobs, and there they are, walking in together, hands on each other's asses.

Then me, climbing down from the lifeguard station ladder in those ridiculous boots, stating to him that I won't tell Nico about Trisha—but we weren't miked! How did they—and there I am hanging out with Nico, saying nothing while she goes on and on about Jase.

And then Jessica Simpson talking about her acne. It takes a second to realize she's not one of us. A commercial.

"*Smile. Smile*," Kara says sternly into my ear. "Everyone is watching you. Turn to each other and talk like you *love* it." I look out at the crowds, who are indeed rapt.

Smiling so hard her lips can't move, Nico beams straight ahead. We all do. And then she minutely tilts her face to me. "Well," she purrs, waving at the crowd, "guess somebody just came into some money."

"I *never* implied I live there," I rush. "Or that I was—"

"My friend?" Nico laughs. "You're not, that's pretty clear."

"And it's *not* real," Jase adds, a Hail Mary pass for himself.

Melanie gives him a sidelong glance. "No shit, dog lover."

"*And we're back in three, two, one . . .*"

REAL REEL 3

"**J**ESSE!"

Rubber-banded stack of mail in hand, I pivot on the porch to the source of the screaming—a Honda slowing to a crawl as it passes our front lawn.

"YOUR OTHER HOUSE IN THE SHOP?!" some guy screams from the driver's window.

"HOW'S DREW?!" a girl screams from the back. "BLOW HIM RECENTLY?" The car screeches away in a cloud of obnoxious laughter and exhaust fumes.

Must stop looking every time someone calls my name.

I see Mrs. Kropel across the street staring out her front door, curlers so tight in her gray hair I can see patches of her pink scalp. I wave my handful of mail.

"Hey, Mrs. Kropel! How are you?"

She scurries back inside.

"And I am now scaring old ladies," I mutter as I twist my key in the lock and push into the quiet front hall. I drop my straining bag to the floor with a thud. Eight more days until the first AP. I wish I could just take it in my bedroom. Wish I could do everything in my bedroom.

Kicking off my sneakers, I watch one sail satisfyingly through the living room and corner off the La-Z-Boy to land dejectedly on the carpet. I fight the temptation to flop there myself and instead head into the kitchen. I grab the cookie jar as I pass and, lifting off the suction top, am greeted by the comforting vanilla scent.

The Post-it on the counter reads, *Jess, chicken out of freezer to defrost. Home by 8, Mom.*

Stuffing a generic sandwich cookie into my mouth, I pull out the tinfoil-covered mound and set it on a plate by the stove. I hear another car slow as it passes our house. So it might be time to acknowledge my if-I-don't-watch-the-show-it-doesn't-exist plan has a huge-ass flaw—everyone is more up-to-date on my life than I am. I flip on the little TV that sits on the counter as Jessica Simpson joins me in the kitchen to share her undying gratitude to Proactiv. I pull open the fridge and take out the milk carton. As I reach for a glass from the cabinet, I hear Drew's voice asking me for hot chocolate. Cold clammy washes over me as I stand with one hand on the glass, the cabinet door blocking my view of the third episode. They must be running it constantly since its original airing last night. Which I managed to keep from turning on by bargaining with myself in five-minute intervals.

I hear the sound of my laughter coming from the TV as Drew cracks a joke. He really is funny.

Resigned, I close the cabinet door and turn to face my XTV self, who, for the next eighteen minutes, will have the carefully edited, flirtatiously promising start of a relationship that's too complicated for real life.

REAL REEL 4

I'm an hour into the AP when I, and everyone else, become aware of knocking on the window. Mrs. Cutler rushes from her desk to yank up the blinds, revealing Kara standing in the spring grass with a giddy expression and a piece of paper pressed to the glass. Which, unless it tells me the speed of this bullet leaving this gun at a thirty-eight-degree vector, I DON'T CARE. I look down and try to pretend I have no idea who that crazy lady is. Even though everyone knows I know. Just like they "know" I love chinchilla slippers. And they "know" I prefer Dom Pérignon. *With Doritos!*

"Jesse!" Kara mouths, pointing at the paper. Mrs. Cutler raps on the glass in Kara's undeterred face and drops the blinds. With the whole room pivoted to me and Mrs. Cutler distracted, Bobby Latman wags his tongue between his V-ed fingers. I quickly flip him off before she turns around. If this keeps up until graduation, I'm going to start walking around with my middle finger permanently erect.

Two miserable hours later, I emerge, twirling my wrists, my neck, and everything else that's cramped. BlackBerry in hand, Kara jumps up from the row of lockers where she's apparently been levitating over the floor this whole time.

"Oh my God, *what*?" I cry, releasing four hours and thirteen years of academic frustration. The test room empties behind me, and for once people are too drained to care about me and the XTV producer.

Oblivious to my ire, Kara thrusts the paper in my face. I squint down at it, trying to see through the little circled letters still swimming in my vision. It's a web page printout. With pictures of me that aren't really pictures—more like freeze-frames—from the show.

"It's your own fan site!" She jumps up and down in little hops.

"My own what?"

"And we didn't do it. It's completely fan-generated. It's getting HUGE traffic. Jesse, I'm so psyched for you! We're totally tracking it to shape the remaining episodes. They like a more accessible, slightly less aspirational you."

"More accessible than what? The Nico droid you edited me to look like?"

"Yeah, she's actually not getting the response I thought. People find her kind of cold. Anyway, they loved your chemistry with Drew!"

Ouch.

"I wanted you to know right away. We've only aired four episodes, and it's slaying the time slot. Slaying! It! *And* . . ." She pauses for dramatic effect. "*Good Morning America* called! They want you guys Thursday morning!"

My eyeballs leave their sockets. "For *what*?"

"To talk about being *real* American teenagers. How great is that?!" She claps her hands together, her silver rings clinking. "You're going to be the face of the pressures and hopes and dreams of America's youth."

It's chaos in the ABC green room. Seated on the hard couch out of the path of human traffic, I just watch the building anxiety and try to breathe.

"Melanie, where's the curling iron?" Mrs. Dubviek is digging in her big python bag, enthralled in her self-assigned task of fluffing everyone's hair. Upon arrival we learned that union rules prohibit non-contracted hair and makeup people from being on the premises. So we've all been ABC-ed, and Mrs. Dubviek is underwhelmed. She returns to tugging at my bangs, practically falling into the laps of my uncomfortable parents, who bookend me on the couch, spreading cream cheese from miniature silver Philly tubs. The coffee table beyond our knees is laden with platters of shiny baked goods and wilting fruit. I look down at the doughnut in my hand. But I don't know how anyone can eat right now—I'm one hiccup away from hurling.

"This is crazy," Mom says with a full mouth as her phone buzzes. Swallowing, she reaches down to the coffee table and tilts it up to her. "Oh, that's Aunt Pat. She wants you to know Providence is watching and rooting for you."

I give her a wan smile.

The blonde with the headset, who met us at the front door and perkily escorted us up here, peeks in. Mr. Sargossi lunges from the chair where he's been flipping loudly through the *Post*. "Is Robin doing the segment? I want to confirm that Nico'll be sitting next to her."

"I have noted that, sir," she chirps through her exasperation. "And as soon as our segment producer comes down from set, I'll let you know, and you can take it up with her."

Giving her an insincere smile, he returns to his chair next to Nico's. "I'm not having you pushed down to Siberia like Ed McMahon," he says, patting her leg.

She nods, slightly pivoted away from him, her gaze out the windows at the sun rising pink above Times Square.

"And you'll mention the dealership?" he shouts to the departing blonde.

She turns in the doorway, all pep. "Robin has a note on it!"

"I don't understand," he says to Nico, raising his *Post*, his voice just as audible through the newsprint. "Explain to me again why Jesse has her own fan site and you don't?"

"Ask the fans," she says, her voice light, hollow.

Mrs. McCaffrey sits beside Jase on the couch opposite me, taking spit to his bangs. "Mom!" He twists away, his voice rising as he drops his cashmere hoodie string from between his teeth.

His dad reaches for a Danish and bites into it. "How much longer is it gonna be? Unlike *some* people, I have a real job. One that doesn't require wearing makeup and having my hair done." He gives Jase a look of withering disgust.

"*Man!*" We all turn to look to where Rick has spilled Swiss Miss mix on the beverage counter and a small cloud onto his shirt. Nico takes advantage of the distraction to slip from her father's immediate radius, only to look momentarily lost now that a seat next to Jase has been officially deemed publicly humiliating. She busies herself touching up her lipstick with Mrs. Dubviek's proffered gloss while Rick's mom taps at the chocolate powder to release it from the fabric.

Kara comes back in from the hallway, slapping her cell shut, her face bright, even though her peasant shirt looks particularly slept-in. "That was Mr. Hollingstone, himself, guys. He's watching." She looks around the room, taking us each in, stopping at Drew, whom she walks over to. He sits alone by the ficus in the corner, the only one of us without chaperoning parents. She bumps her leg into his. "Hey, you okay?" she asks.

He looks up and gives a nervous smile.

"Folks couldn't make it?"

He shakes his head. "They're watching from home. My mom was worried my little brother might be a distraction."

"I can get a sitter for her next time—just let me know."

"Oh no. I mean, it's cool," he rushes. "They've got it covered. But—I'll let her know."

Fingers gripping the door frame, the woman with the headset sticks her blond hair back in. "Okay, so we're moving into the seven o'clock hour. We have a segment on Iraq, commercial, a segment on the new cholesterol drugs, commercial, and then you. Six million watching, and I'll be back to mike you in ten."

And all at once it's like someone just shouted *Fire!* in my abdomen and half my organs are scrambling over my other organs to leap for safety out of my mouth, while the rest are tumbling over one another to race out my ass.

Robin smiles warmly at us as we mike up around the coffee table, which holds a cheerful low bouquet of silk Easter tulips. "Good morning," she says, looking impossibly crisp and well rested in a dark pink suit.

The blonde points us to our seats. "Melanie, on the end, then Trisha, then Jase, then Nico, Drew, and, Jesse, you're next to Robin."

Nodding, I ignore the glares on my back and take the yellow chair.

I look out from the colorful half-room to the dark industrial off-set side, where Kara stands next to the cameraman, making little U shapes next to her mouth with her pointer fingers. "*Smile!*" she mouths silently.

"And we're back in four, three—" The camera guy shoots two and one with his hand.

"Welcome back." Robin smiles at the camera. "We're very excited to have some very prominent teenagers in the studio with us today. Many of you know them already. And if you don't, you soon will. Picked to star in a new documentary series on XTV, these young people agreed to have their lives opened to the camera."

We sit for a few moments while the clip rolls. The clip "documenting" the nighttime spa day. Only I now have a line of spliced dialogue about how I hope Drew likes my new look.

"In just four short weeks since the first episode aired, these kids are becoming a real American phenomenon. This morning we're going to get the inside scoop, the answers to the questions everyone's asking. So, Jesse." Robin leans in, resting her thumb and pointer fingers beneath her chin. I try to resist the pull of my own image, pulsing at a two-second delay from the monitors on either ends of my peripheral vision, and focus on smiling into Robin's eyes. "Let's start with you. When did you first know you had feelings for Drew?"

FIRE!

"This is bullshit!" We can hear Mr. Sargossi as soon as we pass out of the soundproofed studio and into the hallway. "Where is that Kara girl?! Where's Fletch?!" he bellows from the green room. I press my arms in against the rivulets of sweat gushing down my side. I can't look at Drew. I can't look at anyone. What did I even say? I stuttered and repeated myself and, oh God, babbled about Doritos Delights. I sounded like an idiot without taste buds. I just want my parents to take me home.

Kara moves each of us aside by the shoulders and motors down the carpeted hall so she can be the first one in, bless her. "I'm right here. What seems to be the problem?" we hear her ask from our unnerved huddle near the threshold.

"The problem *is*"—he spits as he talks, the corners of his mouth turning white as the rest of our parents look away—"*I* gave Fletch the idea for this show when I sold him his Porsche last summer. A show centered around Nico. *Nico* is the next big thing. He agreed. She didn't even mention my dealership." We turn to Nico, who stares at the floor, her jawline turning pink.

"They ran out of time," Kara says patiently. "You and Fletch may have shared an ah-ha moment about Nico, but

Park Avenue Confidential was the genesis of this show."

"I want to see Fletch!" he shouts at Kara. "I cut him a deal on that Porsche! He owes me!"

Nico walks in to put a tamping hand on his arm. He whips it off. "Don't touch me. You didn't even try." He storms out of the room, breaking apart our huddle, and all at once everyone disperses.

Mrs. McCaffrey stands from the couch. "Great job, Jason. And Nico, you looked really pretty." She squeezes a stunned Nico's shoulder, then pats Jase awkwardly. "Your father had to get back," she tells him. Without so much as a glance to me, Drew darts in for his jacket and leaves with Rick and Rick's mother, who's still prattling on about hitting the Hershey's store. Taking Nico's hand, Melanie leads her over to the table to help Mrs. Dubviek pack the curling irons and makeup into her snakeskin bag.

Dad rises from the couch to hug me. "Great job," he says stiffly into my hair. "But I don't understand. Is he your boyfriend? Are you not telling us stuff anymore, Jess?"

I look up at him, not even knowing where to start.

He pushes up his glasses. "I'll get the car."

As he walks out, I sit down next to Mom, who's staring into Kara's laptop—her face aghast at the familiar freeze-frames from the show on its screen. I silently watch as she scrolls through the postings discussing every aspect of my body, every word I've said, every edited thought I've shared on camera. Woven throughout the smiley faces and gushing observations about my friendly smile, my shiny hair, my funny jokes, are comments that are at once mercilessly vicious and gleeful. It's evident the girls? women? men? boys? writing this stuff couldn't be having more fun.

My voice makes someone want to "kill themselves," my ass looks "dimpled" in a tight skirt, olive green turns me into "homeless-man vomit," and my "attempts to seem human are pathetic." My eyes sting. Who *are* these strangers who are so over me? Are they in my school? In this room? Has everyone always thought my voice was suicide inducing? The multiple exclamation marks and all caps slice straight through me.

"Can we go, please?" I ask, and Mom raises her shocked eyes.

"This one says you're a Paris-in-training who hangs with a jet-set clique." She flips to the next tab. "Here they say you're carrying your books in a ten-thousand-dollar tote. And here—they point out your thin frame might suggest a coke problem—readers should keep their eyes peeled. Who *are* you?" she asks with a tight voice, pointing down at the picture, a pose I'd struck for Diane's files in a Chanel jacket against a paper backdrop in the RV.

"I'm the star of a job you wouldn't let me quit."

REAL REEL 5

*D*ear *Fancy Lady, I don't want to intrude on your valuable time, but if you could possibly let me and your father know how many tickets we have for graduation—if you're even planning to pen it into your whirlwind social calendar next month, that'd be great—Mom.*

"Can I help you?" the waitress behind the counter asks as I toss the note I'd shoved in my pocket on the way out my door in the trash. She rests her hands atop the speckled counter, and the morning light streaming in from the window makes the hairs on her meaty arms glow yellow.

"A double wafer cone of Coffee Almond Fudge, please?" Craft service Twizzlers, my on-set breakfast of choice, have now been replaced by green room doughnuts. Because, on the rare morning that I'm not doing a press event, microwaved eggs just aren't cutting it. In the two weeks since the *Good Morning America* interview, Fletch has pretty much yanked us from school completely to, quote, "fan the flames into an inferno." Whatever. Just hand over the sugar and tell me where to smile.

"You want a bagel with that?" she asks with a glance at the clock over the kitchen.

"Just the ice cream, please." I watch as she scoops out my breakfast—brunch?—struggling against the months-old frost. Just then the door to the diner jingles behind me, and a gaggle of grade schoolers piles in with one of their mothers bringing up the rear.

I watch uncomfortably as their eyes pool into saucers. "Jesse!" they squeal, the pom-poms on their pigtails jig-gling. They pluck lollipops out of their mouths as they crowd around, their sneakers squeaking on the linoleum. "Can we have your autograph? Please? *Please?*"

"Um, sure." I blush.

The waitress rolls her eyes, probably figuring I'm a Hollywood celeb in town for some preseason R&R, not a local who's spent the majority of her Saturdays scraping out Smucker's jars down the street.

"Jesse, we love you! Your hair is so pretty! We love your clothes!"

The waitress takes one more look at the scene my presence is generating and dumps my cone in the trash. "Freezer burn," she mutters with barely concealed con-tempt before walking back to tend to the locals finishing their morning coffee.

The mother appraises me over her sunglasses.

"Mom, we need a pen and paper!" One of the girls tugs at her arm.

Keeping me in her tinted sights, she removes a pen from her purse and what looks to be a receipt, which she tears into small strips for each girl. "You know," she says as she hands them to me, "it would be nice for them to have a local role model who doesn't behave like the summer people."

"*Mommmm,*" her daughter groans, going as pink as her velour hoodie.

"Oh, it's not—uh—you know, it's edited," I say, scribbling my name on each strip of thin paper, my handwriting messy as I try to hold my palm still.

"Hm-hm." She's not buying it.

I shift my attention to the girls, who gaze up at me like I have fairy dust puffing from my ears. "Here you go, thanks! So, why aren't you guys in school today?"

"Parent-teacher conferences! Why aren't you in school?" they sing in response, giddily hugging my hips.

"She's too famous for school," I hear from behind us.

My third-grade entourage and I spin to see Drew standing in the front door.

"DREW!! Oh my God, Drew! It's *Drew*!" The girls go nuts, running to pull him inside by the hand.

"What is this, the Bridgehampton chapter of the Jesse Fan Club?" He laughs as they tug at him.

"I always try to attend in my best sweats," I say sheepishly.

"Me too." He gestures down to his running pants.

"I was hoping to grab a cone on the down low, actually," I comment on the obvious futility. Although I'll take awkward autograph signing over being stuck in the house where the most recent episode, in which Drew and I seem finally about to get together, is perma-running like some haunting breakup song playing whenever you turn on the radio. But I have to give it to them for cobbling it together when we were pretty much never alone on camera—or off.

"Are you on a *date*?" "Do you *love* him?" "Is he your *boyfriend*?" Giggling, squealing, and hopping, the girls drag him to my side and then try to join our hands. We awkwardly hold sweaty fingers as the entire diner stares at us, adults confused, girls riveted.

"Um . . . " Drew fumbles.

I let go. "It's complicated, ladies."

Drew's turn to blush.

"Look, if you two aren't going to order . . . " The over-it waitress returns to free up the traffic jam we've created by the register.

"Okay, you have your autographs, now let's sit down." The mother corrals her giggling gaggle into a booth.

"Actually, I'd love a sugar cone of strawberry, please?" Drew leans into the ice cream case.

"Would you mind getting me the same?" I whisper. "I'm not welcome."

He nods and I walk outside to the bird-chirping sunshine on Main Street. After a moment, Drew slaps through the door. He walks over holding out my pink-topped cone, and I try to pass him three dollars.

"Forget about it."

"Really? Thanks," I say, shoving the cash back in my pocket and taking a satisfying lick. "So . . . what brought you out here?" For ice cream. At ten a.m.

"First really warm day," he says, unzipping his fleece vest with his free hand. "I was going stir-crazy cooped up inside with the TV—" Busted, he stops short and, looking away, sits down on a bench next to a curbside bed of pansies in their May prime.

A passing car rolls down its windows—"RICHIE ASSHOLES!"—and speeds off.

Drew tilts his head. "They never stop and, say, give us their names and home numbers."

I sit tentatively beside him. "You'd think they'd recognize me from the Pear."

"Or that I'm their friendly neighborhood bag boy."

"Yeah, a couple of hardworking locals . . . fresh off an international TV satellite tour."

"God, I hated that! Talking to a taped-up paper smiley face on a three-second delay. I felt like a total idiot. And then my earpiece gave out in the middle of the U.K. one."

"No worries—mine was working loud and clear, and I couldn't follow a word. Did he call Trisha a 'minger'? What's a 'minger'?"

"My favorite was 'slapper'—I've gotta look that up online."

"You chosen a school yet?" I ask, relishing that he's actually talking to me again, yet watching us as if from a TV screen. Feeling weird that we're not being filmed by some interview crew. Feeling weird that not being filmed is the new weird.

"I only got good aid at my safety. So that's good. I'm safe. But not—"

"Jumping up and down?"

"Congratulations on Georgetown. Sorry Cancun kind of stole your thunder."

"Thanks. It's the only thing keeping me from confirming my mother's worst fears—that this whole time I've secretly been a Golden Globe–winning, product-hawking, cookbook-writing, benefit-hosting, full-time celebrity, and just want her to clean my toilet."

He lets out a quick laugh. "So, they're having a hard time with it?"

"That's an understatement. I've betrayed the movement. It was fine if I worked *for* XTV. That's what we've always done, toiled for the glamour machine. I just think I was never supposed to be glamorous in my own right—as if." I roll my eyes. "How are your folks dealing?"

"Well, my little brother's autistic," he says uncomfortably.

"Oh—I had no idea—"

He carefully peels the paper wrapper off the sugar cone. "Yeah, it's not really something I talk about. . . . "

"I'm so sorry. How old is he?"

"Five. He's cool, just—I don't have people over because

it freaks him out. And them out. So, yeah, my parents are happy for me, but they kinda have their hands full with how much his therapy costs. I wish there was some money attached to any of this. I mean, the scholarship is great, but I wish there was something I could give them to help."

I nod, fully shamed out of myself and my petty problems.

"It's weird," he says, "talking to you after . . . you know, seeing us . . . "

"Yeah." I nod again. "I was feeling the same thing."

"Jesse," he says, twisting to face me on the bench.

"Yes?"

"I've been thinking. . . . "

You love me? "Okay . . . "

"We got off on the wrong foot."

"I totally agree!"

"Good." He exhales with relief while I get a giddy shot of joy—this isn't ruined! "Because I think we're better off as friends."

No! "Of course."

"I mean, if we could just be friends, that would be great."

"Friends, sure. No, that's great."

Suddenly the XTV-mobile screeches to a halt in front of us, and Rick opens the door. "Wassup, bitches!" he says in his best Trisha imitation. "Ready to hit the city?"

We both stand, polishing off the last of our cones, and look into the van. Arms crossed, Nico is seated in the front row, staring out the left window, and Jase, arms also crossed, is seated in the far back, looking out the right. "Kara," Drew greets her as he offers a friendly hand to help me up. "Can't you ever park like you're not about to rob a bank?"

"How much do you love that you both called to tell me to pick you up here?" Kara bubbles from the driver's seat. "I love it. Who called it? Who called it? Me!"

"Yup." I nod emptily at her before Drew and I both turn to our own opposite windows.

Three hours later, the van pulls up in front of XTV's Times Square headquarters. In the Broadway meridian the fans are already lining up for the afternoon's live all-request broadcast. Running late after a Jase-mandated highwayside hot-dog run—complete with chili and onions he had to eat and then belch my way—boys and girls are whisked in opposite directions for hair, makeup, breath mints, and wardrobe. Apparently the less aspirational me prefers BCBG to D&G. And peachier cheeks.

I'm sitting in my chair under the brown plastic sheet, head down, watching the whiffs of steam going up from the curling iron and wondering when I can cut my damaged hair off and if my new *friend*, Drew, would even notice, when Nico says, "Mel's running really late. You want me to call her?"

"No, that's okay," Kara replies from the couch behind us, where she sits nervously scrolling her BlackBerry beside Mr. Sargossi, who taps his Ferragamo loafer, today's *Post* rolled tightly in his hands.

"So if Nic does well on this, you think the traffic to the site I created for her will improve?" he asks her. Again.

"Yes, Mr. Sargossi, that's what we're hoping," she says through gritted teeth.

"Is Mrs. Dubviek driving her in?" I ask Nico.

"I think so," Nico says, extending her arms out from under her own protective smock to grab her cell from the makeup counter. "She hasn't texted me back."

"Okay, guys, I have a very sad announcement." Kara stands. "Unfortunately Fletch can't make it today, so it has fallen to me—of course—to inform you that Melanie is no longer with *The Real Hampton Beach*."

"*What?*" Nico stands right out of her chair, the stylist jerking up with her as she tries to release a blond curl from the iron. "She *quit*?"

"We can quit?" I ask, ready to rip off my plastic cape.

"Oh, no, no, no. No quitting." Kara shakes her head and scissors her forearms. "So long as the show stays in the top twenty in the cable ratings, you're under contract. No, sadly, Melanie just didn't have any traction in the blogs."

"So she was fired," I say, stunned.

"Well, she wasn't attracting advertisers." Kara sighs, her eyes not meeting ours.

"Well, she should've had me," a man says, strutting through the doorway with Trisha in tow. In a navy-blue silk dress with a 1940s-For-the-Boys-Betty-Grable-Dita-Von-Teese kind of shape. And hair to match. She strides in and perches in the empty makeup hair, one spectator pump crossed over the other at the ankle. She hasn't been this covered up since Bobby Feinstein's bar mitzvah.

"Tom. Tom Vogel." He extends his card to Kara from the pocket of his pin-striped suit. "Trisha's publicist." Trisha's *what*?

"You want *more* of this?" I choke as I'm engulfed in yet another cloud of spray.

Trisha looks right past me like she's busy concentrating on keeping her carefully rolled hair from moving.

"Um, Mr. Vogel," Kara says without bothering to look at the card. "The show has a publicist, has one in every country XTV airs, as a matter of fact. And we put out a singular message about the show and the cast."

"It's pretty clear where the network wants to take her, and it's a one-way ticket down," he levels back evenly. "Trisha has natural gifts, and they need to be managed for longevity. You let your own U.K. interviewer brand her as a slapper. She can hire me. I read her contract." He snaps his French cuffs over his wrists. "It's time to tweak the message."

"I feel underutilized," Trisha adds stiffly. "My fan site is getting almost as much traffic as Jesse's, but I have no way to reach more people."

"It's not a pie-eating contest." I shake my head, Tandy's mascara wand chasing after me. "You want my fans? Take 'em. Especially the middle-aged bald guy who re-creates my outfits and models them on his blog."

"Can I see that, please, Kara?" Nico pulls out a beaming smile for Tom Vogel. All thoughts of Melanie seemingly gone, she swipes the card from Kara's hand and turns to

Mr. Sargossi. "Dad?" She lowers her voice. "Can I have him? I think it would really help—"

"First you prove to me that you can be front-and-center, then I will hire you a publicist." Her father plucks the card from her fingers.

"What?" she says, echoing my own bewilderment at his logic.

"You become someone worth publicizing, Nico. Make me proud, and then I'll throw more money at this. I'm not going to keep looking like a chump." He drops the card into his empty Starbucks cup and snaps open his *Post* in disgust. Blinking, Nico shakily retakes her seat.

Fifteen minutes later, we line up in the wings, waiting to go on, our adrenaline revved by the live component—no chances to do over any tripped tongue or mispronounced words. Then the VJ announces, "And now, the stars of *The Real Hampton Beach*!" and the chanting starts. But instead of "Hamp-ton Beach," they're saying something else. I hear it before I believe it.

"Jes-se! Jes-se! Jes-se!" Holy crap. As the two hundred members of the live studio audience chant my name, we shuffle onto the circular set in front of the windows over-looking Times Square. With Tom Vogel just off camera, I nervously take my place behind Trisha, as instructed. She and Nico have matching tight smiles as they actively try to ignore the chants. I give little encouraging waves to as many jumping girls and guys as possible, hoping no one feels unappreciated. I can't believe they're so excited to see me. Or the me they think I am.

Despite Tom Vogel's vision, the VJ reaches into our huddle and maneuvers me in front to introduce the Rihanna video. And then we "chat a bit," but I'm so distracted by the kid in the front row's homemade Jesse T-shirt that I forget the question mid-answer. At the commercial break, to my relief, Tom Vogel climbs onstage to re-position Trisha front and center. "*Jesse!*" The T-shirt kid lets out a strangled sob, his arms outstretched toward the stage. Awkward, unsure if I should climb down to comfort him or run far, far away, I instead hide my widening sweat stains behind Jase and Drew. Back from commercial and trying to ignore the kid's wracking sobs, we watch clips from the first six episodes, which Trisha has been edited into with about the same finesse as Forrest Gump meeting JFK. Mostly she whimpers about how *she* could give Jase what he needs. A de-Axe'ing hose down? Etiquette lessons?

But that's not why she's here today. Oh no. Today she has a much loftier purpose. "And then I realized," she intones to the VJ with the gravitas of an oncologist, sticking out her demurely sheathed boobs, tilting her head to light her nose. "After *Us Weekly* called me, that I could share my story about my struggles with weight loss and food issues, and it could inspire others to get help."

Drew reaches around behind Rick to pinch my arm. I turn my listening smile to him, telegraphing, *Yes, Trisha is full of shit.*

"That is so brave of you to come forward," the VJ says

earnestly. Perfect. Let them each get publicists one by one, sharing their trumped-up stories of dyslexia and arachnophobia and glue addiction, and I'll get to retreat from the limelight and go to sleep at night knowing my mere presence isn't reducing anyone to sobs. "Okay, so before we go to commercial break we have a special surprise for Trisha and the cast. Guys, go to the windows and check it out!"

Following Trisha, who teeters at breakneck speed in her pencil skirt like a mad geisha, we go to the glass and look down. One lane of traffic in front of the building has been cleared, and there are six gleaming Lexuses parked with humongous red bows on the hood.

"Courtesy of XTV and the great folks at East Hampton Luxury Motors, you have each been given a *brand-new hybrid car*!" I stare down at the row of bows, my face hot. Rick, Trisha, and Jase pump their fists. Drew, his forehead against the glass, just pivots his head to me and gives a small smile. Because he finally has a way to make some money for his family. And I know this. Because I'm his friend.

"Thank you so much, Mr. Sargossi!" Trisha squeals, holding her new vanity plate, courtesy of XTV, TRHB-TRISH, in her hands. "I'm going to take this one to college so my Beemer doesn't get dented."

We're all piled into Mr. Sargossi's office, where Jase is the last of us to fill out his paperwork. "No shit. With the gas money I save shelving the Hummer, I can score a Ducati."

While Jase waxes on about his future crotch-rocket, I pull yet another makeup-remover towelette out of my bag and continue wiping down my pancaked face. "At least that went well," Mr. Sargossi says to no one in particular, his loafers up on his glass desk, an unlit cigar in his teeth. "I have a solid market with the parents, but I want more kids to think of our dealership as a place they can come and get something cool."

"I was thinking maybe we could lease one to Melanie at a discount, Dad," Nico implores hopefully.

"Maybe . . . " He takes the cigar from his mouth and studies it, not even saying good-bye to her as she leaves.

"So, I'll actually need to speak with you about reselling this, Mr. Sargossi," Drew ventures.

"Oh no you won't," Kara jumps in. "You will be in possession of and seen driving around these cars for at least twelve months from today's date. Or XTV will revoke responsibility for the tax on this *gift*. It's in the contract."

"But it'll lose value"—Drew's face darkens, his plan unraveling—"over a year."

"Oh God, *dude*," Kara breaks in, her exhausted exasperation exploding. "It's a car you didn't have this morning. *Please* try to see the bright side on this one." She stands from where she's seated on the radiator cover by the window and squeezes through our cluster out the open door. "Get some perspective, all of you."

Drew manages to refrain from telling her how much perspective he, in fact, has, and stays behind to find out how to preserve as much of the resale value as possible while still satisfying the contract.

Jase gives a two-fingered salute, hops in TRHB-JASE, and peels out, followed by Rick and Trisha. I, on the other hand, looking both ways three times and, at no more than two miles an hour, ease TRHB-JESSE gingerly off the lot and probably only get up to fifteen the whole drive across town, my sweaty hands gripping the wheel. *I am sitting in my parents' combined annual salaries. I am sitting in my parents' combined annual salaries.* I check the rearviews every two seconds. There is no way I am driving this thing in high season; I will have a cardiac.

Awash in relief, I turn off the ignition in the parking lot behind the spa, feeling like I should check in on Melanie, even though I don't know what I can say. Unable to see clearly as the sun drops behind the trees, I fumble with the power lock. I notice the twin car farther down the lot with TRHB-NICO on the plates. Maybe I should leave? No. Mel should know we're all here for her.

Tentatively I open the door to the salon and can hear the sobbing from the treatment rooms in the back. I walk past embarrassed-looking clients at the manicure tables and pedicure chairs, murmuring to one another as I pass. Down the hall, through a cracked door, I can see Melanie balled up in Nico's arms on a massage table, the uprooted fountain Zacheria could never get to work defunct on the wall behind them.

"Shhh," Nico murmurs, stroking her hair. "It'll be okay. There's so much more than this."

"No . . . there . . . isn't," Melanie chokes out. "I'll be

scrubbing people's feet the rest of my life. I d-don't understand. I did e-everything they asked."

"Enough, Melania." I hear Mrs. Dubviek order over the clomp of her espadrille mules on the basement stairs. I turn to where she marches up from the storeroom, pushing past me to throw open the massage room door.

Nico reaches out for her. "Mamma D—"

"You, both of you—" She points an accusing red nail at me. "Get out. You dead to me."

Stunned, Nico unfurls herself from a silently weeping Melanie. "This wasn't my fault."

"You supposed to protect her, fight for her," she says, her accent thickened by rage. "Melania will make new friends, ones she can trust. *Both of you, get out of my store. You not welcome here.*"

Nico looks to Melanie, but she just pulls her knees deeper into her chest and twists her face into the table.

Nico walks shakily right past me. I hurry behind her, averting my eyes from the openly staring clients, as she lets herself out, a steady stream of Polish invectives at our backs. I follow Nico around to the dark parking lot, and she looks at her car, the hood still sticky where the bow was. She drops her forehead on the top of the roof and starts to cry.

"Nico," I say softly, awkwardly touching her arm. "It'll be okay."

"I just lost my best friend," she bawls into her arm. "What could you *possibly* know about it?" She turns her head to me, the unleashed disdain shredding my sympathy.

"Plenty." I step back. "You might not have noticed, but I wasn't newly born the day Kara forced me on your lunch table. I had a best friend before this started. And your *dad's show* didn't pick her."

"It's not his show!" she yells. "Just his idea. And at least *I* have someone looking out for me, someone who's invested in me, someone trying to make something happen for me."

"Sending you to college is making something happen! Not getting you a publicist!"

"What world do you live in?" she spits contemptuously. "You're just jealous because I have *everything*." Her face splotches red beneath her wet eyes.

"Jealous?"

"You're nobody. I'm Nico. Jase *loves* me. He has some growing up to do, but he *loves* me," she sobs. "My dad *loves* me." She pauses to fill her convulsing lungs with breath. "And I have star quality," she chokes out.

Shaking, I step around her to the other side, unlocking my new car. "Nice reality. I, however, am willing to admit that I've lost my best friend, my life, a chance with Drew, my senior year, *and* my parents' respect. Now, if you'll excuse me, Oh Perfect One, I have to go home and cry about that."

REAL REEL 6

"**H**ello?" I rasp into my cell, still breathing deeply into my pillow, my finger hovering to click the off button, braced to hear that I'm a bitch, a slut, that I give good head, bad head, that my panties smell like fish. And these lovely classmates of mine shockingly weren't deemed XTV material.

"Jesse?" Her voice is so quiet and it's been so long it takes me a groggy moment to place it.

"Caitlyn?" I sit up in bed, exaggeratedly blinking to wake myself up. "Caitlyn, what's wrong?" I check the glowing clock on my night table—only 11:08. I must have passed out after the last round of pre-finale interviews. Four a.m. start times are turning me into a senior citizen.

Eating dinner at five, passing out by eight—pathetic.

"Jesse, I need you to come pick me up," Caitlyn says furtively. "Can you? Can you just come, please, right now?"

"Yes, of course. Yes!" I jump up to tug on my leggings, simultaneously pulling a hoodie over my T-shirt. "Where are you?" I grab my wallet and keys off my desk.

"At the mini-mart. Down the road from the hospital."

"Are you okay?" I whisper as I sneak down the stairs in my bare feet, careful to jump the creaking step.

"Just come." She hangs up.

I screech into the Qwik Fill lot and am relieved to see Caitlyn immediately push through the glowing double doors. I start to get out, but she jogs directly to the passenger side, where we have an awkward misstep of locking and unlocking her door before we get in sync. She drops into the seat next to me, and I take her in under the harsh flickering lights of the pump overhang. Her face is drawn, her eyes puffy.

"Sorry, I haven't figured out this thing yet," I comment too late for it to make sense because I'm distracted by how much I want to hug her, but don't.

"Can we just drive?" She rests her elbow on her door and leans her temple into her fingers.

"Sure!" I back up and then turn us toward the exit, only to slow to a stop by the neon arrow. "Um, where do you want to go?"

"I didn't get any financial aid from American," she states to the dark road before us.

"Oh, Cay—"

"Or GW, or Trinity. My dad refused to submit a letter saying he wasn't contributing. So even though his, quote, *support* has been sporadic, at *best*, they're accounting for his income and have decided we can afford the close to two hundred grand in debt."

"That's awful! What an asshole—"

"So my mom moves right into the now-you-can-go-to-community-college-and-live-with-me thing, and *I can't*. I mean, I couldn't before, but now I really can't. I *can't* stay in this town. And we got in this screaming fight while I was driving her to her shift, and she started crying like she always does when it's about Dad, and it was horrible, and she was late for work, and she said if I hate it here so much I should go now, so I get out of the car."

"In the middle of the road?"

"We'd pulled over by the station to scream at each other without getting in an accident. And she keeps calling me, and I don't want to talk to her. I don't want to talk to anyone."

"Okay," I say, focusing on the pale green dashboard glow glinting off the steering wheel emblem.

"So I didn't have anyone else to call." She twists her face to the window. "And I remembered you got this car, and I don't know where to tell you to go."

"You don't have to." I screech us onto the empty road.

Pulling to a stop, I cut the engine, and we both watch as the headlights beam out over the crests of sand to the crashing surf beyond. They fade off, leaving us in the dark, listening to the rhythmic roar. We used to bike here in the summer, back before they carved up the property into McParcels. Back when the Johnson family had just started selling off the estate to developers, and Caitlyn and I were the closest thing for each other to being in someone else's brain.

She sinks down in her seat, pulling her knees up against the glove compartment. "I haven't been here in forever."

"Me neither." I slide my hands between my thighs as the damp May air seeps in.

"I could go for a cigarette." She runs her finger back and forth across her bangs. "I don't suppose Mr. Sargossi gave you a lifetime supply of those."

"Sponsor conflict. A meth lab got there first. Interested? There's a pipe in the glove."

She turns to me, one eyebrow up.

"Kidding."

She shakes her head. "Jennifer Lanford isn't funny."

"Really?" I ask tentatively, hopefully. "She seems like fun."

"She's fun, kind of. But not funny, not like you."

"*No one's funny like you*," I say emphatically.

"What am I going to do, Jess?" Her eyes widen as she searches my face.

"Options." I tick off on my fingers. "Go to community college for a year, work on your dad, and reapply. Or . . . or . . . maybe we could have him offed?"

"*Yes*. Maybe your meth connection?" she deadpans.

I laugh as my cell buzzes in my hoodie pocket. I tug it out, flick it off, open the armrest compartment, and drop it in.

"You can get that," she offers.

"That's okay—they can tell my voice mail it's an anorexic, bitch-faced whore and that *its* boobs are freakishly different sizes."

"Who's saying *that*?" Her eyebrows scrunch together.

"Like you haven't heard."

"I've heard. I just didn't know you had."

"It's a little hard to miss. On my locker, between my windshield wipers, in the mailbox. And every electronic form of communication known to man." I sigh. "And eggs—when they feel like kicking it old school. It's all petty and foul and crazy mean. People don't just hate me. It's become the new Hampton High religion."

"It's not just you. It's everyone in the cast." She looks down at her lap. "Okay, guilty admission. I can't say it hasn't been the teensiest bit satisfying."

"Good. Someone other than Verizon should be benefiting."

"Well, your boobs are a matched set. You can trust me. I'm not anonymous."

"Thanks, man." I touch her arm.

"Anytime." She pats my hand, reminding me how much I *do* trust her, how long it's been since I could just—talk.

"I hooked up with Jase McCaffrey." My turn to search her face.

"Holy. Shit."

"Ugh, it feels good to say it out loud." I fall back against the seat. "It's grown to IMAX-size, rattling around in my head."

"Did you have the sex?" She sits up, tucking her legs and shifting in the seat to fully face me.

"We did not have the sex. We had mad passionate almost, twice. And I know he's . . ."

"A single cell of testosterone."

"But he's also a single cell of testosterone! Which is kind of what I needed, I thought. We were in Cancun, and Drew was hooking up with Nico, and I was drunk. Oh God, I had a bunch of these lethal tropical punch things, and then I was going to tell him about Nico cheating on him just to get back at Drew—"

"Wait." She slices her arm down between us. "Aren't you two going out?"

"Drew? No! I wish, but no. He acts like I played him. Like I was using him to get to Jase. Which is so ridiculous it's almost funny. But not. So we're just friends. Officially. His choice—not mine."

"So why are you getting back at him, exactly?"

I grab her shoulders. "Because I haven't had you to talk to! I am literally going crazy without you!"

"Okay. I need to know everything from the beginning. From the beginning all the way through putting your clothes back on. And I should pause to tell you I hooked up with Rob over break. It was in Jennifer's basement and not Cancun. We are not going out. I had three Coors and it was okay—not great. But, you first. Go."

I reach across the seat and pull her into a hug, my eyes tearing. She grips me to her and then pushes me back.

"So Jase says . . . " She prompts me to tell her everything. And I do.

"Thanks for the ride, supastah." Caitlyn pulls her bag up from the floor as we idle outside Bambette.

"Hey, babe, my wheels are your wheels."

"So you really think your mom's friend can let the dress out in a week?" she asks, referring to the Nanette Lepore we scored for her at the outlet mall. "I don't want to be the only person at the finale party wearing something that looks like a hand-me-down."

"Caitlyn, we're all in borrowed clothing. Everything I wear has someone else's sweat rings in it. Think of that the next time you watch the Oscars." She makes a "yick" face. "And I'm going to have the hottest date there." I squeeze her knee. "But remember, you can't tell anyone who's hosting it—"

"Can I say a *certain* hip-hop mogul? A *certain* hip-hop mogul with a penchant for changing his name?" I laugh, nodding. "I'm so psyched. To be an actual guest at one of those mansions instead of helping my cousin cater. I'm going to take two of everything and look every server in the eye when I say thank you. Oh God, I think I'm getting sick." She rubs her throat. "Or we talked that much this weekend."

"We talked that much this weekend," I confirm.

"I don't want to go." She drops her head to the dashboard. "It sucks not having you to take breaks with."

"Tell me about it! Mine consist of me wedged between Trisha's cleavage and Jase's cologne. Factor in Trisha's new obsession with American Spirits, and it's like every day is Casino Day."

Caitlyn's boss pulls the eyelet curtain back in the front window, fingering her three-stranded pearls as she peers out at us.

"Ugh. Call you later." Caitlyn leans over for a quick hug and gets out. I grin as she rounds the car, waving to her boss with a false cheer only I can detect, and shift the gear into drive. But Caitlyn slaps her forehead before she makes it inside and comes running back over. I lower my window.

"I forgot! I got this for you, like, last November. Sorry it's a little rumpled—and dusty." She digs in her bag before dropping a package wrapped in paper with illustrations of ladybugs into my lap. "The plastic package said it was called Happy Bugs. That's the name of the paper. The paper has a name and it's Happy Bugs."

"They look happy." I reach up through the opened

window to hug her. "Thank you!"

"I want *that* job." She holds on to the shoulder strap of her bag with both hands and jogs backward up to the store. "I want to get paid big bucks to give titles to wrapping paper. I want to judge its emotions."

"You're the *best* best friend!" I yell.

She does a little bow and pushes inside.

Shifting the gear back to park, I carefully open the paper, separating it from itself along the clear tape so that I can save it in my Caitlyn box. Catching sight of the white Georgetown logo, I shake out the navy-blue T-shirt in front of me. I whip off my seat belt, shrug out of my jacket, and pull it on. As my head clears the collar, I see her smiling in the window with a feather duster in hand. I cross my arms over my heart and mouth, "I love it!"

She gives me a thumbs-up in front of her chest and then returns to dusting the pastel bonnets on display with a comical amount of care.

Pulling back into Main Street, I see my reflection in the rearview. For a second it's unfamiliar . . . because I'm not wearing makeup? Or jewelry?

Because I'm a Happy Bug.

REAL REEL 7

"**N**ice shirt, Georgetown."

I pivot in my Tretorns, shielding my eyes against the rising sun bouncing off the car hoods in the Stop & Shop lot, to see Drew jogging up with his red apron in hand. I quickly dart my tongue across my teeth, checking for Eggo flakes. Cleared to smile, I pull the fabric away from my abdomen, to tilt the emblem up to him. "You like? Caitlyn gave it to me a week ago, and I haven't taken it off since."

"Tasty." He laughs.

"I figure as long as I have another T-shirt under it I'm good."

"You should totally wear that to the finale party tomorrow."

"I'm sure Fletch would love that. So, what's with the park job?" I point to where his Lexus sits by its lonesome way over near the drive-through ATM.

"No one ever parks over there—so it should stay nick-free. I'm getting money from that thing, even if it's a year from now." He cups the brim of his baseball hat. "But not having to drive me to work frees up my mom. And I can bring groceries home; there's only so much you can balance on handlebars."

"Kara didn't quit your job for you, too?"

"No such luck. I will be gladly bagging through the summer." He falls into step with me. "Sweet day."

I lift my bare arms to the sun. "I never thought I'd count natural light in my Top Ten List of Awesome."

He laughs. "And personal space. And my own clothes. And, oh, this is my new favorite, watching *other* people do stuff on TV."

"You too?" I stop short.

"Anything." He folds his arms over his T-shirt. "Renovate a kitchen. Raise a dog. Solve a murder."

"Yes!" I reach out and we high-five as a minivan rolls past, the father scanning for a space, the kids scanning us. "I'm having a weird thing for the Food Network. Nobody talks about shopping or who they hung out with or what party they're going to. Just beat an egg and layer it over the Robiola."

He leans into a stray grocery cart. "Hop on. I'll coast you the final mile." I step onto the back rail, and he rolls me toward the double doors. "Truth: Are you here for the *OK!*?" he asks.

"I just want to see how the photo shoot came out."

"What'd you have to do?"

"I was on a horse in full Hermès dressage gear."

"Sounds glamorous."

"Oh, it was. Especially when Fletch's cell rang at air-raid volume, spooking the horse, and I was then on a big pile of shit in full Hermès dressage gear. I'm still bruised."

"That sucks. Get this, I heard Trisha's publicist dude insisted they shoot her at the nature preserve to show how 'environmentally friendly' she is. The whole thing's ridiculous. And yet my mom wants copies for every family member. She's more excited about this than my Stony Brook aid coming through."

"Wooo!" I jump off the cart. "You got it?"

"Yup." His cheeks redden. "A cross-country scholarship."

"Drew! That's so great!" Before I know it I've thrown my arms around him. And his are around me. And here we are. I smell the spice of his deodorant and the salt of the skin on his warm neck.

"Thanks," he says into my hair.

"Yeah." I reluctantly pull back. "Of course, I mean, I'm so happy for you. You know, because you're my friend."

"Right," he says, fingers resting on my elbows. Here, next to the handful of candy for twenty-five cents machine and the free *PennySaver*. "Jess . . . " He leans into me, his

251

nose practically touching mine.

"Yes?"

"Race you to the magazines—loser buys all." He takes off across the parking lot with me at his heels.

Ten minutes later, I have my solitary copy tucked under one arm, while Drew lugs two stuffed plastic bags behind me as we amble toward my Lexus.

"You want a lift to the hinterlands?" I ask as I press the unlock button, hoping my *whatever* tone masks my eagerness to get him in my car.

"Just 'cause you won, doesn't make me a weakling." He lifts the straining plastic and makes a muscle. But then he opens the passenger door as I open mine and we both get in. He lowers the bags to his feet as I start the car and ease back out of the spot.

"So . . . let's see what the real stars of the *Real Hampton* are like!" He slides my copy onto his lap and flips through as I drive us over to his car. "Wow, it's long. Aw, look at Trisha, sad and naked on a moss bed."

"It's her eating disorder. She goes there to think about it. Naked."

"No way! Jase with a surfboard? That kid never went surfing a day in his life."

"You're kidding! Let me see." I brake to a stop behind his car and lean over the armrest. He slides the page to my lap, and all at once our heads are side by side.

He turns to me as I stare down at the shiny picture, not

seeing it, too acutely aware of how close he is. How can he not feel this?

And then I watch as his right hand releases the magazine and lifts to turn my cheek to him. Is this it? Is he going to? His lips land tentatively on mine. Oh my God— this is it. We're really—we're kissing. Deeply kissing. And everything that has come before slips away. My hands reach up around his neck, his hands spread to slide around me. We can't get close enough.

And suddenly—ringing—Drew's cell.

"Sorry." He heavily exhales into my hair, and I don't want him to let me go. But his hands slip from my lower back. He looks past me and across the crowding lot to a man in a red vest standing outside the entrance talking angrily into his cell and staring straight at us. "Shit. That's my boss. I gotta get in there."

"Yes, go," I manage.

His cheeks flushed, he pulls out his keys from his pocket and pops his trunk with his key chain. I force myself to sit back in my seat. Even though what I want to do is rip off my Georgetown shirt. Rip off my everything.

"I'm sorry I've gotta go." You are? How sorry? This-is-no-longer-complicated sorry? We're-more-than-friends sorry? He opens the door, gets out, and flings the bags into his trunk. He jogs around to the driver's side, and I lower the window as he asks, "I'll see you tomorrow at the party?"

"That's my contractually obligated plan."

"And we could hang out after?" He smiles deliciously.

"I think we should, don't you?"

"Uh, yeah." I nod rapidly.

"Take in some Food Network?"

Or get naked. Whatever. "Sure!"

He reaches in to slide his finger gently across my lips. "Cool."

"Cool," I say, breathless.

Grinning broadly, he pivots to jog away. "Hey, O'Rourke, I'm glad we finally got that straightened out!" he yells up to the sky.

Wow. WOW! I tug out my phone to call Caitlyn—then realize I have to pull out of the lot or it'll look like I'm waiting for him.

I rest the magazine on the steering wheel and, putting the car in drive, maneuver to the exit. Mesmerized by the spread I idle there, waiting for the light to change. Surreal. There we all are. But it's like I'm looking at other people. People who are in magazines. God, *are* my boobs uneven? I turn the page to see a huge headline across a shot of me leaving the lunch buffet in Mexico. My stomach is circled like a football replay. *Jesse O'Rourke pregnant with Jase McCaffrey's baby!*

My whole body goes cold all at once. I look up to see in my rearview my last glimpse of Drew smiling as he waves good-bye to me from the sliding door.

"Jesse?"

I lift my head from my knees to look at the crack of

light coming in under my closed closet door. "Yeah?"

Dad clears his throat. "Are you . . . uh, pregnant?"

"Dad, no!" I push the door open and blink into the slanting afternoon sunshine, my eyes adjusting to see him leaning against my bed, tie askew. "Did Mom call you at work? Oh my God!"

"Can you come out?"

"No," I say, back to my small voice. The pull is too strong to remain here, tucked in where no one can take a picture of me and say it's something else. I just need to stay here. Here with my clothes rubbing the top of my head and my shoes piled around me, a bag of old stuffed animals at my back. Here feels good—better. Better than out there.

"Jess . . . " Dad rubs the bridge of his nose. "Hiding in the closet is not a solution."

"Okay," I murmur, returning my forehead to my knees. I reach out to pull the door closed, but he leans over and catches the knob.

"We need to talk about this."

"Really, Dad, really, do we need to talk about *this*?" I hug my legs tightly.

Silence.

I turn my head to rest my cheek on my knee and look out at him. "Did you read it?"

He tilts his head. "Did you?"

"No. Mom was already crying on the phone with Aunt Pat when I got home so I just ran up here, where I intend to stay until I'm dead. Fuck the finale."

"Jesse."

"So?" We both turn to see Mom appear at the top of the stairs, a tumbler of Maker's Mark in one hand, the magazine in the other, and the phone under her arm.

"We've got the closet door opened." Dad waves her in.

"And I'm not pregnant."

Her shoulders slump in relief. "Jesse, I just need to know." Mom walks over to him and sets the phone on the bed. "Why you would tell *this* to a magazine. All these sexual details. Why would you think that's appropriate?"

"I told them I want to major in psychology and my favorite movie is *Don Juan DeMarco*! I never talked to them about . . . about something that didn't even happen!"

"So you didn't, uh, sleep with Jase McCaffrey?" Dad purses his lips and asks the ceiling. Kill me.

"No, I did not sleep with Jase McCaffrey," I moan.

They both stare me down, question marks in their eyes. "Or anyone! Please, just *please* leave me alone." I pull the door closed.

"Jesse!" Mom screeches with exasperation.

"Can't!" I yell back.

"Fine! Fine."

I feel something getting shoved under the door into the side of my Tretorn. "Then you read it and tell me what I'm supposed to tell Aunt Pat and everyone else," Mom says curtly from the other side of the wood.

I wait a moment for them to leave and then snake my hand up through my shirts to feel for the little metal clip on the light string. Tugging it, the bulb clicks on, the yellow light filtering down to where I'm crammed into the free inches of floor space. I push the hanger of skirts back as hard as I can, and a shaft falls directly onto my lap.

Nauseous, I turn the shiny pages past *real* celebrities doing *real* things—like revealing their cellulite in the Maui surf and holding Macchiatos in parking lots. I get to the photo spread and stare at the shot of Drew leaning against Ralph Lauren's pool table. Drew and his family and his forty-two copies.

I turn the page.

And here I am. Straddling that horse in a way that is downright unseemly. My eyes dance over the page, not wanting to land on any of it. "A source close to Jesse says that when things got too hot in Cancun—" A *source*? What source? I've never talked about Jase. "The two shared illicit nights of steamy passion. The source says Jesse readily admits that 'she played Drew, using him just to get to Jase.' Jesse also called her costar 'one big cell of testosterone' and 'just what she thought she needed.'"

Oh. My. God.

Caitlyn shuffles into view in shorts and her graying bunny slippers, grabbing her dog's collar to move him behind her to get to the door. "I've been trying to call you all day—"

"Don't." I lift a shaking finger. She freezes. "Ever again," I spit out, stepping back to her porch stairs. "Call *OK! Magazine* instead."

"What? Why? Jesse, why did you tell me exactly what you told them? Is it just some script the show gave you?" She steps outside as I stumble back to the driveway where I've left my engine running.

"I hope they paid you a lot. I really do." I reach the open car door. "You know, all of this—I can take. The world thinks I'm a pregnant backstabbing slut, fine. I have to talk to my parents about who I'm *not* having sex with, fine. The one guy I might've—the one guy I really like— will never talk to me again, fine. But you, *you*, Caitlyn—" Sliding into the driver's seat I feel a sharp burst in my throat as tears blur my vision. "You broke my heart."

Slamming the door, I throw the shift into reverse and back up her long drive, watching my former best friend get smaller and smaller.

REAL REEL 8

"**I**sn't there a dress with a waist?" I ask the stylist baby-oiling my tanned legs, prepping me for the finale party like a rib roast at Cooper's. Pressing my hands against the white organza baby doll, I stare at my reflection in the massive mahogany-framed mirror through puffy, bloodshot eyes. Exhausted from alternating sob sessions on my closet floor and under my comforter, I'm light-headed from hunger and heartache.

"Be careful," Diane warns me yet again as I turn, stepping off the brown paper and onto the pool house's unbelievably impractical porous Carrara floor.

But even through my misery haze, a voice in the back of my head rings an alarm at this dress. "This dress makes me look—I need to show my waist," I say with increased urgency as Tandy re-pins the Van Cleef & Arpels chains she's woven around my carefully constructed Grecian updo.

"But this dress goes with these." Diane sets down the baby oil and, wiping her hands on her apron, scoots on her knees to retrieve yet another chocolate-brown Gucci bag, from which she withdraws a large box and sets it on to the marble. "These are next season, wait-listed so long your grandchildren won't—" She stops short, her cheeks reddening. Tandy arches her penciled-in eyebrows. The rain continues drizzling outside the slats of the shuttered windows.

"I'm not," I say quietly. As I did at the gas station, the mini-mart, and the hosting mogul's guard gate. I wanted to roll down the window and shout it to the cadre of soaked parents protesting in the rain with soggy signs against our, *my* immorality. Why'd I bother putting on clothes before leaving the house? At least I would look how I feel—naked.

"No, right, I meant . . . So, these are *the* shoes! The Gucci Gladiator Spike." She pulls off the box top and pushes aside the thin tissue to reveal pale gold heels with thick straps wrapping around and around them. Cooing with admiration, she unwinds the shimmering leather and sets them on the floor in front of my bare feet.

"Those have to be four inches." I stare down at the contraptions awaiting me, the me who hasn't been able to keep down more than a glass of water.

"Four and a quarter. You're the Gucci runway bride," she gushes while adjusting the hem of my dress, where it falls a modest centimeter below my crotch. Fine. Finefinefine! There is one mission today: Salvage Drew. Tell him the truth, just like I did with Caitlyn about Josh Dupree in sixth grade. Because this is my closest frame of reference to this shit mess. I mean, what exactly *is* the protocol when one's cheated on someone who's not their boyfriend twice and an international magazine makes a hookup sound like a possible baby conception? Forget a publicist, I need a *Desperate Housewives* staffer. Drew, I'm so sorry for cheating on you twice when you weren't my boyfriend, I hope you can see past the international magazine making a hookup sound like a possible baby conception. Boy, someday we'll look back on this and laugh!

Sigh.

I'm just going to apologize, and if it's as a runway bride, so be it.

Holding Diane's outstretched hand, I step into the shoes, my entire body weight pitching forward onto the balls of my feet. I grimace as Diane and Tandy lace them tightly up my calves, their cooing so fervent I momentarily think they'll lick them. They let go, and I dart my hands out for balance. I'm precarious. Betrayed, mortified, wretchedly exhausted—and precarious. They should sell it as the XTV perfume.

"God, Jesse, you give Gisele a run for her money."

I look back into the mirror to see Kara has slipped in

the side door, headset around her neck, clipboard to her chest, raincoat dripping onto the tile.

"Thanks," I say as I teeter around to face her.

"Eek." She bites her lip. "Can't you guys do anything more about the swelling around her eyes?"

"She's spackled in Preparation H. Any more and she won't be able to blink. But you reminded me about the Visine." Tandy digs in her open toolbox and hands me the drops. "Two on each side."

I obediently lift my head and squirt in the cold liquid while she darts over to pad my cheeks dry with a puff. "Kara." I blink. "This dress isn't helping."

"Sorry, Jess." She looks down, seeing what I see. "Oh God, sorry. But we promised Gucci. The whole cast, head to toe."

"Where is the whole cast? Why aren't we getting ready together?"

"Fletch thought you guys could use some space before the VIP reception. Temperatures have been running a little high."

Oh God, I hadn't even— "How's Nico?"

"She's on her way down to the party now."

"No, I mean, *how* is she?"

"She's quiet." Kara checks her cell and then something on her clipboard. "And Drew hit Jase, so those two are separated. Actually, I need you guys to wrap up and go help with covering the bruising on his jaw." She waves at the women as they pack up their tools.

"Drew hit him?"

"Yup. Jess," Kara says tentatively, lowering her voice. "Is there anything I can do?"

"Besides giving me a fitted dress?"

"I meant outside the show. If your parents are having a hard time with this, I could take you to someone in the city—"

"Kara, *I'm not pregnant*! And at this point, there is no outside the show."

She nods, absorbing the crappiness of my situation. "I'm sorry, Jesse. This has gotten really out of hand. It's not what I signed up for, I'll tell you that much."

"That makes two of us," I say. Her sad face stares back at me in the mirror.

"Let's go," she sighs, pulling her hood back up. "Before it starts to pour again. The golf cart is waiting to take us to the house."

"I really think we should all talk before we're surrounded by a bunch of contest winners, don't you? I never would have . . . " My eyes start to fill again.

"*No!*" All three women rush at me like I'm a puppy circling on white carpet. "No crying! We don't have time!"

"Kara? What's the holdup?" We all pivot toward the door at the sound of Fletch's voice.

Kara whips the puff from the makeup woman and dabs at my eyes. "Coming right out, Fletch!"

"Holy hotness." Too late. The ladies step away from me to let Fletch leer from the doorway in his white suit and

263

dripping XTV golf umbrella.

"Fletch." I take a step toward him. "I need a chance to set things straight with everyone before this VIP thing. I feel awful—"

His face twists. "So let's review. You feel awful. Drew's bummed. Jase is freaked, and Nico's all closed up. Are Rick and Trisha the only ones who got the goddamn memo?! Thanks to that *OK! Magazine* story, the rerun marathon is our highest in the network's history. Tyra wants to book you with Jamie Lynn and Ashlee Simpson. You . . . are the most ungrateful fucking babies I have ever met. *You* are standing in six thousand dollars worth of clothes and ten times that is wrapped around your stupid little head in jewels, for which you have your own private guard waiting to escort you. Do you know how many girls would trade their right tit for this? Get a grip, get happy, and get in the fucking golf cart. *Now.*"

My security guard at my elbow, I inch under his umbrella into the receiving throng of contest winners that line the white carpet leading to the main entrance. White. In a rainstorm. Because everything at this estate is white. "Jesse, Jesse, we love you!" a girl squeals, breaking into tears. I open my mouth to say something, but I'm hit by a barrage of more questions: "Do you love being on the show?" "Is it so perfect?" "Did you plan to get pregnant?" I catch sight of the amoeba clusters around Drew and Nico, who look like deer in front of speeding trucks, and Trisha, who looks like the eager mud-flap silhouette.

"Were you just doing it to get back at Nico for trying to get Drew?" "Are you in love with Jase?" "Are you getting married?" "What are you naming the baby?"

"Jesse, do you have a minute? We need to talk." Jase breaks through his mob of teenage girls, to break through my mob of teenage girls, sending both mobs into collective rapt silence.

"Yes," I say, as I would to Satan himself if he were standing here offering to put an end to this.

"Excuse us, ladies," Jase charms, sending them atwitter. He gestures for me to follow and I do, my Van Cleef & Arpels guard at my wobbling heels as we make our way through the entrance gallery to a side room off the library. The guard closes the door behind us, and I turn to Jase in what appears to be a room solely for a bathtub—no sink, no toilet, no towel racks—as if it didn't play well with the rest of the fixtures and was given a time-out. In the white floor's center, Jase takes a seat on the edge of the chalky marble oval, his bruised chin the only color beneath the crystal chandelier.

"Jase, you have to back me up on this. Tell everyone it's not true, and that what happened between us was drunk and stupid and over."

His shoulders release. "So, it's not true." He lets out a long, relieved breath.

"No, it's not true!" I look back over my shoulder at the guard. "Sorry, could we just have, like, a minute here?"

"I have to keep the merchandise within visual range at all times," he says, staring straight ahead.

"Man." Jase claps his hands together. "That was a close call."

I spin to him, taking a few steps closer to hiss, "We *didn't* sleep together. *How* could it be true?!"

"Well, I mean, I passed out. You could've had your way with me."

"We *both* passed out. And don't flatter yourself."

"Well, here we are in a bathroom . . . " He tilts his head and raises an inviting eyebrow.

"Never. Again." My hands find my hips.

"But those shoes . . . " He smiles, his lids heavy.

"Are not mine and will be going back to Guantánamo as soon as this thing is done. So, you're not going to help me clear this up?"

"It's not like *I* look bad in this. I don't owe Nico anything now, and with the amount of ass flying my way . . . I got fourteen numbers in fourteen minutes out there. It's not hurting me."

"Jase." I totter the few feet to him. "You *have* to help me. You *have* to. Why did you even ask me in here?"

"Fletch told me to." He picks at an errant white thread on his linen blazer. "And to make sure I'm not a daddy."

The adrenaline surges through me. "Okay, one: Get over yourself. Two: I know things about you. Things I never told anyone. I'd hate to have to."

He stands, his face darkening, all come-ons dropped.

He walks past me to the white lacquered door, his shoes tapping against the shiny floor. He stops but doesn't turn around. "You know, you want to be this nice person. This real person. This girl who's better than all the player bullshit that happens here. And just now—what you threatened? It means you aren't. Officially." He walks out of the bathroom, brushing past Kara.

"Jesse—Jase!" she calls to his retreating back. "Your parents are all seated, the audience is in the ballroom—it's time to line up."

As she keeps up a steady string of unintelligible muttering into her headset, we follow her labyrinthine path through the ground floor, Jase using long strides to keep his distance. "Okay, here." She deposits us with the rest of the cast and their jewelry guards in an albino-python-covered hallway serving as the staging area. "On the other side of that door," she says, "is the packed ballroom. In the center of which is a stage where the show's about to begin. Stand by, rock stars, I'll be back to get you in three."

She slips through the door to the ballroom, my chanted name pouring through the wall for a moment before they realize we're not following behind her.

"Nico, Drew," I begin furtively. "I need to say something." The made-up faces of my cast mates turn to me, their expressions withering. Jase leans his body weight forward, primed to take me out if necessary. "Everyone had lies printed about them. You have to understand the same thing happened to me. Jase and I didn't have sex." I try to catch Drew's eye. "I'm not pregnant."

"Well, as long as there was no intercourse!" Nico cheers, then returns to scowling at the mirrored ceiling.

"But there wasn't! Nico, you were kissing Drew in your underwear in a hot tub. It's not like I'm the only one—"

"You're both skanky hos," Trisha pronounces.

"Shut up," the rest of us say in unison.

Drew crosses his arms, his expression pained. "So how do you explain that Jase's been talking about screwing you since Valentine's?"

"Great." Nico nods. "That's just great."

"Oh, *come on*, Nico," Jase explodes. "We're eighteen, for fuck's sake, and you wanted to be married!"

"I *wanted* a boyfriend who was *mine*. Sorry it was such torture."

I look to Drew. "I swear on my grandmother I never said I was playing you. I wasn't."

Drew clears his throat. "It was just the once, right? In Cancun?" Everyone stares me down, and I lose my nerve. I mean, I've apologized. And the "source" didn't mention the limo.

I nod. "So, Jase and I hooked up. Nico and Drew kissed. Trisha has . . . Trisha-ed . . . everyone . . . and that's that, so we're all cool?"

"I'm cool." Rick shrugs.

I look hopefully at Drew.

He bites his lip and nods slowly.

"Okay, kids, you're on!"

In the vaulted room, knees clamped, I sit as far back on the white couch as possible. And here we are: full circle—on a stage, in front of a salivating crowd, another huge screen suspended too close to see things clearly. But the sound is perfect. Crystal. I can hear every one of my gasps as I writhe in the back of the limo under Jase McCaffrey pushing up my pink dress. Then, later in the episode, I hear myself urge him to lock the door as I pull him into the hotel suite bathroom in the dark security-camera-style footage. We were, indeed, being watched. Blushing in front of these fans, in front of America, I hear the soft, low moans that come from behind that door. I hear Drew tell Nico, as he pulls away from her in the pineapple hot tub, that he doesn't have feelings for her, he likes me. And, when I think this could not be any worse, that I could not want to leave my body more, I hear a voiceover of my own voice. My end of the conversation with Caitlyn in the Lexus that night. Edited so that it sounds like I'm telling my deepest darkest to every glitter-eyed stranger watching breathlessly in this room.

They bugged the car.

They had cameras all over that hotel.

And then it hits me so hard I'm light-headed, the spotlights swimming before me into a white blur.

I am the source.

REAL REEL 9

Early the next morning, I'm woken from the respite of a dreamless Ambien sleep by Mom standing in her pajamas, clasping the phone to her chest and holding the other extension out to me. "Who is it?" I whisper, pressing my hand over the receiver as I pull myself up to sit.

"Your guidance counselor," she says, her exhausted eyes flecked with the first signs of hope I've seen in the seventy-two hours since the *OK!* hit newsstands. "I gave the school our new number. Maybe it's about your financial aid?"

I go to say hello and then whip the phone back against my stomach. "Is it safe?"

"What?"

"Do you think our phone is bugged, too?"

"No." She studies me with a whole new level of concern. "I definitively do not think that."

Nodding, I raise it to my ear. "Mrs. Pritchard?"

"Jesse, good morning. Are you both on the line?"

"Yes," Mom says into her extension as she sinks next to me on the duvet with a heaviness that suggests her Ambien didn't do the trick.

"I'm afraid I'm not calling with good news," Mrs. Pritchard says tentatively.

"Is it the financial aid?" Mom jumps in, her voice rising. "It'll be okay, Jess." She squeezes my knee, her face stricken. "We'll figure this out. You have your Doritos money."

"Mrs. O'Rourke, it's actually worse than that. I just got off the phone with Georgetown. They've rescinded their offer."

"*What?*" My stomach lurches. "Can they do that?"

"I'm afraid they can."

"On what grounds?" Mom cries as my mouth wets, signaling vomit.

"Believe me, I begged. I staked my reputation on Jesse. But they're a Jesuit school, Mrs. O'Rourke. And they feel very strongly that this whole reality TV thing, which came to pass after Jesse applied, that it's, well, the phrase they used was, *conduct unbecoming.*"

And at that I do. All over the floor.

* * *

Leaving the key in the ignition so the radio can continue to drown out the mental reverberations of Mom's sobs and Dad's door-slamming, I take a swig of Dunkin' Donuts coffee, trying to wash the acid taste from the back of my throat. From the only car in the sand-strewn lot, I have an unimpeded view of the empty beach, the rough waves slapping the shore in rhythm under the ascending sun.

I tune back into the mental frequency replaying every moment of the last five months, my stomach curdling, the pain sharpest right below my ribs. *Why* didn't I see this coming? And *why* couldn't I just have kept my shit together? Avoided Drew. God, avoided *Jase*. Stayed nice, stayed quiet, listened to my instincts instead of everyone's bullhorned directions. What's the worst that could have happened then—getting cut? Getting fired? *I wish.* Pressing my fingers into my brow bone, I slump over the wheel, every sickening decision pouring past my mind's eye like a horror movie projected on molasses.

Sensing another round of imminent retching, I pull out the keys and open the door, the salty breeze finally tempering my nausea as I shakily stand. I kick off my Converses as my hair whips across my face and, grabbing them up, walk down the planks that snake through the dunes to the sand.

Still damp from yesterday's rain, it's chilly against my feet, but I'm just so relieved to be alone, with nothing but what my senses tell me is real—the cool sand, the sharp breeze, the sun on my face, the salt in my nostrils, the cries of gulls in my ears. My breath steadying, I feel the familiar weight of being here, at once home among these forces and comfortingly small and irrelevant. I bend and pick up a small white stone, egg-shaped and smooth, holding it in my hand as the birds circle overhead, squawking and crying. A sound reaches me in strips as the wind snaps, rising and falling, rising and falling—

I twist around to see Nico sitting at the edge of the dunes, her sobs braided with the birds'. I spin to scan up and down the empty beach, as if I might spot the explanation—but it's just me, her, and the gulls. As I turn to find my own dune and leave her in privacy, she lifts her head from her knees and, spotting me, cries harder. Crap. Girding myself, I jog up the sand.

"Hey," I call out hesitantly as I approach. "I didn't see your car in the lot."

Huddling in a big white blazer she raises her head, her eyes almost swollen shut. "I walked."

I reach into my jacket pocket for some napkins. "Here."

She takes them from my hand and presses them to her wet face.

"Don't worry, they're only doughnut-*scented*—no calories," I lamely joke.

But she lets out a hollow laugh. "Eating for two?" she asks, blowing her nose.

"Yes, in eight to nine months I'm actually going to give birth to a large XTV logo." She pats her face dry while I bite my lip. "I feel truly shitty about Jase, Nico. It doesn't excuse me, but I really thought you were going after Drew."

"And let's be honest, I tried." She shrugs, sending a pang through my gut. "But . . . "

"But?" I try to secure my hair behind my ears.

"He wants *you*, Jesse."

"Wanted," I say ruefully, the pang dispersing to a full body ache as I drop down next to her to face the surf. "Now I think the term is *disgust*."

She starts to sob again.

"Oh God, sorry, did I say something wrong?"

Unable to speak, she extends her hand from the over-sized sleeve to reveal something black and sparkly—a phone. One I've seen before. "*I'm* . . . disgusting," she chokes out.

"Why do you have Fletch's phone, Nico?"

"I took it."

At that I place the blazer she's wearing over her white Gucci romper from last night, her bare legs goose bumping through their spray tan. "Have you even been home? What happened?"

She rakes the sleeve across her face, leaving a wide streak of bronzer and blush in its wake. "You saw how my dad was last night—when the crowd was chanting your name—so totally *done* with me. So I went over to Fletch after the screening and told him it couldn't end like this." She shudders. "Everyone thinking I suck—people at school, Melanie, the blogs. Not with me just—ruined—for forty thousand dollars."

"There's a good price to be ruined for?" I pull my hands into my jacket sleeves.

She lifts an eyebrow.

"Okay, naive. Continue."

"So he says the network wants another season. With shake-ups. And he looks me up and down. And I'm, like, Okay, I know that look, I get that look at the dealership. Reel 'em in without giving a thing. I can do this. So his driver drops us off at the house Fletch's rented down the beach. Fletch makes me a drink. He makes me another. We talk about cars. I mean, he's not unattractive, you know? He pitches the idea of me starring next season." She stops, her watery blue eyes glazing as she replays the events inside her mind. "He says he held me back to let you run your course, but now I'm ready to explode. I show him some leg, I flip some hair. He—" She squints, her voice going flat. "Lunges for me. Like bad seventh grade. Not, like, older guy, with moves and whatever you'd think. This was like getting mauled. Angry mauled."

"Oh my God, Nico." I put my hand on her hunched shoulder, feeling a completely different nausea take hold as she shakes.

"So, I leaped up." She starts to cry again. "It was instinct." Her tears run silently while she talks. "And I saw it on his face—immediately—done—totally done with me—just like Jase, just like my dad. So he left the room to get himself another drink, and I grabbed my clutch and his blazer and ran out the patio door. I'm such an asshole." She hands me the phone.

"And you took this with you?" I ask.

"It was in the blazer pocket. Check the video," she says. I tap the icon and look at the long list of files . . . all of them girls' names . . . Trisha? I tap her name, and in a second her image fills the palm-sized screen. It's dark, but I recognize the Mexican bay. The camera captures her topless from an infinitely closer vantage point than where I stumbled past that night waiting for Drew. Over her unmistakable Trisha giggles, Fletch's voice floats from the phone: "Now you're ready to explode."

A hand reaches into frame, his *Killah* tattoo visible in the moonlight, groping her breast, and the screen goes to black.

I drop the phone in the sand between us and look at Nico, shaking my head in disbelief. "*Shit.*"

"I'm so *stupid*," she says again, flopping her head to her bent knees.

"Why are *you* stupid?"

"Because I *believed* him. He said the same thing my dad's always said."

"That you have star quality?" I take a guess.

"*Yes.*" She blows her nose again into the disintegrating napkin.

"Oh my God. He's the grown-up who drove you back to his house and tried to jump you! It's not your fault. This isn't our fault," I repeat, more for myself. "We've just been doing what we've been told, and they've totally twisted everything to make us look and feel like assholes."

I expect her to take hold of my rage and run with it, but instead she just stares out at the ocean, nodding her head.

"I shouldn't be here." She closes her eyes tightly. "I should be in the city shopping for a prom dress. Or home, taping extra blank pages into my yearbook." She opens her eyes, her pupils round. "Someone lobbed manure on our lawn and wrote *bitch* on our door with spray paint."

"Nico, this has to blow over at some point. Any minute now someone will forget to wear underwear or break up a celebrity marriage or both and we'll be old news. I mean, at least you're going to college—"

"I'm not. Dad won't pay. He says I've had my shot—I didn't fight to do better, and he's done investing in me. *First your mother, now you*, he says."

"Jesus."

"You want to know the truth? He's right. I didn't fight. As soon as the initial response came in, and you were the star, and I saw how he handled it, I just . . . I guess part of me wanted to see what he would do if I failed. Would he still love me?" The question hangs in the wind between us as she turns her raw face to me. "When I was twelve and doing those local beauty pageants in malls, he made me wear the name of the dealership on all my outfits like fucking NASCAR." She looks down at the clump of her discarded white patent Gucci heels. "I got a little famous, so I can help sell cars."

"But if someday you inherited the business, that wouldn't be so bad."

"It's not what I want." She pushes her chin against her kneecap.

"What do you want?"

"I don't know . . . options, I guess." She sniffs. "You?"

"Same." I nod, watching a gull swoop down and then soar back up toward the pink sky.

Suddenly the sand is ringing between us. Ghostface Killah, to be precise. We both stare at Fletch's illuminated cell like it's as viral as *The Ring* video.

"Is it him?" she asks.

I carefully pick it up and check the number. "I don't know. It's local."

"Chuck it in the ocean," she says, but we both just stare at it until it's quiet.

We startle afresh as ringing emits from the pocket of my jeans. Handing her Fletch's phone, I lean back to tug my cell out and check the number. I look at Nico. "Ever imagine the day it would be a relief when Kara calls? I mean, at least I know no one'll scream *fucking bitch* and hang up."

As Nico offers a faint smile, I press answer.

"Hey, Jess! It's Kara."

"Hi." I put the phone on speaker, and Nico leans close to listen.

"Fantastic news! The numbers are in from last night, and they're through the roof! The network is super-stoked about a second season! God, it's *fantastic*. All that hard work has paid off, Jesse! So we're all going to meet at Fletch's rental in about thirty, cool?"

"Sure . . . " I say, staring at the horizon, buying a second to think. "The thing is, actually, I'm with Nico. We're already on our way into the city to get . . . prom dresses, so today won't work. Sorry."

Nico mouths, "*Nice.*"

"Well, Fletch wants to do this now, so . . . "

"Unless you wanted to meet us in the city, I don't see how we can." Nico gives me a thumbs-up as I tap-dance to ensure we don't have to see him today.

"That's not really convenient for Fletch, Jesse."

"What the hell!" he rants in the background. "Tell her to get her ass over here, *now*. I'm sick of her shit."

"Fletch," Kara tries. "She's already in the city with Nico—"

"Nico?" Fletch repeats. Nico grips her hand over mine to listen into the phone. "Fine . . . great. That's great. Well, they both should get in the fucking car and come back."

"Jesse," Kara pleads.

We hear Fletch grab the phone from her and then he's on. "Turn. Around."

Oh, so done. "See, there you all go talking to me in the imperative tense again." I tug the phone from Nico.

"The imperative?" Fletch balks. "What?"

"*Turn* around. *Tilt* your head. *Get* in the golf cart—sorry, the *fucking* golf cart. Oh, and my new favorite least favorite: *Smile*." My anger is roiling now as Nico's eyes bug. "It's one of those fancy Latin things they teach you at a place like Georgetown, only I won't be going there now because you guys *lied* to us. About what was being filmed, what was being used, that *we* were being used. So, uh, Nico and I are almost at the tunnel. I think I'm going to lose you. Fletch? Fletch? Yup—sorry, bye!"

I hang up, my heart pounding.

"Wow." Nico gazes at me with unprecedented admiration.

"Thanks." I bite my lip.

Fletch's phone rings.

My phone rings.

Nico's clutch buzzes.

"They're just going to keep calling." Nico drops her head to her knees. "And then they'll show up at our houses. A stoked network means—"

"A stoked network means they need something from us." The realization that we actually have some leverage fully landing, I whip open my phone and answer it. "Yes?"

"Jesse, it's Kara. I'm *really* sorry about Georgetown. We'll make it up to you. But you guys need to turn around and come back out to the island. Fletch has to speak to both of you—"

"You'll make it up to me with *what*?! A sweatshirt? A beer cozy?"

There's the sound of fumbling and then Fletch's voice is back on the line. "I don't know who the hell you think you—"

"I think I'm the highest rated cable show this week." And if we're going to have to face you eventually, I'm certainly not dragging Nico back to the scene of her mauling. "So if you want to talk to us that badly, meet us in the city. At XTV. Three o'clock."

I disconnect and turn to Nico.

"What are you doing?" she asks incredulously as I reach out a hand to help her up.

"Other than going Katherine Heigl on their ass, I have no idea."

"You have no idea," she repeats, crossing her arms over the blazer, wrapping it around her against the gathering wind.

"Nope." I wipe the sand off my jeans. "But we have a phone we shouldn't have. So that's a start."

In Kinko's parking lot I leap back into the driver's seat and toss the twenty disks, still warm from being burned, into Nico's lap.

"Oh my God!" she snorts. "Back up enough?"

"We're going to leave nineteen behind and take one with us."

"Genius. My turn." She points at the fabric roof, which

has been neatly spliced down the center. Her face glowing, she opens her hands to reveal two microphones and a transmitter. "I ran down the block to the hardware store, bought a magnet and a razor. Once I found the transmitter, I sliced along the wires and found the mikes. We're good to go."

"I don't know about star quality, but if we can rustle up an Asian third I say we give serious consideration to the *Charlie's Angels* thing." I peel us out and, after splitting the disks between each of our garages, book it to the Long Island Expressway, praying we stay ahead of Fletch.

"So, what *do* we want?" I ask Nico as I edge above the speed limit.

"Options."

"Right," I chorus, reaching over to switch on the radio, and a Coldplay song fills the car. The Coldplay song XTV played over the internationally broadcasted limo hookup between me and my riding companion's boyfriend. I push it off.

"So that's not going away," she mutters as she rolls up her window.

"I said at the beach—"

"Oh, I'm sorry, is this getting old for you? Because I, for one, am thrilled to get to watch my ex get ridden every time I turn on the fucking TV."

I bite my tongue to keep from invoking Trisha and try for humor. "How many apologies are required to cover reruns?"

A chilly silence descends as we remember who we're seated next to—the fact that we're solely dependent on each other in this impromptu mission beginning to feel risky at best. I try to ignore the returning image of her walking away from my pleas at the 21 Club, all the more pointed now that she's owned up to it. Try to remind myself that the images she has to overlook fill an entire twenty-two minutes of television, rerunning in perpetuity.

Before we know it, we're crossing the Midtown Tunnel between rush hours. I maneuver us west through stop-and-go traffic, toward Times Square. After counting my money at a stoplight, I find a garage and drive in.

"Did you get some sleep?" I ask as we get out of the Lexus, scanning the tightly packed cars for the attendant.

"A little. Do we have a plan yet?" she asks in turn.

"Not unless you dreamed of one." I flip open the trunk, pull out a pair of jeans and sweater from the mini-closet that's sprouted there, and toss them to her. She opens the back passenger door, leaving her heels on the blacktop. With a quick scan for the still-absent attendant, I turn my back and she slides onto the seat to slip off her G-patterned romper. "But we now have a mantra."

"Which is?" Lying on her back she tugs up my jeans, which are like capris on her, sticks her feet back into her heels, and shrugs on Fletch's blazer over the sweater.

"The thing my parents never had," I answer as she tosses her wadded Gucci into the backseat and slams the door. "*Options*." We both look to where the freight elevator is descending with a uniformed man inside and weave over to drop off my keys.

Murmuring our mantra and keeping our recognizable heads down, we push across Forty-fifth Street through the crowd of tourists staring up at the pulsing billboards. With a little elbow we maneuver to the glass tower's revolving lobby doors and pass beneath the rotating Buick-sized XTV logo and into the relative silence of the atrium. We don't let ourselves slow for even a second, lest we lose our nerve, and beeline across the tan flecked floor for the escalator and up one flight to the guard's desk. Pulling out our driver's licenses, Nico announces, "Nico Sargossi and Jesse O'Rourke for Fletch Chapman, please. He's expecting us."

The burly guard gets on the phone to confirm us with I don't know who and then points to a row of metal detectors. We pass through and, instead of turning toward the elevator for the studio as we have in the past, we walk to the bank for the executive floors. I step in behind Nico and, looking up at the department store–like legend over the doors, press 33 for XTV, which is sandwiched between all the other entertainment networks the parent company, Zeus Media, owns.

"This is insane." I turn to her, my clanging nerves making my pre-*Good Morning America* wooziness feel like Buddhist clarity as the express elevator rattles in its shaft, hurtling skyward. My ears popping, we pass Animal

World on 31, the Fashion Network on 32, and bob to a stop, the door whisking open. "We can't go in there without knowing what the hell we're going to do. What the hell are we going to do?"

Nico suddenly darts her arm across me to press 40. The top floor—Zeus headquarters.

"Nico, seriously, what are we doing?" I ask as the door slides shut.

"What *I* do best," she says with a glimmer of her signature confidence. My stomach sinks farther as I imagine her cartwheeling off the elevator.

The door glides open into a small, white-marble reception space, and we step out beneath a gilt ceiling. "May I help you?" the receptionist asks from behind the white leather desk trimmed with gold darts, her middle-aged face coiled in suspicion.

"Hi. We're here to see Mr. Hollingstone." Nico beams, and I focus on not passing out on the marble.

"You don't have an appointment," the receptionist states flatly, and I sense a finger reaching toward a security buzzer. I step back, ready to make a break for the elevator. Ready to drive all the way back to Fletch's rental. Ready to remember that we are two eighteen-year-olds from a town with a population that probably runs a close second to the workforce in this building.

Nico swans toward the desk. "We're supposed to be downstairs with Fletch right now," she says, putting a slightly conspiratorial spin on the word *Fletch*. The receptionist gives her a blank stare. "Fletch Chapman from XTV?"

"Fletcher, yes, of course," she concedes, her expression no less dubious.

"We're on *The Real Hampton Beach*," I find my voice to explain, the statement forever holding its uncomfortable charge. "Jesse O'Rourke?"

"Oh my gosh!" she says, a smile breaking her face open with a twinge of embarrassment. "Nico, Jesse! I'm such a fan! Apologies."

Nico perches her perfect ass on the corner of the white leather. "We couldn't let this opportunity pass without coming up here to thank Alistair in person for *everything* he's done for us."

Yes, this is what she does best.

"Thank him?" The receptionist blinks. I blink. "Of course. That's . . . lovely of you ladies." She presses her phone. "Mr. Hollingstone? Two stars of *The Real Hampton Beach* are out here, and they'd love to thank you."

"Who's with them?" a gravelly voice echoes out into the marble.

"No one, sir. They have a meeting with Mr. Chapman."

The intercom goes dead.

"I love your sweater," Nico coos, staring admiringly at the woman's boxy rose twin set.

"Thank you." She touches her pearls as the door behind her opens, and there stands the octogenarian emperor of the thirty-nine-floored media conglomerate stacked beneath our feet.

"Ladies," he says warmly as he extends his hand to Nico. "You're unescorted?" he looks behind us to confirm his receptionist's assessment.

"Yes, hope you don't mind," Nico says, boldly kissing him on the cheek as she passes into his office, eliciting her second blush on this floor. She is full-wattage now. I am not. I shake his hand and smile like a clammy idiot.

Realizing that he is not going to have us thrown out, I notice first that Mr. Hollingstone's old-fashioned wood-paneled office has a view clear to Central Park. And second, that every square inch is crammed with best-selling books, Emmys, Oscars, and Tonys, promotional posters, signs, and cardboard stands, footballs, Frisbees, and beer cozies. And right next to his desk, sitting atop an easel, is a large mock-up of an ad for *The Real Hampton Beach: Season Two!* Each of our individual pics from the *OK!* photo shoot is positioned along a beach at sunset, the pool cue Photoshopped out of Drew's hand, the horse Photoshopped out from under my ass.

"So what can I do for the current jewel in the crown of XTV?" he asks, leaning back against his desk and glancing so fast at his watch I wonder if it actually happened.

"We just wanted the chance to meet you in person!" Nico gushes. "And thank you. Oh, look!" she says, pointing at the poster like it was a kitten wrapped in puppies sprinkled with ducklings. "That's so exciting!"

287

Where is she going with this?

"It is!" I nod up and down, up and down. "So exciting! Yes."

"You know, Jess and I are supposed to be downstairs *right now* discussing season two. Hey! Do you want to come?" she inquires with a verve reserved for a Playmate asking if someone wants to see her naked.

Again, another flash watch-check, impressive for a man of any age. "I'd be delighted," he says, taking her proffered hand and wrapping it around his cashmere'd bicep. "How is old Fletch? Shaving yet?" He chuckles as we pass back out into the waiting area. "Eudora, hold my calls. I'm just going to escort these lovely young ladies to Fletch's office. I'll be back in ten minutes."

"What's your plan?" I mouth as he pushes for the elevator.

"*What's yours?*" she mouths back. Again the flash to 21, the question of trust. Is she going to throw me under the bus, save herself? Will I do the same if it comes down to it?

We step inside with him and the car drops down, while Nico keeps up a steady stream of chatter about how much we *love* the show and how *happy* we are. The doors open onto a metallic-blue hallway that runs the length of the building, with only one door at its end. Lights along the perimeter of the floor transition from red to blue to green under the framed platinum records and pictures of Fletch with everyone from Kid Rock to Charlotte Church.

Finally, Mr. Hollingstone raps on Fletch's door with his freckled knuckles.

"Fletch, they're here," Kara says, swinging it open. "Mr. Hollingstone!" She leaps back. "What a surprise!" She continues walking backward, and the three of us follow her into Fletch's office—metallic wallpaper, lots of white leather, gray carpeting, zebra prints, and an actual conversation pit. It's impossible to discern if he paid a fortune to make it look like this or inherited it directly from someone who wore slit sweatshirts the *first* time around. At the sight of his boss, Fletch hangs up the phone and swings his high-tops to the floor from his shiny desk. At the sight of Fletch, Nico wavers.

"Find the perfect prom dress?" Kara asks, her eyes darting from us to her boss's boss. "They were prom dress shopping today, Mr. Hollingstone! Fletch, why didn't we think of that?! Prom dress shopping! Or an online contest—let viewers pick your dresses! Or a design contest—partner with Bravo!"

Fletch scurries forward, acting for the first time like what he is—a kid who's not much older than us—one hand extended to shake, the other to pat. "Alistair!"

"Fletch." Alistair tolerates being shaken and patted. "Our *enfant terrible*. You've redeemed yourself this quarter. This network is one of our top earners again. It's nice to see her regaining prominence instead of dragging us under."

"We're happy to be of service." Nico shakes her hair,

the color returning to her cheeks.

Alistair chuckles. "Well, I just came to see the girls here safely. Take good care of them, Fletch. They're valuable."

Emboldened by the validation, Nico slips off the blazer and tosses it across Alistair to Fletch. "Speaking of taking care of me, thanks for the loan," she says, pulled back up to her full height, her eyes sharp in her luminously cried-clean face. Kara does a double take.

"Right! Well, good to see you as always, Alistair." Fletch extends his palm to the door to usher out his boss, his recovered jacket clenched in his other fist.

"A pleasure, ladies."

"Bye! Thank you!" We wave.

Fletch closes the door with a click, listening attentively to the receding echoes of Alistair's loafers before whipping around. "*Sit.*"

Nico doesn't. I don't. She extends her arm at him, holding out his god-awful phone. "Lose this?"

"That's not mine," he says fast. So this is Fletch flustered—I like.

Confused, Kara tilts her head at the sparkly skull and crossbones. "Yes it is."

Nico and Fletch glare at each other. I take the phone from her hand and go down the three gray carpeted steps to the white leather couch that runs the circumference of the conversation pit. "Kara, you know Fletch is an excellent producer, but did you know he's also an amateur director?" I stress the last word to bring Nico back. She turns from Fletch and steps down to perch on the couch arm next to me.

I set the cell in the center of the black Lucite coffee table.

Fletch ambles down the steps and, running his hands through his choppy bedhead, sits on the curved couch across the pit from us. "Look, Kara, I was going to tell you." He lifts an ankle to rest on the opposite knee and fingers the hem of his jeans. "Nico partied a little hard at the finale last night. I lent her my jacket and drove her home. No big deal." He tosses his hands with a casualness that makes Nico stiffen.

"Is that what happened or how you edited it?" I snap.

Kara looks down from an incredulous me to a glaring Nico to a stone-faced Fletch, concern starting to register. She leans tentatively on the radiator cover, her back smushing the blinds against the window. "Look, Fletch," I continue, my voice quivering both from outrage and the fear that I won't do it justice, "Nico and I have given up a lot, everything actually, to do your show, a show that has made you a *ton* of money."

"It's made you celebrities," Fletch counters, slouching to communicate that I'm as riveting as the Weather Channel.

"With no options," Nico adds icily.

"Georgetown *dropped* me." My voice rises. "Nico lost her . . . financial aid. I wasn't looking to be a celebrity. I was looking to be . . . " What? I look past Kara, where the blinds have spread to reveal the top executive floors of the surrounding midtown buildings, each filled with people like Fletch and Alistair, the people who make the decisions, call the shots. And suddenly I know. "We'll sign on for another season . . . " I pause for a moment, still needing to make abstract "options" into a definitive choice. Kara and Fletch wait. "*In exchange* for a full ride at . . . NYU for me, Nico—" They lean forward. Nico is wide-eyed. "—and my friend Caitlyn. Who will join the cast. She really is funny. And you know what this show could use, in between the shots of sunsets and people saying next to nothing? Some funny. Seriously."

"Seriously," Nico murmurs.

"Wait, were you even accepted at NYU?" Kara shakes her head in confusion.

"I didn't apply."

"Me neither." Nico shoots me a furtive look. I push on.

"But I'm sure donating a building like the Hollingstone Library, which I did take a tour of, earns this company one free phone call." I sit back and cross my clammy hands.

Fletch stares straight into me, taking his time, because he can. "You fucking idiots. You think Alistair gives a *shit* about what's on that phone? You haven't done a single thing that I didn't set in motion. I put the drinks in your hands. I put the boys in your reach. Jesse, I knew I could get you and Jase to hook up; it was just a matter of getting the ingredients right, and Nico, *you* and your insecurity were the perfect ingredient. You think you're acting on your own now? How do you know you aren't doing exactly what I've planned?" He grins, his eyes flashing as he leans forward to drop his elbows on his knees. "Affording me the pleasure of looking you both in your pathetic faces to inform you that we own you *already*. Your parents signed you away in perpetuity for forty thousand dollars and some snack chips. You will continue to go *where* I say and do *what* I say or find yourselves in breach of contract. Your families sitting on a few million they'd like to cough up? Get up, go back to Long Island, and we'll call you when we have our shooting schedule."

There is an airless silence in which I can hear hope drain into the gray shag. Options die. I can feel Nico struggling to breathe beside me, see her fist tighten on the armrest. I look from Fletch, smug as hell, to Kara—

"What *is* on that phone?" She walks down the steps.

Not waiting for Fletch to redirect, I snatch the cell off the table, scroll, and press play. I reach it up to Kara, who watches as the color leaves her face.

"Trisha's barely eighteen," I inform her.

"Exactly! Perfectly legal," Fletch spits.

Kara straightens, stunned. Her expression blank, she holds the phone out to Fletch. "Wait!" I stand to take the phone back and scroll a few names to something that hadn't registered in my initial viewing. I hit *Mel*.

And I hold the phone out so we all can see and we watch for twenty mortifying seconds, as Melanie, half-naked on spread knees above Fletch, looks so eager to please. We all listen as he gives her his shtick. "—*ready to explode*."

"Mel's seventeen, which *is* illegal," Nico says evenly,

reining in her rage. "And I'm more than happy to smile for our new friends at *OK!* and tell my story."

"Jesus, this is getting blown completely out of proportion." Fletch stands, crossing his arms protectively over his Chrome Hearts shirt.

Still pale, Kara sits on the carpeted steps. "This is not what I signed up for."

"Kara—"

She cuts him off. "Hollingstone will care, Fletch, because *the media* will care. There's too much attention on these girls for a story like this not to have legs. And I think—I *know* you crossed a *huge* line, here."

"Which brings us to our last demand." I glance at Nico now that we're driving the bus we could've thrown each other under. "Fletch is out. Kara takes over. You two can explain that to our new best friend, Mr. Hollingstone." I lob the phone to Fletch and climb past Kara with Nico in tow.

"No worries, we have plenty of copies," Nico tosses over her shoulder with satisfaction.

"One question, ladies," Kara asks, still catching up as she takes off her glasses to rub her eyes.

"Yes?" we answer from the door.

"Do you want to live in the dorms or an apartment?"

Nico and I look at each other for a split second and then turn to them both. "Whatever works best on camera," we say in unison.

PART IV
THE REAL REAL

"**J**esse, wait!" Mom calls down to the living room as I grab my white suede Gucci bag—a souvenir from the finale to remind me of the value of nice and quiet—and retrieve my car keys, ready to head out into the warm June night. "Wait!" She comes running down the stairs with the camera, jogging right past me to call to the basement. "Mike, she's leaving!"

Patting my shorts pockets, I glance around the living room for my phone, fairly sure I was channel surfing the last time I had it.

"That's it?" Mom asks me as Dad emerges from the basement in his new NYU sweatshirt.

"What do you mean, is that it?" I ask, wriggling out

my cell from between the couch cushions and checking the display, happy to see that no one's called. I must be part of a very small club of eighteen-year-olds who get giddy at an empty call log.

"You're not changing?" Mom hands the camera to Dad and crosses her arms over her tank top. "Is someone from the show going to at least do your hair?"

"I told you, I'm borrowing a dress from Nico. She's the one who decided we might as well go. No hair, no nails, no 'doing.' It's not a big deal—"

"*It's your prom!*" I look up as her eyes go to the framed picture of my smiling, heavily banged parents on the bookcase under the banner Caribbean Carnival Hampton High Prom 1985.

"Yes, this is not working out like that," I acknowledge, dropping my phone in my bag.

"I know." Her shoulders slump.

"I'm sorry, Jess." Dad puts his arm around her. "You didn't want to go with Caitlyn?"

"She has a hot date, and we're going to the beach together tomorrow. Really, guys, it's fine. I'm okay with just swinging by. You should be, too."

"But, Jess, you don't *know* what you're missing."

I take a deep breath, take her hand, and lead her over to the couch, while Dad starts fumbling with the camera. "Okay, Mom, you're right. I won't ever know what it feels like to have the boy I love, *future father of my children*"—we watch Dad accidentally take a picture of his fingers—"pick me up to take me on the most romantic night of my young life." I squeeze her hand. "But starting in the fall I'll be having a lot of experiences you didn't have."

"And that's great. That's what we wanted for you," she says, her voice breaking. "Just not as—"

"A semi-celebrity? I know. Me neither. But I get a full ride at an amazing school, close to you guys. And I have to focus on that and let it outweigh any trade-off, anything I might be losing." Gazing at the picture of my 1980s' parents, my heart twists at the thought of Drew in a tux.

"Then I'm giving you the camera, and you two take a picture once you're dolled up." Dad walks over to pass me the Olympus and offer me a hand up off the couch.

I drop it in my bag. "Okay, but I'm not promising one under the banner."

"I've seen my daughter under enough text to last a lifetime, thank you very much. A nice tree or shrub will do fine." Mom stands to walk me to the door.

"Well," I say, unhooking my seat belt over the gold Stella McCartney gown Nico loaned me, a gift from her father last year that I've been instructed to wear into the ground or set on fire.

"Yes?" As the Lexus headlights slowly fade over the Hampton Country Club's full lot, she withdraws her keys from the ignition and turns to me in her red Dolce.

"I wouldn't have called this twelve months ago," I say. "Make that twelve grades ago."

"What?" She unwraps a bottle of chilled champagne from its safekeeping in an NYU sweatshirt, one piece of the full range of gear we've promised to wear in exchange for our tuition.

"You being my prom date."

She opens her car door to the lull of crickets and looks back at me. "Really? *That's* the surprise?"

I laugh, getting out on my side into the balmy night.

"Nice parking job, maverick." I look back at the tire marks she's etched into the golf course grass as she swerved us to a stop a safe distance from the pillars of the main building.

"Thanks." Rubber band around her wrist, she leans over to flip her hair up and down before letting it dangle into the grass. She smoothes it into a high bun and rolls up her long spine. "I mean, my ex-boyfriend's in there with some actress extra wannabe who's, like, thirty—"

"I bet she's having the time of her life. I bet her whole career has led her right to this very moment."

"And my ex-best friend is in there with her agent."

"Trisha's multitasking."

"And I am as far from Prom Queen as a girl can get." She leans against the car. "Screw the shoes." I watch as she kicks one strappy heel and then the other into a sand trap.

"Nico, you could have sold those on eBay with the others for your fund," I admonish, as she's putting every penny into renting a tiny studio over the Bridgehampton

300

dry cleaners until we move to Washington Square this fall.

"You mean my Fuck You, Dad, Freedom Fund."

"We have to come up with an acronym for that—FUDFF? And yes, no more throwing away profitable accessories."

"But my toes are so happy now." She lifts the feathered hem of her dress to her knees and does a little jig in the lush lawn.

"Did you hit the champagne already?"

"High on life. Come on." Pausing to hold on to the car for support, I step out of my snakeskin heels and pick them up to walk over to her.

"Nice, right?" She sticks the bottle between her knees.

"Yes." I wiggle my toes in the cool grass.

POP!

We scream as the cork goes flying and white foam bubbles out onto Nico's extended arms. She takes a long swig and passes it to me. I imbibe a fizzy gulp and pass it back. We continue our sips as we meander a little closer toward the white columns.

"So what's the plan?" I wipe my chin. "Are we slow-dancing?"

She takes another mouthful and points the bottle to the windows, where purple light slants out to the terrace, the sound of laughter and music growing louder. Suddenly Nico stops at the periphery of the pool's flagstone deck and fills her chest with breath. "I'm not going in," she says with certainty. "I'm done."

"We faced down a multimedia corporation; we can face these losers. They barely remember us—when's the last time you got a call?"

"Monday. You?"

"Two days ago. So we're making progress. I hear one of the Olsen twins might get a place out here for the season. Maybe she'll bring a Jonas brother. Then everyone can give them shit and we can go to the beach. Nico, we can just walk in there and dance. We can."

"I know we can. I just"—she smiles serenely, flopping down on a wicker deck chair—"realized I don't care."

I turn and look back, across the length of the glistening pool and the covered veranda, through the big picture window at the crowd of silks and satins, the jewel-tone hues moving under the circles of electric color. It's dizzying. And beautiful. I step up on an adjacent wicker chair. "Okay, I just want to say hey to Caitlyn, take a quick picture for my folks, and then I guess I don't really care, either—" My voice catches as I see Drew in a tux milling around with his teammates as they talk to one another and their dates but not to him.

"He looks miserable," Nico confirms, standing up beside me. He does. His shoulders slumped, he fidgets with his cell.

"He went stag?" I ask. "Caitlyn heard he asked some sophomore. What happened to the sophomore?"

"Food poisoning," we hear from behind us.

We both pivot to Caitlyn.

"Oh my gosh, you look *so* beautiful!" I hug her.

"Thanks! You two are pretty decked out for reconnaissance."

"Well," I demure, "not having dates—"

"Or friends," Nico adds. "Present company excluded."

"We didn't get our hair done or anything," I explain. "But we did doll up."

"Is this XTV standard issue?" Caitlyn asks, fingering the shimmering fabric of my dress.

"No, it's mine, actually." Nico lifts the bottle out to her. "Champagne?"

"Don't mind if I do."

"So how's it going in there?" I ask as she passes back the bottle.

"Oh, it's like gym class with a sound track. But, looks like Melanie's going to snag Prom Queen. Everyone I've talked to voted for her."

"That's awesome." Nico nods. "Good for her. I'll send flowers tomorrow and her mom can flush 'em, but this should be celebrated."

"Mrs. Dubviek won't flush 'em." I shake my head at her. "Maybe grind them up for a body treatment . . . And how's the hot date?" I push Caitlyn lightly with my elbow.

"Not so hot without the three Coors. I think I'm saving myself for the men of NYU."

"Here, here!" Nico lifts a fake glass, as do I, and the three of us fake cheers. "Ch—" We all freeze, noses up, ears cocked as we wait to confirm that the bu—bu—bump

303

is the right bu—bu—bump.

"*Nah nah nah nah nah nah nah nah—Nah nah nah nah nah nah—*" we squeal at the opening lines of a defiant Pink, and, scrambling, take one another's hands as the three of us start dancing right there at the golf course's edge. "I've got my rock moves!" we scream, tears of joy in the corners of our eyes.

As the song winds down, we catch our breath and Nico picks up the bottle.

"Caitlyn, you can go back in," I say. "We're cool, really."

"You sure?"

"Yeah. The night is young—there may still be Coors and hotness in your future. And one of us should get to have this."

She nods and starts to walk away, but stops and pivots to me. "Jess, Drew is not having the fun. Come in. Rescue him."

"I don't think that'd be appreciated."

"Jess, it's prom night—"

"*Un*prom night," Nico chimes from her chair.

Caitlyn walks back and takes my hand. "It's still your senior prom. Don't let them take that away from you, too." I stare through the window at him. Wondering for the millionth time if I'd just taken a different turn I could've been pointing to him in that tux and me in this dress captured in a yellowed photo on my own mantle, explaining our haircuts to our kids as they roll their eyes. A couple dances in front of him, blocking my view.

"Hey, loser," I hear Nico suddenly say from behind us. "It's Nico."

We both spin to Nico, who's backing away from us as she continues talking on her cell. "Because prom can suck my ass. Well, hi to you, too." She falls back on a chaise and sticks her legs up in the air, fabric and feathers sliding down to her butt. "Listen, I've got some friends here from the city, and we're having our own party, just decided. We're at the new school pool. Come hang out. . . . Don't even try to front that you're having a good time. *Please*." She gives a self-satisfied grin. "Thanks, Drew. You're a love. See you in ten."

"What are you doing?" I cry as she clicks off her phone. "What is she doing?" I turn to Caitlyn.

"You a favor," Nico says, throwing me her keys.

I press my hands against the tiers of gold fabric fishtailing onto the metal risers and listen to the string symphony of crickets outside the recently completed pool. I can't believe the school actually got it out of them. Then again, the school probably had a lawyer or two review that contract. I look up at the waving lines of light that undulate and ripple across the plaster ceiling. What am I doing here?

Maybe he won't even show. Or he will.

Which is worse?

I turn to the sound of footsteps echoing across the tile.

"Nico?" Drew's voice bounces off the hard surfaces

encasing the shimmering water.

Swallowing, I stand. Blazer off, tie loosened, he looks up, his expression hardening as he spots me. "In my defense, this wasn't my idea." I walk down to where he's stalled near the starting blocks.

"Okay. Can I go?" He shoves his hands into his pockets.

"Drew."

"What, Jesse?"

"I'm sorry."

He nods, the moonlight glinting off the pool making waves across his pursed lips.

"So that's that?" I ask.

"What do you want me to say?"

I step closer to him. "I want you to say you forgive me."

"Jesse," he sighs, slipping his hands through his hair and looking away.

"Drew! I haven't got this all figured out. I made mistakes like everyone. I just get to watch mine on reruns."

"You lied to me!" He shakes his head. "To my face."

"I didn't know what else to do! The minute you thought I hooked up with him—"

"*Did* hook up with him."

"Yes, you were just so . . . so *disgusted* with me. Like I was ruined or something."

"He's such a dick, Jesse. I don't know how you could have—"

"So let me ask you, is it just Jase, or would you feel this

way about anyone I was with?"

He stares at me long and hard, his voice barely audible over the whir of the filter. "Anyone."

Right answer. I step forward. "Then why didn't you *do* something?"

"I tried. But there was always some Fletch-planned thing interrupting us."

"Well." I look up at him. "There isn't now."

He crosses his arms. "There's too much . . . too much has happened."

I bite my lip and stare at him, incapable of accepting that, unwilling to let this be it. "Okay. Well, then, let's start over."

"What?"

I walk to the edge of the pool, my heart pounding under my rib cage.

"What are you doing?"

"Clean start. Right here in these XTV-underwritten waters. I'm jumping in and washing off the last five months. When I come out, I expect you to smile at me in a snowbank and ask me for a muffin and tell me we're in this together."

"You're crazy."

"Maybe. But if you don't have the balls to take the plunge this time, then it's officially your problem." I turn away from him, one more glance to the moon hanging low in the window, one huge breath in—and dive. As I sink into the bracing water, the sound of my splash recedes, my soaking dress weighing me down in the dark silence.

Alone.

I stay under until my chest feels like it's going to burst and then kick to the surface, gasping for air. I wipe the water out of my stinging eyes to see him standing on the pavement where I left him, his hands on his hips. He glares down at me.

I twist, pushing against the weight of the dress and the cold of the water to reach the other side of the pool, desperate to get away from this. I grab the tile and whip around. He's still there—staring.

"Is this entertaining you?" I yell through the torrent of drips running down my face. "Too bad the show's over. Show's over, and the episode summary is posted—I like you and you used to like me and it got royally screwed up. I get it." I try to lift myself up but just can't, the unheated water, heavy gown, and heartache have conspired to zap my strength. "So just . . . fucking . . . *go* and let me drag myself out of this pool without an audience." But he doesn't move. "Please?" I am crying now.

And all at once he dives in.

Oh God—could he—is it—I kick my legs against the clinging fabric, searching for where he'll surface.

Drew's arms circle around my waist as he lifts up in front of me, his lips finding mine. We kiss, slow and deep. "So," he says, releasing me so we're nose to nose as he swims me to the wall, pressing me back against the tile.

"So." I smile from my toes, suddenly warm.

"No more surprises? No lost episode where you and Jase secretly marry in Vegas and then do the entire Playboy Mansion together?" He puts his forehead to mine.

"Airing only in Jase's mind. I swear."

"And now the Three Musketeers at NYU, huh? *The Real Washington Square Park*?" he murmurs as his warm lips move down to my neck.

"Mm-hmm," I murmur back. "All the glamorous homeless people and drug dealers XTV could want." I raise his head, my hands cupping his gorgeous face. "You sure you want to be with a girl who has so many blogs devoted to her?"

"I've got blogs," he balks, pulling back from me to tread water. "I've got a nine-year-old in Missoula who thinks I should run for president."

"So, I have competition, is what you're telling me." I kick forward and circle languorously around him.

"Think you can handle it?" He grabs me by the waist.

"I don't know. I'm a very jealous person," I say, letting him float us to the wall, the pool at my back.

"You should work on that. I don't believe in jealousy." He releases me to extend his arms over the edge and tilts his chin up to the ceiling.

"I see. And what do you believe in?"

"This." And at that, finally, we sink into each other.

Best.

Prom.

Ever.

ACKNOWLEDGMENTS

With tremendous gratitude to: Our phenomenal editor, Farrin Jacobs—should she ever be casting a reality show, we're first in line. Suzanne Gluck and the rest of our spectacularly hardworking team at William Morris, Erin Malone, Alicia Gordon, Sara Bottfeld, Ava Greenfield, and Lauren Heller Whitney. Our rock-star lawyers, Ken Weinrib and Eric Brown. Sarah Mlynowski, for being a great cheerleader and even better friend. Evi Kraus for proofreading at the zero hour. And last, but not least, our husbands, Joel and David, for the real.

What if your ex was adored by millions and you had only one chance to make him regret his entire existence?

MEET KATE HOLLIS.

She's about to have that chance in *Dedication*, a novel by EMMA McLAUGHLIN and NICOLA KRAUS. Turn the page for a peek at Kate in high school, before her future-ex, Jake Sharpe, was all over MTV with songs he wrote about *her*. . . .

Laura crosses her eyes in my direction from the alto section of the risers. I scrunch my nose in response. "The concert is three weeks away and you don't want to embarrass yourselves." Mrs. Sergeant waves her man-hands at the baritones, and a sad trickle of "We Built This City" ekes out into the choir room for the millionth time.

Little Mrs. Beazley attacks the piano keys, her pink beads jumping against her blouse. A row beneath Laura and me sits Jake, and I watch as his finger slides along his song sheet.

"Sopranos, let's see those 'ooo' faces, big and round! *Say you don't knooow me ooooooor recooooognize my face.*" Sergeant stops us with a frustrated shake of her Play-Doh beauty parlor perm, but Mrs. Beazley joyfully continues.

As does Jake. Pitch perfect, his voice fills the air like light unearthed from beneath the soil of all our breathy singing. Everyone twists to watch. He's good. Really good. Buy it at the mall, listen to it in your car, good. And much, much better than molar-mouthed, oversinging, doing her best Valkyrie, Mrs. Sergeant. Red splotches appear on her jowls. Jake clears his throat and Laura takes the moment to make a huge "o" face. I snort.

"You think this is funny, Katie Hollis?" Mrs. Sergeant spins to me, seething.

I freeze. "No—"

"You think someone trying to steal the show from forty-eight of his classmates is worth laughing about?"

"No, I—"

"You *what*? Or were you just trying to get his attention?"

I sit at the edge of my chair. "No, I just . . . remembered something . . . funny someone said at lunch."

"What?" She raps her music stand. "What was the funny thing someone said?"

"Nothing." I shrink. "I'm sorry."

"It takes years of work before you can just sing wherever and whenever you like." She narrows her eyes. "I want you and Mr. Sharpe to take your huge egos and put together a presentable duet with a descant of your own devising. To be performed for all of us, let's see . . . a week from this Friday seems fair. That should be something two freshmen can handle if they think they're prodigies." A sneer forms her last *s*. "And Katie?"

"Yes?"

"Enough flirting." A blast of heat explodes in my face. With a satisfied smile, Mrs. Sergeant nods and Mrs. Beazley begins again.

Benjy bounces a Hacky Sack from one hand to the other as he sits slouched against the locker next to Laura's. "It's 'cause Sergeant's not doin' it."

"Shut up," Laura and I chime. "Neither are you," she

adds, to clarify her sexual status for anyone in earshot. He tugs at her bare calf and she collapses into his lap shrieking, "Ben-jy!"

"It's not like we can just use the sheet music," I say, starting to panic. "We have to devise a descant. I have no idea how to do that!" Craig, slumped with me against the lockers across from them, doesn't even look up from the car magazine he's leafing through. I ruffle his hair. "Hey, I need advice."

"What? You have to do a song." Craig flattens his bangs back the way he likes them.

"A duet," Laura corrects as Benjy's hand tries to push under her sweatshirt. Giggling, she grabs it through the fabric, holding it at bay below her under-wire. Craig drops his arm around me in an attempt to keep up, and I pull my legs in so I can curl against his sturdy frame. The tallest frame in the class. The frame that for the last four months I am proud to call my boyfriend's. A cute frame, a nice frame, an honest frame. The frame of someone who would never, ever, in a billion years, say they don't want to go out with anyone and then, less than a week later, start going out with Annika Kaiser.

"Should I be jealous?" Craig asks.

"No!" Laura and I cry in unison.

Three days later Jake Sharpe has not done anything. I walk over as Biology ends and inch in between his friends. Closer than I've been to him in the five months since our "date," I try to ignore the lingering freckles from his spring break tan. "Jake?"

"Hey." He fidgets with his pen.

"Hey. So we should plan to practice or something."

"Cool. Whenever."

"I have fourth period free on Monday. Do you think it'll be enough time to prepare? That's only five days."

Suddenly his eyes land on mine and he smiles like he just remembered the idea of me and likes it. "Yeah."

"So, fourth period, Monday. Think the music room'll be free? I think the gym is free. What do you think?"

"Whichever." He shrugs.

Yeah, I get it, you don't care. "Fine. The gym."

"Cool." He nods.

I get into the gym at the start of fourth period. I get a sore butt from sitting on the hard wood for three hours. I get detention for skipping fifth period in case I had the time wrong. I get annoyed on a whole new level.

"Jake." I tap him on the shoulder at the drinking fountain. "What happened?"

"Hey." He pulls back like I stung him.

I drop my offending hand. "Hey. So, what happened?"

"What? Fourth period, Wednesday."

"Monday. That was yesterday," I say. "So, what do you want to do?"

"How about Wednesday, you know, fourth?"

Of course I can't fourth on Wednesday. "I can't fourth on Wednesday." I switch my books to my other hip. "How about after school? The music room should be free."

"Cool."

So not. So far from cool. So very far. Mrs. Beazley stops in some time after dark to pick up her forgotten fuchsia glasses and wakes me on the risers, my hands asleep from resting under my hair to keep it fluffed.

"Hi, Jake?"

"Hey."

"This is Katie Hollis." I lean against my kitchen wall.

"Yeah, hey."

"Hey." I repeat.

Laura rolls her hand at me, helpfully prompting. I take her cue. "I'm calling because—so, what happened?"

"Right," he says like he knew I was going to call.

"Oh my god!" I mouth to Laura. "Yeah," I try to relax my voice so as to avoid further fulfilling any expectation of me as psycho. "Well, we only have two days left."

"I know. After school?" he volunteers.

"How about before, just to be safe. Too early for you?"

"No way. I'm there." I hear the twanging of a guitar being tuned in the background. "Sam, dude, hold on."

"Okay, Jake, so, seven A.M. tomorrow. Music room. You sure?"

"Definitely."

"Stood up! Again! Detention! No sleep all week! Three chapters behind on *House of Mirth*! And I have to get up in front of everyone tomorrow and try to wing a descant with Jake Sharpe, who may actually, now that the evidence is in, be clinically retarded." I grip my books to my chest as I stomp up the hill home with Laura.

"I'll pull a fire drill. Or Benjy can call in a bomb threat? I think he'd be up for it, I really do."

"No! This is now officially Jake Sharpe's to fix."

"Agreed." We nod at each other.

"Except I'm the one who's going to sound like a beaten cat."

"That's so sad!" She stops her stride to ponder. "Such a sad picture, a cat that's being beaten, who would do that?"

"Laura!"

"Katie! Just, I don't know, march over there and tell him what a retard he is!"

My eyes widen as the reality of the idea passes between us. "What if I do?" I murmur.

"You'd be my hero and I'd bake a whole batch of devil's food cupcakes just for you."

"Step aside."

I tug one arm free from my backpack, raising the other shoulder against its load, because I need every ounce of cool right now and will not risk precious points for proper spinal alignment. I push the glowing doorbell again. I'm going to stay here all night, that's what. I'll just wait for him until he comes out in the morning and we'll practice this stupid freaking duet all the way to stupid freaking school—

"Hey." Jake slouches inside the doorway, holding a box of Kraft macaroni and cheese.

"Hey."

"So, come in." He waves me inside with the blue cardboard. Thrown by his expectant demeanor, I dumbly follow. His socked feet sliding Tom Cruise–style, he's already retreating through the door on the other side of the living room. I try to keep up, but I'm mesmerized by the wood paneling, Chinese pottery, and little smushed-face porcelain dogs on the mantel. The closest I've been to a house like this was the lobby of the Boston Ritz-Carlton, where we met my cousins for tea when I was nine.

I find him in the kitchen, which is wallpapered in a lilac pattern with matching fabric in the breakfast nook. But no pictures. No tchotchkes. No art or good grades stuck to the fridge. Sitcom kitchens, trying to look like real family kitchens, have more stuff in them than this.

Jake is stirring in the cheese powder on the stovetop. I stand behind him, gripping my books. Finally satisfied, he turns around, slides the pot onto the counter of the island, and hops onto a lilac cushioned stool.

"You going to put your books down?" he asks, taking a big, wooden-spoon mouthful. I rest them on the counter and slide off my backpack. "Sorry. Want some?"

"Sure," I say automatically and he leans to grab two forks from a drawer, bouncing one over to me like a skipping stone. I catch it as he shoves the copper pot between us.

"Where're your parents?" I ask, taking a forkful of orange noodles.

"My dad's traveling for work. Somewhere west. Texas, or New Mexico this week, I think. Mom's asleep. Upstairs."

"She doesn't work?"

"No," he half-laughs, stabbing his fork around in the pot, his hair flopping down.

I nod awkwardly and try to figure out how I suddenly found myself in this intimate activity. Because in the two feet between us, mostly what I am doing right now is not throwing our forks across the room, grabbing his face, and kissing him. Right now I am the girl not kissing Jake Sharpe. I am the girl not kissing Jake Sharpe who will now clear her throat.

"So, Jake, I'm really pissed. I mean, I pretty much got roped into this stupid duet because you couldn't keep your mouth shut, and I've wasted, like, half the week waiting for you and you just completely blew me off."

He has stopped eating and stares intently at me. "You're going out with Craig."

Wha—"I am."

"For how long?"

I can hear the blood in my ears. "I don't know.

November sometime." I stare back. "You're going out with Annika," I return evenly.

"Yeah." He nods down into the pot. "I am."

"So . . ."

"So, I'm not that good at schedules."

"Okay . . ."

"But you're here."

"I am."

"So, let's practice."

"Okay."

He pushes back from the counter, the stool tipping as he jumps off to place the pot in the sink, running water into it as someone must have told him to. "Sam and I have been working on some band stuff with Todd. I think we've rigged up a descant. Want a Klondike?" He holds open the freezer, steam billowing out over a few boxes of pops and at least five gallon bottles of vodka.

"Thanks, sure. Your parents having a party?"

"What?" He glances back at the stocked wire shelves. "No," he bristles.

"Oh, I just thought—"

"It's cool." He grabs two bars and swings the door shut. It makes a shushing sound as it seals.

"Um, I'm not really a singer," I say, needing to divert. "I mean, I like doing it in a big group, but I'm not really a soloist or anything." Understatement of the century.

"I know. That's cool. You've got your whole science thing. This way." No time to stop and absorb that he knows what my "thing" is, or call Laura, or take out an ad, once again I'm following. I catch sight of him disappearing into a doorway halfway down a long corridor running the length of the house. I find it leads to a flight of tan-carpeted steps.

"You coming?" He looks up at me standing on the threshold, his face illuminated by a low-watt bulb. "I have to practice in the basement." He pauses. "My mom gets headaches." His eyes implore me.

"I'm sorry," I say, finding myself replying, not to his words but to the look on his face asking me to understand.

Sergeant towers above the spindly black music stand, arms crossed over her polyester turtleneck dress as she waits for us to fail. Behind her, the entire chorus shifts in their seats along the risers, studying their nails, scrawling notes to each other. All except Laura, who stares straight into her lap, hands balled in shared horror. As Mrs. Beazley pounds out the opening chords, nervousness is being redefined in my lower intestines. To my left, Jake, redefining relaxed, lightly taps the top of the piano percussively as if this were a real performance and not just straight-out torture. Will falling into a coma get me out of this? Could I drop chorus right this second? Or should I just start dancing, as if that was the assignment, just take off doing *West Side Story* moves around the room. Really throw myself into it. Or just turn and walk out. I picture Sergeant chasing me through the parking lot, dragging me back through the halls by my hair—and suddenly Jake is singing. He nods his head in encouragement and I feel my lips moving, sound pushing out. I realize Jake has subdued the strength of his part so that mine can be heard. I breathe more sound out, letting my shoulders drop like he reminded me when we practiced. The more I sing, the more he sings, and suddenly we're halfway there. Feeling prickles of relief, I notice then that the edges of Jake's eyes and mouth are curled into a smile as he continues guiding me, lifting me, helping me survive this with his voice.

From DEDICATION, by Emma McLaughlin and Nicola Kraus
Published by Washington Square Press

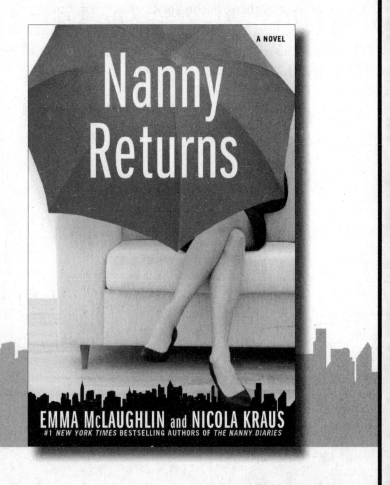